Trans-4-ma-tion

Austin P.

ISBN # 978- 1515371052

Contact Information:
KBA Publications
P.O. Box 2863
Phenix City, AL 36868

Printed in the USA.

Special Dedication

I wrote this with the notion of my baby son, Keiron, in mind, but, as I re-read it, I discovered that due to my absence, it applies to my daughter, Keiara, my other sons, Desmond, Keith Jr., and Terrell, as well.

When God created you all, Allah definitely was in a great spirit, because all of you are equipped with all the right tools, talentedly gifted, intelligent, and loaded with incredible skills.

Y'all are my pride and joy, as well as on the journey to a successful, bright arisen future. If one of you get the butterflys in your stomach, don't allow them to reach your head. You're too smart for that. You're a thinker. Meaning, don't fight the situation, don't entertain the negativity! Don't hold hostage the frustration that you can easily over come, because you have the key, knowledge, and education. You struggle with understanding, but master patients and travel the world, without an ounce of the law of nature. Each one of you have carried the weight of the world, you endured and became stronger, When you think you're weak, that's when you are at your strongest stand point. Don't allow pessimistic views to block your blessing. I love you all more than I love life itself.

Love Unconditionally,

Daddy

DEDICATION

I dedicate this book to the good brothers for all the knowledge and foresight they have shared with me. I would go to these brothers with my dilemmas, like a baby brother would run to his big brother, and like always, these positive and knowledgeable brothers would bail me out, with their advice and wisdom. I ran the idea across to them that I was going to write this novel for my community and for the younger generation. They advised me, that it was my duty and also took on part of the responsibility.

Uncle Pete showed me it was his obligation by supplying me with facts and furnishing me with evidence mentally. He actually baby-sat and spoon-fed me when and where needed. Brother Curtis Muhammad and Yahya Dillard took the time out to translate and polish up my language. I owe these brothers a lot for allowing me to intrude upon their tranquility. I would also like to thank my homie, Romero Q. Caesar Jr., because he participated in a major way. He forced me to utilize certain parts of my brain, that I felt didn't exist. Playa upgraded my imagination. My true brothers, thanks a million for the nutrients!

ACKNOWLEDGEMENT

Now, to all the aunties and grandmothers, who deserve the recognition, because back in the day, as well as nowadays, they are left alone to raise the kids. Only God knows what all those knuckleheads are taking them through. You strong Queens all around the globe are well-loved, respected, and appreciated.

Even though we didn't finish school or became the positive person that you tried to raise us to be, know that you didn't fail us. We failed you, because we became addicted to the negative aspect of life. We were affiliated with our lower self. We allowed the evil of money to entrap us, instead of standing firm on what was righteous. A lot of us don't face reality, until we hit rock bottom and wake up at the bottom of the tunnel. Unfortunately, some people weren't blessed with the opportunity to redeem themselves. When you're young, you have a young mind. Sometimes, we have the tendency to make a bad decision, and that decision can affect our family, while we have to pay the consequences with our freedom or our lives. My peeps, think, before you speed into motion. A coin has two sides, and every action has a reaction. There are consequences for everything, whether good or bad.

1

We can change the world with one youth at a time. I feel like Dr. Martin Luther King Jr., "If I can change one single individual's negative pattern of thinking, then my life will not have been in vain."

Keiron, thanks to you, I no-longer consider myself as a Daddy, because any male will and can be considered a Daddy, but it takes a real man to step up to the plate and be a father. Once you gave me the opportunity to play my fatherly role, along with your mother claiming, I couldn't be a daddy from in jail. I began searching for the positive things, that I could attain from my negative situation. I had you, Keiara, and Ja'Myra counting on me. I had to pull a rabbit out of my hat. I took trials, tribulation, and misfortunes and converted them into a message. Plus, the Temptation's song, *Poppa was a Rolling Stone,* gave me the drive, as well because I don't want to be like the song say, "and when he died, all he left us was alone." I don't live for me anymore, I live for you guys, so I can raise y'all kids and be there for them, as big momma held the family together.

INTRODUCTION

These individuals came into the prison system in total ignorance. During the course of their incarceration, individually, they started evolving, growing into complete human beings.

Through, their growth, they awakened. They knew that it was their ignorance that had led them to their destiny. They also knew it was only right to awaken the people to the things in life, that they had been awakened to. Their whole message was to tell everybody to wake up. However, they knew their message would only reach the chosen ones!

Every second...

A vehicle is reported stolen.

A child is born.

For every one person being released from prison,

Ten are coming to prison.

The death toll rises.

A crime is being committed.

PROLOGUE

April 17, 1998, 7:00 p.m.
Detroit, Michigan

Sten Peabody stood in the alley of Highland Park North, West of Detroit. He had been selling heroin, since the age of fourteen, but had recently changed his hustle to murder-for-hire. He thought, if they caught him dealing drugs, they would lock him up and throw away the key, but if he caught a murder charge, he'd get a lesser sentence.

The black Benz turned down the alley. Kingpin Big Ro sat in the back seat smiling, as he saw Sten, thinking about how well his lil homie had successfully handled the first lick for him.

Sten had gone up to the victim's door and rang the doorbell. The victim's wife answered the door, "Yes!"

"Ma'am, would you like to buy some candy? I'm selling it for my school, so I can buy some tennis shoes. I play on the basketball team."

She looked down at his 5'5", 120-pound frame and innocent face, and couldn't turn him down. She let him in, without bothering to ask for the candy bar's price.

5

"Honey, bring me a beer, and who is that at the door?" Sten heard the victim ask. Sten drew his 9mm, with the silencer fitted on it. He shot the victim's wife in the head twice, then he traveled in the direction the victim's voice had come from. The victim was watching the Houston Rockets and Atlanta Hawks playoff game.

"Hey, sir!" Sten said.

When his victim turned around, Sten fired twice into his face. As he was headed back to the door, he saw a poodle beside the victim's wife. He put the dog to sleep as well. There was nothing breathing, when Sten left the house.

He walked down the street, with his candy box in one hand and the basketball under his arm.

Ro had used Sten to put many of his enemies in the cemetery. Ro was proud of young Sten and to a degree, realized that he had created a monster.

Within a two-year period, Sten had committed five murders for Big Ro. Big Ro treated Sten more like a son than anything else. Sten was blowing his money on clothes, drugs, and partying, not saving anything. Before any big job, Big Ro would drop a few jewels on him and would always tell Sten, he loved him like a son. Big Ro never played Sten or beat him out of his money. After one of the jobs, he had surprised Sten with a Camaro, to go along with the payment.

The Benz stopped in front of Sten, the tinted windows casting his reflection back to him. Sten had a caramel complexion, and he rocked a season haircut. He wore an oversized black hood and black saggy bag, Sean-John jeans. His footgear was a pair of Jordans that wouldn't hit the market, until tomorrow. The back window lowered.

"What's poppin', lil one?"

"Me, if you got anotha job."

"While on my way over here, I got a call sayin', that boy Scott is over there on Liver Nosey and Pearton. Lay 'em the fuck down," Big Ro ordered. "You carrying?"

Sten always carried his pistol. He had a .40 cal, with an extra clip, tucked away in the lower part of his back.

"What you got?" he asked.

"A Glock 40" Big Ro replied, as he displayed the gun in his right palm.

"Yeah, let me get that up offa ya," Sten said. Any man in his right mind wasn't going to turn down more iron. The more heat the better, who knew when it might come in handy.

"After you use your heater, you can throw it away and still be armed," Big Ro announced, smiling.

Sten liked what he had just heard. Big Ro was looking out for his best interest.

"Give me a call, soon as the shit is over," Big Ro requested.

"For sho!"

Ro exercised his trigger finger on the door panel. The tinted window rolled back up, giving Sten another opportunity to look himself over once again. Big Ro knew deep within, Sten was dealing with addictions and demons. Young Sten walked around, with the weight of the world on his shoulders and still managed to hold his head up high. Big Ro beat Sten to his destination, having his driver park in the college pharmacy parking lot. He went into Coney Island, a restaurant that let you order whatever you wanted, any time of day. Even if it wasn't on the menu, they'd prepare it for you. Sten parked at NBD bank and made his way through the Mobile gas station.

Big Ro's motive for wanting Scott murdered was simple. Scott was trying to eat off a Big Ro's turf. Big Ro had a spot that would generate thirty thousand a day in bags. He was making grand theft over there. The spot had been like that for years. Big Ro lived in that spot, and he wasn't lettin' anybody who didn't live in there come and get a piece of the pie, crust, or crumbs. From Big Ro's perspective, that would be like another lion trying to bogart his way into another lion's den.

Sten's mother was aware of his M.O. and drug addiction. She'd been in the same projects all her life, but from youth, she had always kept a job to keep her children's heads above water. She knew Sten was a night flyer. He would usually sleep all day and be out all night, so before she left for her night job, she would always kiss him on the forehead and drop a jewel on him. She was no stranger to the streets.

"Baby, please be careful out there, cause the night don't have no eyes," his mother always lectured him. He knew what she meant. When someone was killed, no one knew nothing, saw nothing, or heard nothing! Sten's mother stayed on her knees praying so much, you would have thought she scrubbed floors for a living.

Sten paced up and down the sidewalk. His seventh lap, he saw his target, Scott, walking out of the dope house. Scott went to the   trunk of his Lexus. Sten picked up his pace and caught Scott bending over in the trunk. Sten grabbed Scott by the back of the neck and shoved the pistol into his temple, firing two slugs into his head. He grabbed Scott's legs, threw him into the trunk, and slammed it shut. Sten had no way of knowing at that moment, two undercover cops had Scott's house under surveillance. The detective on the passenger side of the car immediately reported the incident. "1-8-7 in progress. Black male suspect, wearing a black hood and black jeans. About 5'4" to 5'6", approximately 130 pounds, age 13 or 15. We are pursuing target on foot at corner of Liver Nosey and Pearton. Requesting backup, immediately."

Both detectives quietly exited the vehicle and split up. One walked down the sidewalk, and the other walked in the street, as close as possible to the row of parked cars.

Sten was heading in their direction, with both hands in the pocket of his hoody.

"Hey you, get your hands out of your pockets and hold 'em up, so I can see 'em!" the detective on the sidewalk shouted, with his revolver aimed at Sten.

Sten pulled out both guns and started firing. The detective only got off a couple of stray bullets, before being gunned down. The other detective raced back to the sidewalk, where he saw his partner laying face down on the concrete, blood pouring out of his neck and head. Knowing his partner was dead, the detective sprinted down the sidewalk after Sten, exchanging bullets, until Sten's baggy pants fell to his knees. As he bent over to pull them back up, he felt bullets explode into his shoulder and chest. While he was falling to the ground, hot lead continued to penetrate down his body. When the detective reached him, Sten was palming only one of the weapons. He kicked the pistol out of Sten's hand.

"You fucking nigger!" he spat, as he shot Sten in the head. Before he was able to squeeze off another round, as he had planned, a pair of headlights caught his attention, as a luxury car sped toward him.

The Benz came to a complete stop and Big Ro jumped out of the back seat, screaming, "That's my son! That's my fucking child!" He ran past the detective and knelt down beside Sten. He squeezed Sten's hand and didn't receive a return grip. Big Ro reached under his shirt, locking his strong grip around his Glock 40, as he began to stand. Patrol cars closed in on him. He left the gun where it was.

ॐ - ॐ

April 17, 1998, 7:00 p.m. Pacific
New Orleans

Justin Chase walked out the front door of the B. W. Cooper projects, also known as the Calliope. Killer chirped him, as he parked on the curb. C-murder lived a couple doors down from Chase and was standing in front of his apartment. Chase respected how C-murder still kept it gutter. Killer's Cutlass was candy-apple red, sitting on 22's, with Lambo doors. Soulja Slim's song, *My Jacket,* showered the small group of people standing out front.

"My jacket consists of batteries, armed robberies, pistol charges and murder. I know I'm the realest nigga ya heard of since Pac, got niggas screaming Soulja from the streets to the cell block."

Chase was dressed in Red Monkey jeans, with Bathing Ape on his feet. His shirt was thrown across his shoulder, protecting it from the gumbo he was eating, as he walked towards the car.

"What's up, woady? What it hit for?"
"Coolin', coolin' like an Eskimo. 'Bout to hit Canal Street, because you know they got a line of females down

there from all over," Chase replied, back to the hustler. "Be cool, my nigga," he added, getting into the car.

"What's up, round?" Killer addressed Chase.

"The playas better hide their women and the women better guard their daughters, cause we on the loose, ya heard me?" Chase spoke, before filling his mouth.

The traffic was just as they predicted--hectic, because of the Bayou Classic game. Everyone wanted to get to the live event, before their team crushed the opponent.

As the Cutlass finally touched Bourbon Street's French Quarters, Killer decided that they should go to club Utopia, where he knew there would be lots of hot girls. As Killer and Chase arrived, P-N-C music pumped the party and embraced the club crowd. They walked through the courtyard past the fountain spouting fire and settled for the bar, that was stationed beside the giant dance floor. The hot girls in the cages suspended above the dance floor were shaking what their mother gave them, and what their fathers worked so got-damn hard for. When the DJ played Juvenile song, *Back That Ass Up*, they danced like Rick James girls--super freaks.

Killer and Chase ordered drinks and joined the party. Countless drinks and hours later, they decided it was time to hit the road and relocate. The party wouldn't stop, until 5 a.m. They were both intoxicated, so Killer was driving carefully, observing all the rules of the road. He kept checking the mirror, as headlights appeared behind them.

"Don't look back, but I think 5-0 behind us," Killer finally said to Chase. "Round, I don't have a damn of license, and I got this burner on me. I already got three strikes, round. Shit, any lil thing I do will put me behind bars for life."

Right on cue, the police car's blue lights went to work and Chase's counseling began.

"Round, give me ya heat, and I'll jump out and run with it. Tell 'em you don't know me, and that you were just giving me a ride," instructed Chase, knowing Killer was in no shape to take the law enforcers on a high-speed chase as usual.

Chase secured the pistol in his waistline, and before the car even stopped, he slipped out the door, running like a runaway slave. The blue and white immediately got on his trail.

❦ - ❧

April 17, 1998, 7:00 p.m. Mountain
Memphis, Tennessee

Zeek Wilson and his partner in crime toured the city looking for a Lexus LS400. The chop-shop man had put in his order, and Zeek refused to let a day go to waste.

"Pimp, swing through German Town, and if we don't find our ride up there, then we'll go get that slow money. Ho money, for sho money," Zeek sang out.

"You sho know what to say," his partner, Hammer, fired back, as he made a U-turn, heading back towards the prestigious neighborhood.

While they sat at the red light, they scanned the business ahead. There was a bank, two restaurants, and a Food Giant grocery store.

"Man, drive through them parking lots," Zeek directed.

Hammer had been thinking the same thing, but Zeek just beat him to the draw, by saying it first. He pulled slowly into the bank parking lot. It was full of vehicles, but no Lexus.

"Hit the restaurants," Zeek said.

The place was loaded with foreign cars, but there was no Lexus. Hammer really wanted to leave the place of business with something, instead of leaving empty-handed, because some money would beat no money any day.

"Man, if we don't find one at the grocery store, then that's a sign for us to be a mothafucka gofer and get what the fuck we can get," Hammer stated.

"Shit, I think I agree wit' cha," Zeek replied.

Vakeita walked out of the Food Giant grocery store, with her one-year-old slumped across her shoulder. The bag boy strolled beside her, pushing the buggy. Expecting another child, she was almost eight months along, and feeling tired.

"Nice car," the bag boy said, as they walked up to her spotless burgundy LS400.

"Thanks," Vakeita smiled. She unlocked the trunk for the bag boy and as he put the groceries in for her, she secured her son in his car seat. She handed the bag boy a handsome tip, thanking him for his service, as she sat down behind the wheel of her car. She was rummaging through her purse for a piece of candy, when she heard someone snatching on the door handle. Vakeita looked up at Zeek like he was crazy, not frightened in the least.

"Okay, bitch, you got the door locked, huh? Oh, I got something for that," Zeek gritted, pulling the pistol from under his shirt. He drew back and swung hard at the window, shattering the glass all over Vakeita. Reaching in, Zeek hit the unlock switch and opened the door.

"Get the fuck outta the car, bitch," Zeek growled.

Vakeita gripped the steering wheel with both hands, screaming, "I ain't giving up my car for no fucking body!"

She didn't have a mustard seed of fear and totally disregarded the weapon. Her child's father had been murdered two months before, during a drug deal gone bad, and his mother had tried to take the car from her soon after. Then she'd had a run-in with his brothers and sisters concerning the car. Now this! The car meant a lot to her and was their only transportation.

Zeek grabbed a handful of Vakeita's sandy reddish hair, snatching her out of the car. She came out swinging and hollering at the top of her lungs. She missed Zeek's face, but hit him in the chest, clawing wildly with her fingernails. They dug in, leaving five long marks on Zeek's chest, which started bleeding, immediately. As he threw her to the pavement, some of the blood splattered on Vakeita's white sundress.

"Fuck!" raged Zeek, as he gave her a swift kick in the chest, causing her 160-pound body to lay spread out on the parking lot.

Hammer did not like how this operation was going down. Yeah, he was down for the crown, but that didn't include assaulting a pregnant sister. He stood there helpless. As he looked at Vakeita laying on the ground, his tough-man image went straight out the window.

"Oh, my stomach hurts," Vakeita cried out.

Hammer knelt down beside her, "Please, just stay down, and I promise I'll call an ambulance on our way outta here."

Zeek brushed the broken glass out of the car seat and fired the car up. "Nigga, let's get the fuck outta here!" he commanded his partner.

Still on the ground, Vakeita was sobbing, "Please, don't take my baby. Please, don't take my child!"

Zeek already had the car in drive and was about to pull off, when Hammer ran up to the car. The baby stared at him, with a hateful glare from the rear seat car carrier.

"Man, hold the fuck up. Let me get this baby outta the fucking car! Old wild-ass nigga!" Hammer said, as he unlatched the car seat. "A nigga ain't try'na catch a fucking kidnapping charge on a humbug."

When he handed the baby to Vakeita, she whispered a polite, "Thank you."

"Ms. Lady, you're most welcome," Hammer said.

Zeek reached over the seat to slam the back door closed. "Fucking soft-ass nigga... I'll meet you back at the spot," he said, with an attitude.

Spinning out of the parking lot, he headed down the highway. Zeek hadn't even gone a mile, when he came up to a line of stopped traffic. Zeek immediately knew what was happening. Every month, the law enforcers set up a roadblock to check for license, insurance, and registration, and he had just been unlucky enough to run upon the damned thing. They had set it up so that there were no streets or driveways to turn off into, without the cops seeing exactly what you were doing, trying to avoid them.

Zeek only had one choice, *Plan B*. He pulled the burgundy Lexus over to the side of the road, popped the hood, and turned on the hazard signals. After looking under the hood for a minute, he closed it. Zeek took one more look at the car and calmly deserted it, walking up the road, like he was headed to the nearest gas station.

ॐ - ॐ

April17, 1998, 8:00 p.m. Eastern
Beloit, Wisconsin

Shakur Douglas sat on the corner of Porter and Hull smoking weed. He watched Peanut get pulled over on the switch track by a patrol car. *Geez,* he thought. *Everybody oughta know the damn cops are going to pull you over when they know ya don't have a license...*

His observation was interrupted, as his father's Suburban crossed the switch track, the moment he had been anticipating. Shakur raced back home to their empty house, carrying the blanket full of guns down the stairs and spreading them out on the kitchen table. He set up shop like he did every day, when his father was gone to work.

Shakur lived with his mother in Chicago, but would spend his summers with his father. Since he was his father's only child, he loved being here.

A blue-box Chevy pulled up in the driveway, and three people got out. One of them was his cousin, Reese, along with two other guys, he had never seen before. Shakur immediately got a funny feeling, like something wasn't right. For the first time in his eighteen years, he felt butterflies in his stomach. For some reason, he felt in his gut he should not sell these two dudes anything.

You're trippin', Shakur told himself. *Since these people done come way over here, I'm gonna stick with the plan and serve 'em.* He let the curtains fall back into place, as he made his way over to the front door. He opened it, before they could knock.

"Y'all come on in," he invited.

"Shakur, what's poppin', cuz?" Reese greeted him. "These my people, the ones I was telling you 'bout. They tryin' to shop with ya. I told them you got the quality and the quantity."

Shakur didn't even bother glancing at the two guys, just wanting to get this business over with as soon as possible. "Y'all follow me," he said, as he led them into the kitchen, where the merchandise was laid out for display.

"Cuz, you got some new merch, right?" Reese asked, as he trailed Shakur.

"Yeah, you know... a lil sumpin' sumpin'," Shakur replied.

When they reached the kitchen, he studied the two men, as they were busy letting their eyes sweep the table, full of the finest brand-new weapons on the market. The bad feeling returned, and if anything, was worse. However, they weren't paying him any attention, too taken up with all the toys on the table. Everything he had was laid out: an AR-15, an AK-47, a SKS, a M-16, complete with a grenade launcher, a Mossberg pump shotgun, a Calico, Mac-10, Ingram-11, and an M-90.

"Damn! You got some good shit here!" one of the guys said, obviously impressed by the lethal arsenal.

"Yeah, this is some pretty good artillery," the other guy echoed his sentiment. "Brother, is these pretty babies sellin' good on the street?" he asked, holding up the M-16 with the grenade launcher.

"Better than sex and drugs," Shakur replied.

"What's the hottest guns they buyin' on the streets?" he questioned, placing the M-16 back on the table.

"Street sweepers, M-90s, Mac-10s, and Mac-11s," Shakur answered.

"Cuz, where unk?" Reese fished.

"Gone to work, Reese. Y'all gotta hurry the fuck up." Now the butterflies were really beginning to act up. Shakur could feel them trying to get out.

"How much cash you got on you?" one of the guys asked, as he reached behind his back, as if to pull out a wallet. His partner also reached behind his back, and before Shakur realized what was happening, he was staring done the barrels of two large service-issue pistols.

"We finally got your good gun-sellin' ass!" one of the undercovers stated.

"Damn, cuz. Man, what kind of bullshit is this?" Shakur demanded, with both hands held in the air.

"Man, I have a two-year-old daughter, and my wife eight months pregnant. I can't go to jail for fifteen years and leave them like that," Reese tried to justify.

Shakur has heard the street rumor, that his cousin was no good, so now, he could only fault himself, he thought, as the officers snapped the handcuffs on his wrist. As they led him past Reese, Shakur aimed a kick directly into

Reese's testicles. To his satisfaction, Reese fell backwards, hitting his head on the wall. Shakur hawed up a nice wad of spit and spat it in Reese's face.

"You snitch-ass mothafucka! It don't matter. You still gonna lose your woman," Shakur berated, knowing the real reason for his cousin's actions.

IN THE
BELLY
OF THE BEAST

Chapter 1

Six months after his arrest, Shakur arrived at USP Petty Rock. During his time waiting to get to the penitentiary, he'd had plenty of time to think about his life, and how he had strayed from the Islamic teachings that had been ingrained in him since birth.

When Shakur entered Petty Rock and settled in, his top priority was to get back on his Deen. He asked Allah to forgive him of his wrongdoings, to continue to guide him and to increase his knowledge, as well as to do the same for the other Muslims around the world.

Shakur promised himself, Allah, and his mother that he would do his best to do Allah's will, and Allah's will only. He had determined in his heart, that he would live a good, clean life and be a servant of Allah in trying to bring other young people into the fold. He wanted to help them avoid some of the same mistakes and bad decisions, he'd made in his life.

The prison was jam-packed. It was not that way, because men were jay walking or not going to church. You had to keep your eyes focused on everyone, especially the ones in your car, because the majority of them had snake traces in their DNA. Shakur sat in a huddle on C-Yard with his Muslim brothers, after they finished offering Salat.

Musa, the second imam in charge, counseled the group, "Brothers need to stop backbiting and envying one another. Whoever is doing this needs to stop, because it is not Sunnah. We as Muslims are not to be jealous of one another. That is the way of Kufers. Allah has cleansed our hearts, and we need to love each other for the sake of Allah. A Muslim's blood, property, and honor is sacred. We've all held onto the rope of Allah."

Gray-Top nodded his approval. Abdul Qawi continued cleaning his teeth with the miswak stick, trying to get them as white as possible.

Raheem backed Musa's speech, "The brothers know if they are doing this, and they know it wouldn't be Islamic, and they wouldn't be following Qur'an and Sunnah."

"They need to divide it, not hide it," Halim popped slick, while massaging the knot on the back of his head.

Khabir immediately put his two cents in. "That's something we shouldn't even be discussing, because that's not conduct for the Akhs. That's something done only by the Kufers. Everyone among this circle, as well as every Muslim on the yard, should want for his brother, what he wants for himself."

Abdul Malik raised his hand, indicating he was ready to speak. He addressed the group with the proper greeting, "As-Salaamu 'Alaikum."

"Wa 'Alaikum Salaam," they returned the greeting in unison.

"Musa, you are the imam, and if you know of any brother or brothers participating in this un-Islamic act, you need to pull that individual to the side and show him in the Qur'an and Sunnah, that it is not Islamic and Inshaa-Allaah it will stop. You mentioned this in the Friday Khutbah and in the Khutbah the Friday before that, so everyone should understand by now. It should be a dead issue." Abdul Malik's eyes roamed over the other Muslims.

"Inshaa-Allaah," Abdus-Salaam said.

Shakur made a mental note to make Du'a for the brothers, as he sat back watching his surroundings and silently asking Allah what he had gotten himself into, as he watched everyone on the yard scatter and hug the fence.

"Allaahu-akbar," Musa said out loud, attracting the attention of all the Muslims on the yard. He waved them over, so they would be out of harm's way, as a group of people cleaned up their car. There were people on the yard, who didn't belong. They had done something at their last prison, had come in as a street snitch, or were a jailhouse snitch. They were going to get punished. Blood would be wasted, and they would be placed in protective custody, until their transfer. They wouldn't be seen on the compound again.

The taffy man set up shop. He was guaranteed to sell out of candy. He would make so many stamps, he'd feel like he was only a few stamps away from being a stampanaire.

The only problem was, Swag would eat up all of his own supply like it was popcorn, once the blood started to fly. Blood could be smelled from a mile away, and it drew bystanders like flies on shit. It made some guys have nightmares, dreaming they were the victim, but others were always going to be around waiting for the action to start, because the tension in the air stayed so thick, it could be sliced with a knife.

"What we need to do is make Du'a for the brothers and ask Allah to remove the disease from the brothers' hearts," Egg Yoke mumbled.

Rasul nodded once. Du'a was a prayer that a Muslim would make for his brothers, asking Allah for forgiveness.

Allah said if you hide one of your brother's faults, then he'll hide two of yours, Halim wanted to say, but knew it was not the time or the place, even though he swallowed the slick comment. The brothers knew that he had been thinking of some mischief or a sarcastic comment, because of his foolish smile. He was constantly backsliding and going back to his ungodly ways.

≈ - ≈

A Nation of Islam brother pushed Sten across the Bloody-Bloody Beaumont compound to the other side of the pen, where the recreational yard was located. Sten offered to pay the guy for his assistance, but the knowledgeable brother assured him, that he was content with the blessing he was getting from Allah.

"I used to buy bean pies and final call newspapers from the brothers in my neighborhood to contribute to their cause, when I was a free man. They stayed suited and booted and wore bow ties," Sten revealed to the brother. It was the God-honest truth; he had supported the brothers with money, even if he didn't follow their teachings.

The brother parked Sten's wheelchair by the gate, so they could be the first through the gate, when yard recall was called…

Sten had been in another cell, but the brother had told him he could move into the cell with him, so he wouldn't be moved out of the large penthouse cell, because he wasn't handicapped. He treated Sten as if he was family and did all the cooking and cleaning.

Sten had many problems, but a dollar wasn't one of them. Big Ro put more money on Sten's account, than he could spend. The institution had informed Sten, the six figures on his account needed to be sent home. They threatened to freeze his account, if he kept receiving so much money. Sten kept them eating good. He bought his celly shoes, sweats, and had money put on his account. Sten showed him love, as if they had come out of the same womb. The brother didn't try to force his religious views on Sten.

They had many good conversations and that day, Sten told his celly about his ungodly lifestyle, and that he thanked God for still being alive.

His celly added an X to Sten's name without consent. Sten did not know what the X meant, but he did not reject the title. "Brother Sten X, you know everyone has a purpose in life. Allah spared you for a reason, and neither you nor I know what that reason is. It is a mystery to us, but I truly think Allah wants you to minister to the people."

Sten looked surprised. "I'm no minister," he replied, to his celly.

"You could be. Allah would lead you."

"Brother, I told you what I done for the money. I use to kill people and sell heroin," Sten reminded. For the first time in his life, he felt embarrassment and shame for his unlawful conduct.

"There are people who have done worse," the brother said, letting Sten know he wasn't the only one in the world to commit sinful acts, and Allah was their witness, that he wouldn't be the last human being to break one of the Ten Commandments, thou shall not kill. He assured Sten that from this day forward, they would both make their good deeds outweigh their bad deeds. "Brother Sten X, you think, because of your past criminal history, that Allah would not have a use for your worship, but you're wrong. Actually, Allah would have a great use for you, because your testimony would be an eye-opener, and because of your reputation, people would listen to you. They will see

28

the difference in you, and that would be a great message to the people."

"The people won't listen to me, because I wouldn't know what to say to them."

"Don't worry, Sten X," the brother said, patting Sten on the shoulder. "Allah can speak through us all."

As Sten thought about it, the brother's words gave him hope that maybe, he could be of use to Allah, and he began to study and listen to the brother's teachings. He started seeking out the brothers on the compound and asking them questions. That is how he came to get under the umbrella of Islam.

He enjoyed the brothers' company. They were always polite and respectful. The thing he liked the best is, how they always stayed the same. They didn't change; they were always humble and peaceful with a good vibe of energy. They made Sten want to be around them, because they never did anything that would make him want to run away from religion. He decided to join them and serve the brotherhood. After he made the decision, he was amazed, because it was as if a huge weight had been lifted from his shoulders. More importantly, he felt at peace within himself and felt happier than he had in years.

One of the brothers was talking with Sten one day and asked, "Brother Sten X, when will there be a day we can come out on the yard and enjoy some fresh air, without seeing all the senseless killing?"

"They say that misery loves company, but I was always told that, if you are not pleased with the conditions of the people, you do something about it. If not with your hands, then your mouth," Sten said, repeating back words that had been told to him. "You replace the people's ignorance with knowledge. You teach them better, so they will do better."

They watched, as two large groups of brothers, who had been having a disagreement, ended up going to war with each other. The black-on-black crime and violence was a terrible sight to see. At least a dozen of the guys fighting had knives taped to their hands, so they would not lose their grip on them. It was bloody, violent, vicious, and happened all the time.

When it was over, staff rushed around tending to the injured guys. Many were taken to outside hospitals. Sten found out later, that several of the inmates had died.

The ones that got away promised to finish the job, when they came off lockdown. It was a never-ending cycle of violence, where one war led to the next. The losing side said that, as sure as there was a God in heaven, they would avenge their brother's death.

The newspaper, TV, and even NPR on the radio broadcasted news about the tragedy. Violence took place every day within the prison walls and made the news headlines from time to time.

Sten was on one of the deadliest prison grounds. He thought, *Allah, the people done sent me here to get killed.*

He did not have the guts to allow the words to slip from his lips.

ॐ - ॐ

When Zeek finally reached his destination at Florence USP in Colorado, they escorted him straight to the SHU, as they were currently doing with everyone, who came into the system. The prison officials would lie and say, they didn't have any bed space right now, but would have some by the weekend, due to the violence. Actually, they needed time to get Zeek's paperwork together. His Pre-Sentencing Investigation (PSI) told all the details about his case and told them a lot about the individual, where they came from, and who his immediate family members were, as well as his past criminal history.

It was also this paperwork that his celly and homies would want to see, when he arrived on the compound. It would be very important to them to make sure that, he had not assisted the government in any form or fashion.

Three days later, Zeek was released from the hole. The CO. gave him a bedroll and a copy of his PSI. Zeek didn't pay the paperwork any mind. He went to his assigned unit and cell, placing everything on his bunk. He had only been there a few seconds, before he had a homie come looking for him, giving the opportunity to his celly to put the towel over the door window. His celly claimed he needed to defecate, but it really allowed him the time needed to

31

thumb through Zeek's paperwork, to make sure that he was not a snitch or Chester, the child-molester. When he came out, he gave Zeek's homie the thumbs-up, and they welcomed Zeek into the car.

While Zeek had been in the county jail, transit centers, and other holdovers, he found he had been drawn to the Moors. He was invited, as a guest, to a number of their meetings in the county jail, and that had gotten his mind on a mission. He was hungry for knowledge, and now that he was finally at the prison, he continued his search.

He found himself craving to know more about this religion, that he had not even known existed a few months before, when he was a free man. He asked questions to every Mo that he came across, and they spoon-fed him the beauty of their religion. The more his ears were lubricated, the more his soul craved. He tried to divide his time equally between the Moorish-Americans and his homies, but the scale began to tip in the Moor's favor.

Zeek's celly was with the Grand Sheek, so Zeek sat with them in the chow hall and stayed in their company, until eventually, he decided to become part of their family.

Zeek and a couple of his Moor brothers sat on the concrete table, looking up into the mountain tops. The prison sat in the shadow of a mountain, and the elevation was higher than Zeek was used to. The air was so thin, that by the time he made it to the chow hall, he would be short of breath.

Two towers sat on the compound. There was one in the center of the compound and another one over close to the lieutenant's office. The recreational yard was in the center of the compound as well.

As Zeek and the brothers were talking, some action on the other side of the yard attracted his attention. A mob was assembling on the basketball courts. The court was known to be a blind spot and hard to see from the towers. Brothers were abandoning the weight pile to join the group. The peace treaty between the brothers and the Mexicans was in jeopardy, because of several incidents that had recently happened, and there was no way around them bumping heads. The Mexicans were the largest group. They outnumbered the brothers by probably five to one, but the brother's strength and fighting skills gave them the edge. However, the Mexicans weren't backing down and the chosen ones weren't tucking their tails or turning the other cheek.

Damn, what have I gotten myself into? Zeek Bey thought. *Why can't we all just get along?*

It was an all-out war and the prison staff was completely overwhelmed. It wasn't long before a helicopter dropped off twenty National Guard troops, and they finally got the compound back under control. Since it was a battle between two different races, Zeek Bey knew it would be a long time, before they came off lockdown.

Sure enough, the compound was closed for almost six months. Eventually, they started letting inmates out to go to chow, but there were so many officers in the tunnel, it looked like the edge of a President street parade. They wore shields, vests, and carried shock sticks. If someone tried to rekindle the war, it would end before it started, because the officers would attack them with the shock sticks. They had them set to a level that would knock King Kong to the ground, and if they continued resisting the officers would turn it up, until it would permanently fry the brain.

There was a convict called Tarzan, who had once tested the guards and found out what could happen. He was 6'8", 400 pounds and could bench-press double his weight. He had kept fighting them, and they turned up the power on the shock sticks and kept hitting him, until they almost killed him. Tarzan had never been the smartest man, but when they were done with the Tasers, he had the mind of a 12-year-old child. He could barely remember his age, birthday, and name. He would say *yes ma'am and yes sir*, which he had not done his whole life. Once a man, twice a child!

When Zeek had seen the giant and heard the child's voice, he had witnessed the friendliest smile he had ever seen. He could not believe that Tarzan was the same monster he had heard all the stories about, before he arrived on the compound. One of the Moors alerted him that Tarzan had come from the ADX, and the majority of guys there had high profile cases. Zeek's eyes bucked, as his heart beat like crazy.

"Big guy was ruthless," he mumbled.

"Mo, there's guys on the pound make the big guy's crime look like child's play. Mo, we in the big house, but we don't have nothing to worry about, because we're here chasing knowledge and walking in the footsteps of The Prophet, Noble Drew Ali."

A CRIMINAL'S PLEA

By: Ras. Zupi

Crown Heights, Brooklyn, New York

My life's kinda hard, it got me stressin'

Compared to the paradise, I'm far from heaven,

I thought about a God so long, I'm second guessin'

And I know I ain't the only one who made this confession,

I fall to the same traps created by the next man

Never thinkin' 'bout a way to formulate the best plan,

Too busy losin' all my goods to the Jets fan

Or slammin' dominoes signifyin' I'm da best; and,

I ain't gotta clue wit' what's goin' on around me

Never been the type to have a million dudes surround me,

Never been lost so you can never say you found me

And pardon me, if you don't like the way that I'm sounding, Brother's workin' hard for every penny in this place

Compared to what his son's makin', Dad's a disgrace,

Feels like the whole world's spittin' in yo' face...
What happened to the million dollar man dealin' base?
He converted to a five dollar man without a dream
And he don't give a damn 'cause life ain't what it seems,
With vivid visions of goin' home and livin' like a fiend
Just to come right back, he took a body for the "Team",
I gotta break the cycle or my son gon' pick it up
Can't be the dude in the bank tryin' to stick it up,
Kind' a hard fo' me to make the vow and just give it up
When that was a guaranteed way for me to live it up,
Yes! I'm a criminal, but I'm try'na make some changes
Like who to - and who not - and why not to hang wit',
The crew my pride was dedicated to bang wit'
I guess 'cause now we ain't speakin' the same language...
Hands on my chest -- so I hope you all can get this
The words that I speak today we all can bare witness,
But how many men gon' vow to make it yo' business,
To understand the struggles we now leavin' da kids wit'?

Chapter 2

July 21, 2002, 6:00 a.m.
Oklahoma City, Oklahoma

At the Oklahoma holdover facility, the officer stood in the center floor demanding attention. "Everybody whose names I just called, pack up... you have five minutes to meet me by the door." Chase's name was called with the others, and he was ready to desert the holdover. The twelve days there had been beautiful, but he was ready to get to his destination, so he could get more comfortable.

Chase had enjoyed the last eight days of his stay. He could look out of his cell window and look into the females' windows. What a lovely sight to see! The girls kept Chase weak at the knees and up all night. He spent the entire 192 hours in his cell, by choice. He could exercise his freedom by roaming around in the unit, using the telephone, watching television, or playing cards with other inmates, but Chase chose to spend his time becoming better acquainted with the ladies. He met a Mexican chick named Silver and a sister named Monica from the MIA. Monica looked like Da Brat. Chase really got a kick out of another sister named Mary. Mary was thirteen years older than him, and was a large and possessive woman. She was jealous as hell, and carried on as if their relationship had developed on the street, and not through a pumped-out toilet.

They would sit on the floor talking over their toilets, sometimes for twenty hours a day, using the toilet for a pillow to rest their head, while listening to the other person talk. It was even better than talking on the telephone! They could hear each other as clear as day. It was so clear they could hear a needle drop. The toilet worked like a giant loudspeaker. Chase could talk to people above or beneath him. Since Chase was on the second floor in cell 222, he could talk to Aggressive Mary on the first floor, cell122, or Nature, from Nebraska, on the third floor in cell 322.

Chase and Nature hit it off big time. Nature would listen to Chase and Mary's conversation day in and day out. It was a wrap, once she learned Chase was her age. She intervened with Mary, since she knew that Chase was a hot boy and was looking for a hot girl. Chase melted her heart, and in no time, Nature was pouring out her heart and proposing through the shitter. She vowed to be with Chase through thick and thin, for better or for worse, until death did they part.

Nature grew tired of them having to use other people's rooms to talk on the toilet. They both had to pump out the toilet and clean it out really good, before they talked on it. One day the CO. caught Nature talking on the commode, and warned Nature that she could catch hepatitis. Nature completely disregarded the warning, since the only thing she was concerned about catching was Chase.

Nature told Chase he needed to choose between her and Mary. She threatened that she would start talking to him from her room, from her toilet, and if he didn't man up and tell Mary, then she would.

Before the shit could hit the fan, Chase had them both sit by the toilet. The two sisters screamed and shouted back and forth through the toilet calling each other B and H words, until Chase finally stepped in, putting them both in silence, as they waited on his verdict.

The girls both made it firm and clear that today, not tomorrow, he had to choose.

"Nature, you're going to be my woman, until Mary runs off, and Mary, you're going to be my woman, until Nature runs off," Chase stated, and he left it as simple as that.

Chase stood on the black carpet box with fifteen other transport inmates. One U.S. marshal was shackling up his ankles, while another marshal put the cuffs around his wrists. They all took baby steps and boarded the plane. For some of the inmates, it was the first plane ride of their lives.

"I ain't never rode a plane before," Fifty freely came clean.

"You keep fuckin' with the Feds, you might fuck around and be on a boat," RE-O predicted.

"Shit, it wouldn't surprise me, if they start shippin' mothafuckas around on a hot air balloon," someone else said.

"Back in the day, they used to transport us by horse and wagons," stated an older brother.

"I'm an '88 baby. I wouldn't know about all that," Chase said.

"Damn, playa, you only twenty-two?" a guy asked Chase.

"Yup!"

"How long you been down?"

"Four and some change. I done walked my nickel down."

"Shit, you shorter than a mosquito peter. By the time you go to sleep and wake up, them little months done flew by."

"I hope you right," Chase smiled, now walking slower, because the cuffs around his ankle were cutting into his skin.

"Where you headed to, playa?"

"To some joint called Petty Rock. It's close by, where I come from."

"Man, I just left that mothafucka. They just had a black on white riot. I jumped in the shit, just so I could get the fuck away from that bullshit spot. Ain't nothing there, but a bunch of broke, miserable mothafuckas. Playa, soon as you get there, please get you a knife. Them cats will catch you slippin' and will rock you to sleep. It's hard on the yard," the guy related. "A nigga need that iron, believe dat!"

"It might be hard on the yard, but it's sweet in the streets," Chase replied, thinking about how in 180 days, he'd be swallowing real liquor and not the jailhouse fruit wine. Drinking the prison wine was like slurping on a daiquiri. The sweet alcohol would sneak up on you, and the end result was you'd feel like you had been drinking store-bought liquor. When you encountered wine that smelled like rubbing alcohol, you were in trouble, because that was that gas, the best wine on the market.

The guys boarded the plane and the females were sitting in the front, like usual. A couple of the plane marshals stood in the aisle directing the guys to their seats. The marshals made sure everybody was well secured in their seat belts. If you couldn't put your seatbelt on, the marshals didn't have a problem with putting it on for you. Everyone had to be buckled up, before the plane took off.

Once the plane was in the air, the restroom section was kicking. All the girls, who had a so-called boyfriend on the plane, would claim they had to use the lavatory. If her guy was fortunate enough to be seated by the aisle when she came back by, he would be blessed with the scent of a womb.

स - स

Zeek was led from his Terre Haute holdover cell by a female CO. While Zeek slowly trailed her, his mind was completely in the gutter, as if all his religion had abandoned him. He was thinking about the positions they could experiment, while going half on a baby. Zeek's four years of incarceration and celibacy did not make him believe he had the power of a monk. It was impossible for Zeek's conscience to even produce an image that the CO was a nun. His imagination wouldn't allow it. He automatically became excited. When they reached the R&D section, it caught the female CO's attention.

"Did I do that?" she asked, innocently.

Zeek didn't reply, ashamed for giving into his weakness. It wasn't too often that he was thrown off balance and captivated by lust. Once the eyes lust, you have already committed adultery, he coached himself. Zeek overlooked the fact that he was a male, and his reaction was normal.

There were several CO's stationed in R&D, each attending to an inmate. They strip-searched Zeek, giving him the proper size of clothes. No inmate could escape the room with their pants sliding down their hips. Inmates could get away with T-shirts a size too big, but the pants absolutely not. The staff would show their ass and raise all kinds of hell about trying to get a pair of pants a little wider in the hips, so most likely the guys would end up traveling in skin-tights. Some CO's played vicious games. They could ... they were the boss. You would wear the pants they selected for you or sit in the holdover, until your turn came back up to transfer.

The steel chair that sat on a four-inch circle concrete slab spooked Zeek. To him, the chair looked identical to an electric chair. The only difference, he could tell was that it didn't have straps on it.

"What's that chair for?"

"To take your nature," the female guard joked, smiling. "It removes your hormones!"

Zeek's imagination ran wild. He wondered how many people had died in that chair. How much flesh had been scraped from that chair? How long would it take him to die in that chair?

The female guard knew by Zeek's silence what kinds of thoughts were running through his head, and that he was giving it a great deal of thought, so she said, "Nobody has died in that chair. We do have an electric chair here, though. It's in another building. Now everybody that come in and out of Terra Haute has to sit in this here chair."

"That's crazy!" Zeek blurted, in a child's voice.

"Crazy! What's so crazy about it?"

"I ain't try'na sit in that chair!"

"Then you ain't gonna get transferred. Come on back here, so I can put you back in your cell," she stated.

"What's up with that chair?" Zeek asked, still looking crazy.

"That chair is just a big X-ray machine, man. Once you sit on it, it'll tell us, if you've keistered anything."

"I ain't keistered nothing! Ain't nothin' going up my butt!"

"I'm not saying you're one of them. You wouldn't believe some of the things people will shove up their butts."

"Like what?" Zeek asked. This he wanted to hear.

The female guard started listing off the things she was expected to be on the lookout for. "Drugs, syringes, tobacco, matches, jewelry. You never heard about the guy, who had the 22 pistol stuck up his butt?"

"Cut the BS, lady."

"I'm serious! How long you been in the system?"

"Four years."

"How much more time you got to go?"

"Sixty-one more years."

"Then start asking around. Before you finish your bid, you'll find someone who's heard about the pistol being keistered. Now come and sit in this chair, before your bus seat is filled with someone else, son. You know one monkey don't stop no show." She wanted to tell him about the guy, who keistered the cell phone and had to go to the hospital to have it removed, but she wasn't ready for that news to travel.

"Damn boy, I sho gonna miss that dark and lovely." The female guard caught the hint. She knew Zeek was talking about every square inch of her 5' 11" and 140 pound. Her jet-black hair was the perfect combination for her dark brown complexion. "What, you use to wear a perm, before you cut your hair off?"

"I never wore a perm. I don't need to imitate the Caucasian with the stringy hair," Zeek stated, while rubbing his bald head.

❧ – ❧

Sten stared straight ahead, as the transport marshal cuffed and shackled his ankles. He couldn't wait to leave the Atlanta holdover. To him, the marshal wasn't moving fast enough.

Being on lockdown twenty-three hours a day, with two and sometimes three guys in a cell designed for only two people, caused more problems than Chinatown. If one celly wasn't defecating, another was passing gas. Most people would say, it was being cruel to animals, if you locked up four dogs in a space that small, so how inhumane was it for someone's husband, brother, father, and son?

"How did you enjoy your stay in Hotlanta?" the marshal asked, as he cuffed Sten's right wrist to the wheelchair.

Sten mean-mugged the marshal. "Why complain when it never does any good, and besides, no one wants to listen? But since you asked, I'll answer your question. I ate in this chair, I showered in this chair, and I'll be damned, if I didn't have to sleep every night in this chair. How do you think I enjoyed it?"

"Anything else?"

45

"Yeah man, the food is some slop. I feed my dog better meals. Y'all got green eggs, the only thing that's missin' is the green ham," Sten added, as the marshal pushed him down the ramp.

"The way you sound, I take it you didn't like Atlanta."

"The only thing I like about the urban city is the Artist and the variety of radio stations," Sten replied grimly, thinking he could see where this shit was going. The old fart was trying to be funny.

"So, you're not trying to spend one more night?" the marshal sarcastically asked, as they approached the transport van. It rocked his boat to hear the inmates pouring out their complaints about being uncomfortable. Sometimes, he wanted to tell them that this wasn't McDonald's or Burger King, where they could have it their way. If they had wanted to be comfortable, they shouldn't have committed the crime and stayed their butts at home.

"Shit, you couldn't make it past the tail end of the twenty-three hours of lockdown. Before three hours surfaced, you'd been done committed suicide. You know how you people do it," Sten said, loud and proud.

"Mr. Detroit, we'll see how you like your new home. Just don't be in for a rude awakening," the marshal cackled. "You'll have a lot more to worry about, besides just dropping the soap."

"What you mean by that?"

"You'll see!"

"Yeah, they try'na send me somewhere, hoping I get killed. Hoping I take a life and trap myself behind these walls forever. I'm aware, the system plays for keeps. It's designed to destroy my people," Sten said, observing the marshal's wrinkled hand, as he lowered the steel plate for his wheel chair to be lifted into the van. Green and blue veins spider webbed across the hand.

"Young men have dreams. Old men have vision," the marshal threw at him.

"Once a man and twice a child," Sten lectured. "When I was a child, I thought like a child, and once I became a man, I put all the childishness to the side. And marshal, for the record, I don't fear nothing, nobody, but God."

This handicapped joker is sitting here trying to play tough. I know he's scared. He's wasting his breath, while trying to fool me. I got over twenty years tied into this job. He needs to save that breath for someone, who doesn't know any better, the marshal thought. *"Very cute, I'm impressed"* he patted Sten on the shoulder.

Sten smiled, "I have the greatest protector in the world."

The marshal laughed, "And who's that?"

"The same one that parted the Red Sea," Sten smiled again. "The same one, who protected Moses from Pharoah."

"Someone has to keep the hope alive," the marshal said, still laughing, as he continued to try to verbally assault Sten. "And have faith the size of a mustard seed."

Chapter 3

Unit manager, Nicholas, stood by the microwave waiting on his 8-ounce Styrofoam cup of coffee to get two minutes of heat. Nicholas liked his coffee hot, but not to the point of burning his tongue. The microwave bell beeped, and Nicholas retrieved the cup. Just a little steam rising from it--perfect. Nicholas claimed he only drank coffee to speed up his metabolism, but he was addicted to the caffeine buzz.

Thirty-one people had arrived. *They should almost be done interviewing them by now,* Nicholas thought, as he looked into the holding tank, where the inmates were piled up eating their bag lunches. Two bologna sandwiches, a bag of chips, and a green apple would have to carry the guys through the night, until breakfast the next morning.

The system was broke, and they were on a tight budget. They couldn't afford to put mustard and mayonnaise in every bag. Some bags had mustard, and others had mayonnaise. No one used the Kool-aid packs, because it would spread through your system like wildfire. Those Kool-Aid packs were only good for dying clothes or cleaning grills and toilets.

Nicholas stuck his head through the door and asked, "How many of you have not been interviewed yet?"

The frivolous conversations among the guys came to a halt. Their eyes searched their small crowd, along with Nicholas. Only one hand was raised.

"I haven't," said Chase.

"Okay, thank you," Nicholas replied, as he politely closed the door back to seal off unnecessary noise.

A moment later, Nicholas reopened the door, sticking his head back in for the second time. "Please bring your trash out with you," he added. "I will do an inspection, before y'all leave. I don't want to see any food items or bags. If I do, I promise all of you will sleep in here tonight. This area needs to be clean, just like you found it."

"Man, trash was already in this bitch, when we got here!" Kansas shouted.

"Nigga, take off that tight, cheap-ass pinstripe suit you got on!" another brother hollered.

"Mothafucka, you look more like a maid, than I do," said a white guy.

The unit manager heard every word that was said, but he didn't entertain any foolish thoughts. The guys could cuss, until their tongues fell out for all he cared. He walked over to Counselor Peggy's work area.

"Excuse me, do you have the last file?" he asked.

"No, he's my last case," Peggy stated. "I have no more files, thank you, Jesus."

"Say, Slim, how long it'll be, before we make it to the unit?" asked DC. He didn't care who answered, he just wanted to know.

"Not long," Nicholas answered, as he glanced at the clock on the wall, that read 7:47. "Y'all will be outta here, before recall," he promised.

"What time is recall?" DC asked, ready to break camp, look for his homies, and get that care package. The cosmetics and little bit of food items would do him good, after a hot shower.

"Recall is 8:30," Counselor Peggy responded.

DC smiled, knowing now that he'd get to see his homies from other units. On days that the yard was crowded, everyone wanted to see who all was coming in off the bus. Guys needed to see if their victim or enemy was on the bus, so they could catch them slipping and rock them to sleep.

Nicholas made his way over to Counselor Temesha's office, where she sat behind her desk with her head down. She read off question after question. She was tired; she had read this same sheet eighty-eight times today, since this was the second bus to arrive. Temesha intentionally skipped over some of the questions. Most of the questions needed to be asked, but others were completely ridiculous. Nicholas pecked on the office glass, and Counselor Temesha gave Nicholas an exhausted look, as he stuck his head in.

"Please tell me we're almost done," she pleaded.

"Actually, I came back to inform you that you have the very last file," Nicholas confirmed.

"Ooh ... why me, Lord? Why me, every time? Why do I always end up with the last inmate?" Counselor Temesha exhaled, with both hands raised up towards the ceiling.

"Be easy, Ms. T. This last guy isn't going to be a knuckle-head," Nicholas predicted, trying to brighten her up.

"Huh, speak for yourself! You don't have to sit up in this chair all day. I probably have butt sores."

"Shit, me too," threw in New York, referring to the 14-hour bus ride he had endured.

Counselor Temesha had five more questions to ask New York, before her boss interrupted. "We're through. Now go on back and tell that last guy to come on, so we can get this over with."

Counselor Temesha huffed, laying her head down on the desk. Her head was pounding, as she tried to look at the questions. She was so tired, they were making her cross-eyed. It was a good thing she knew them all from memory. New York went back into the holding tank, looking for his bag lunch. It was nowhere to be found.

"Damn, son, what happened to my sack?" he questioned the DC guy, that had been sitting next to him.

"That joint long gone, Joe. That fuckin' nigga came in hollerin' 'bout a mothafucka can't leave outta here, until the shit is clean as a mothafucka, so we was forced to smash that. Brothers in here try'na get to the pound tonight, Slim!"

"Man, I still had two boiled eggs in there. I was going to make me an egg sandwich. Word up, son."

"I'm pretty sure your celly would thank us for it, Slim. Them eggs would have had you fartin' all night in your sleep."

New York sat down on the solid concrete slab, where his sack had disappeared from. "Man, whoever the last person is, the lady said send'em on back there. Man, the sooner you get done, the sooner we can hit the pound."

"Yeah, round, let me ease on back there and holla at the hot girl," Chase stated.

He pulled up his light brown pants a little, but not enough to keep them from sagging. He walked on the heels of his blue bus shoes. Chase had a clear view across the hall to Counselor Peggy's office. She was removing the pile of files from her desk putting them back into the cart.

Why carry them, when I can push them, she thought. *I work smart, not hard.* Seeing Chase, she mumbled, "No sir, not me, not tonight. Down the hall, mister. Hook the first right."

"Say partna, I go to the lady across the hall?" asked Chase, looking back at New York.

"Naw, son. Down the hall and make the first right you come across," New York instructed.

"Word up, son?" Chase uttered, being playful.

"Word is bond," New York chanted.

"Where you from, the Bronx?" Chase queried.

"Naw, son, I'm from Brooklyn," New York told him.

"BK is in the house," Juke shouted.

"Can you say New York City?" Chase's homie blurted, doing his best LL Cool J imitation.

Chase slowly started walking, looking straight ahead at Counselor Peggy. "Down the hall," she hissed, with an obvious attitude, as she pointed toward Counselor Temesha's station.

"A nigga ain't try'na holla at'cha, Grandma. You got a daughter? An old woman can't do nothing for me, but point me in the direction the young one done went, ya heard me?" Chase growled, as he continued trucking down the hall.

Counselor Temesha's head was still on the desk, when Chase arrived. "Knock, knock, knock," he said.

She raised her head, her face exposing her youth. She looked to be a few years older than Chase.

"Ready or not, here I come. I'm gonna find you and make you mines, ya heard me?"

"Inmate, sit down in that chair, and let Lauryn Hill and the Fugees sing their own song." Counselor Temesha scolded. She rubbed her eyes. "I'm going to ask you a few questions, and then we'll be finished."

"Naw, I ain't got no kids, yeah, I'm single," Chase volunteered.

Counselor Temesha rolled her eyes at him. "Boy, please. You try'na stay up here all night? I sho ain't. I have

Jikesis, JaTavis and JeQuavis to go home to. Now, are you ready to answer these questions?"

"Bring it."

"Have you ever been sexually molested?"

"Woman, hell naw! What kinda sick-ass question is that? A nigga ever try them homosexual games with me, you'll read about it."

Counselor Temesha had heard that line many times and continued with the next important question. "Have you ever aided and assisted the government or testified in court against anyone?" The questions were similar, but had a small difference. One part just meant had you ever given information to the government about anyone. The other part meant had you ever openly testified in court for the government against someone.

"Woman, that's the second time you done asked me some crazy-ass shit. Do I look like a hot-ass nigga to you?" Chase spat out. He stood and leaned over the desk, looking the counselor straight into her eyes.

"Nothing personal," she said. "We just have to ask those questions."

"You shoulda read my jacket, before you asked me some bullshit like that."

Counselor Temesha sat up straight in her chair. "I know, but we don't have all your information right here. Besides, I didn't have time to read the jackets of everyone that came through here today. To ask you bus guys these questions is a part of my job requirement."

Chase sat there listening to what Counselor Temesha was saying, but as soon as she fired off another crazy question, Chase got up and walked out of the office, dismissing himself. Class was over; the school bell had rung for him. Chase went back into the holding tank, regaining his same spot on the concrete bench, beside his homie.

"Shit, I'm ready to get outta this stuffy tank, ya heard me?" his homie said.

"Say, round, you didn't tell me the people ask you, did somebody run up in you. And you didn't tell me they ask did you aid and assist the government. They didn't think you was, right?" Chase interrogated, with a good sense of humor.

"That's when I snapped on her for askin' me that dumbass shit, ya heard me? How you know she asked me that?"

"She told me," Chase lied. "Yeah, round, I know you went the fuck off. She asked me the same shit, and I went berserk, ya heard me? That's when she mentioned your name, askin' me is you my friend or co-defendant. I ask her why, and she said, you acted the same way about them questions."

"She know we some 504 boys, huh? Round, she know we gonna keep it gangsta, until we die, ya heard me?"

Unit Manager Nicholas entered the holding tank, looking around. "Y'all ready to go to the unit and get yourselves a nice hot shower and kick it with your homies?" he questioned.

"Hell yeah, we been ready," someone snapped.

"We stay ready, so we ain't gotta get ready," DC spoke.

Nicholas pointed to four slices of white bread, two boiled eggs, and a dove green apple, from New York's bag that had reappeared. "Y'all can't be ready. What is that?"

"Don't worry bout that son, I got it, kid. It will be well taken care of, word is bond. I'm gonna punish all of that, when I get to the unit," stated New York.

"Can you say New York City?" Chase's homie shouted.

"Ya heard me," New York teased back.

Nicholas had heard enough of the guy's mouth. "All you inmates line up by the door. On your way out, there's a big blue waste basket with bedrolls. Grab one set and not two. There's only enough for one each, so if you get two, someone's sleeping on a bare ass mattress, and it ain't gonna be me."

"Is the yard still open?" Memphis asked.

"Trust me, whoever you looking for will find you. You won't have to find them," Nicholas assured him.

Twenty inmates walked towards the door, while eleven others remained seated. They had no intention of going out onto the compound. They had informed Counselor Peggy and Counselor Temesha right out of the gate to lock them up; march them straight down to the hole for protective custody, known as P.C. The counselors assured them that it would be arranged, once they were finished with normal procedure. She advised them to stay seated, and an escort would arrive to safely escort them to special housing.

The eleven inmates had different technicalities, that would prevent them from living peacefully in general population. They could be street snitches, jailhouse snitches, told on someone who assaulted them, sex offenders, had ripped someone off in the past and found out they were at this spot, or maybe just scared to death from hearing about the blood-shedding events. When the group reached the Lieutenant's Office, there was a dozen COs and several PAs posted up in the hall. Some of the inmates studied the medication boxes and the stretchers.

"What the fuck is that? The A-Team?" DC said, laughing.

A lieutenant stepped forward with a walkie-talkie in his palm. "Inmates, if you ain't right, then don't step through those double doors. I'm here to ensure your safety. Once you step through those doors, you are on your own. Only you know, if you are right or not. This is your last and final warning. If you want to go lay down, step aside and line up beside my office door and my staff will take care of you."

"Say, woady... everybody here straight, ya heard me?" Chase blurted. However, Chase's words must not have applied to everyone in the group, because eight of the twenty guys took heed to the lieutenant's message. They shuffled over and formed a single file line beside the lieutenant's office door.

"Officer Foot, would you take these inmates to the SHU?" The lieutenant said in a question form, but everyone understood that it was a direct order.

Officer Foot stood about 5'2" and weighed 101 pounds, soaking wet. The lieutenant had tried to guess his weight, and had figured around 120 pounds, but in truth, Officer Foot wouldn't even weigh that much with a couple of bricks in each pocket. When Officer Foot had weighed in for the Bureau, he had put everything he could think of in his pockets and barely tipped the scales at 110 pounds. He was embarrassed enough at his small size; he refused to be embarrassed about his weight. One of them was enough.

As 23-year old Officer Foot led the guys down the hall, he was all too happy to be out of the way. He was glad to be a key-turner on bus days. On normal days, he'd get upset, because the SHU inmates would tell him he wasn't nothing, but a fuckin' key-turner.

"Bus inmates are being released. I repeat, the bus inmates are being released," the lieutenant announced into his walkie-talkie.

I shall walk
through the valley
of the shadow of death. I will fear no evil.

Chapter 4

"Buzz." Officer Foot pushed the Special Housing Unit buzzer. The steel door made a clicking sound, and Officer Foot opened it and stepped in, along with the check-ins. Check-ins were the guys, who go to the hole for protection. When the steel door closed behind them, another one opened in front of them. As they walked into the room, they saw two correctional officers on standby.

One of the officers greeted the group with "Y'all follow me." He led them to a dry tank, a cell that contained nothing, but lights.

A SHU orderly rushed in with a pen and paper in hand. He was ready to do the officer's job instead of his, since his main responsibilities were sweeping, mopping, folding, and washing clothes, and stacking the food trays back into the hot box.

The kitchen inmates fixed trays for the hole three times a day. They pushed a hot box to the SHU and returned to pick it up, before the chow hall closed. Their first trip would be at 5:30 a.m., second trip at 10:00 a.m., and the final and last meal delivery at 2:30 p.m. A SHU officer would plug the hot box in to keep the food hot, until they decided to feed the inmates.

"I need all your names, numbers, and whether you want pork or no pork," requested the orderly. The inmates that did not eat pork would receive a substitution like baked beans, boiled eggs, cottage cheese, or peanut butter and jelly.

"Say, orderly, I want no-meat trays," a guy among the crowd shouted. "Yeah, I don't want no flesh, period, on my tray."

"Hold that thought, until it's your turn, bro." said the orderly.

"Orderly, I don't want no beef or pork on my trays," another guy yelled. The orderly was well aware that sometimes, these guys could be like little kids. They refused to listen and follow instructions. Some could just plain refuse to go along with the program.

"Man, did I not just say hold that shit, until you get to the gate?" the orderly snapped.

The guy who had requested no beef and no pork trays was trying to put some security on the days, when fish or chicken was served. While he didn't eat pork or beef, he did eat seafood and chicken.

After the orderly had gotten all their info and walked away, a husky CO. walked up. "Do any of y'all have somebody you can cell up with?"

"Man, I'm trying to get in a cell with my partner, here," announced a short stocky guy. He had met the guy he wanted to be roommates with in the Oklahoma holdover, and they already had it planned out.

"Shit, I'm trying to get in a room with my man here, that I came on the bus with," requested someone else.

Truth is, all the check-ins wanted to be cellies with each other. They would feel safer and more comfortable in the cell with someone in their same predicament, rather than someone who had come off the compound for fighting or something else.

"Who do y'all know here that you can cell up with?" asked the CO.

"We don't know nobody. We just got here," chanted a couple of guys together, like they were rehearsing in choir practice.

"Well, y'all gotta find somebody," the CO said, ready to get this problem off his hands. He unlocked the tank door. "Y'all follow me."

"Where we going?" one of the guys asked. The fear in his eyes would have caused him even more fear, if he could see how he looked in a mirror.

"We're going to find y'all a cell," the CO answered. His intention was to lead them down all eight ranges and let them see the other SHU inmate's names and picture ID's, that were posted on each cell door. He wanted to give the check-ins the opportunity to see if they saw any familiar faces.

As soon as they arrived on range 100, the guy in cell 101 was standing at his cell door. "Y'all mothafuckas keep it movin' ... ain't no hot mothafucka coming in here!"

At cell 107, the inmate got off two questions, "Man, where y'all from? Anybody out there from Mississippi?"

They left the first range without having any luck. As they reached the 200 range, the SHU inmates started hollering through their doors. "Here come some more hot mothafuckas!"

"One of you try'na suck and get fucked can come in here," cell 222 invited.

"Freaksome say, he'll hit a pig in a wig and screw a rattlesnake, if someone will hold the head," cell 212 said, because he knew Freaksome was going to put that out there on the range, every time a new group of inmates came to the hole and needed a cell.

"I said this is room 222. If you try'na get pregnant, then holla at your boy, Freaksome."

"Freaksome still try'na get his nuts outta the sand?" asked cell 228, helping to entertain the range.

"Not the booty bandit," someone instigated.

The officer stopped by Freaksome's door, "Cut it out, man."

"When you give me them two wide-leg, butt-ass naked Barbees," Freaksome replied. The COs could get the same invitation as the check-ins.

"If there's a smart guy out there on the range, tell me what these two things have in common? A womb and a booty hole?"

"They both looking for a pole," Freaksome answered cell 236's question. The joke was originally formulated by Freaksome, but he didn't even ask the question anymore. He got a bigger thrill out of giving the answer.

"Man, ain't you afraid you'll catch AIDS?" the CO interrupted Freaksome's conversation.

"Shit, I gotta die of something," Freaksome replied, thinking that justified his ignorance.

"Man, where the hell we at?" whispered one of the check-ins.

After they had walked through all eight ranges, not one check-in had found someone, who would take one of them in the cell.

"I'll give y'all a mattress and you'll have to sleep in the dry tank," the CO said finally. He put them in a common area to sleep in. They didn't have a sink, toilet, or running water in the room. They had to use a cup to urinate in. They would have to wait, until another bus came in to relieve the over-populated hole, or take the SHU inmates to another holdover area.

I need to get me a book of stamps from somebody, from somewhere, Yank, a.k.a Gank-Ain't-Got-No-License thought, as he patrolled the rec yard. He covered every section several times for two hours straight and still had not come up with one wrinkled, beat-up stamp. Everyone on the compound knew Yank's activity was to lust after the women and steal out of the kitchen. You couldn't loan him a dime, because he wouldn't even pay back a nickel.

Yank posted up by the softball field, scanning the crowd. Determined to find a prey, he refused to go back into the unit without a book of stamps. He saw the dice game players as his victims, disregarding the fact they had won the ninety stamps, he'd made from muling the cereal and oatmeal out of the kitchen that morning. Yank used Carmouche, as the scapegoat.

Yank thought he would have won if his homie hadn't kept standing over him, asking for the few stamps he owed him. Dealing with Yank, you couldn't loan him any more than you could afford to give away. The only thing you'd get in return were a lot of promises. *I promise you, you'll have it by tomorrow, I got you,* was his favorite line, as he shook your hand.

You'd know that Yank had lied to you again, but all you could do is stand on your threat. *Man, have my shit by tomorrow.* Yank was going to pay you on the thirty-third of the month.

Yank's radar picked up Shakur coming out of the unit. He needed to catch Shakur, before he reached the crowded sidewalk. Shakur noticed Yank's fast movement, so he slowed down his pace. Yank met him on the bottom step.

"Akh, let me holla at cha."

Shakur laughed. He didn't have to brace himself; he already knew that Yank was going to bring some propaganda to the table. It wouldn't be Yank, if he didn't try to run some watered-down game on you. A five-year-old would have realized that.

"I'm listening," Shakur said, giving Yank his two minutes of fame.

"Akh, I need a book, until tomorrow. Come on now, this me now," Yank said, spreading his hands wide. "I got'cha tomorrow, I promise."

Shakur's laughter surface. It overflowed his system, to much to be caged up. "Yank, I know better, but I'm going to give you this book, because of your Niyyah."

"What is a Niyyah?" Yank questioned, hoping the word Niyyah could be used to con a couple more Muslims out some books of stamps.

"Niyyah means good intention."

Good intention? Yank thought, as he watched Shakur separate fifteen stamps from the loose stamp pile. Only at Petty Rock was a book considered to be fifteen stamps instead of twenty.

"Yank, now I'd like to share a Hadith with you. This brother paddled ten miles down the river to his neighbor's house to borrow some money from his neighbor. He promised to pay it back on a certain date, but when that date arrived, the brother didn't return the small sum of money. One day, the neighbor saw a bottle washed up on the bank. There was a note, along with the borrowed money. It had been so long, the neighbor had forgotten about the money, but the brother did hold up to his promise. Yank, your word can only carry you, as far as you allow it."

"Thank you, Akh, I got'cha," Yank said, as he leaped up the stairs two-by-two.

Yeah, I know you done got me, Shakur thought, as he yelled, "Yank, I know you are not going to play dice with that money I gave you. If you do, it's like I'm a part of your wrongdoing."

"Come on, Akh. Allah already know you ain't gonna bet that water is wet," Yank replied out of breath, as he raced up the stairs.

The rec yard was swarming with people. They were branched off in large sections, like Baby Shaka Zulu Warriors, ready and prepared for war if necessary. No group wanted to be singled out by the tower. The tower guards were trained to watch the people and the movement of the people. They could read the expression and body language of the people, as a group would come together. The tower guards would watch to see, if it was a social gathering or an aggressive gathering. Until they determined the mood, they would be on alert for this group activity. If they did not detect aggression, they would dismiss them and zone in on another group's activity. A family of guys swirled by Shakur.

Dirt acknowledged Shakur, because they had been at another prison together, "What's up, big Akh?"

"Dirt, I see you got your gloves on, you gettin' ready to put in that work?" Shakur asked.

"Naw, big Akh, I don't kill people no more," Dirt replied. He had misunderstood what Shakur meant.

Shakur was only asking if he was getting ready to do push-ups, as he walked the yard.

"Al-hamdu lillah," Shakur mumbled, the Arabic word meaning, *surely all praises be to Allah,* (Allah is the proper name for GOD, who is the Creator of all that exists), and may his peace and commendations be on his Messenger (Muhammad), as well as his family, companions, and those who follow his guidance. Shakur thought, *If it's the will of Allah, brother Dirt will report back to his rightful place in Islam.* All Muslims praise Allah and seek Allah's aid. They seek refuge in Allah from the evil of their own souls and from the wickedness of their own deeds. Whomever Allah guides shall never go astray, and whomever Allah allows to go astray shall never find guidance.

The crowd on the yard started creeping, easing, and sliding up the sidewalk. Shakur's eyes settled on the double doors. By the crowd's movement, he knew the new arrivals were coming out. "If you ain't never seen hell break loose before, you'll see it today," he said to himself.

People were lined up on both sides of the sidewalk, like they were waiting on their hometown parade. Sten led the flock in his wheelchair, every push he gave himself carried him ten steps. As he wheeled between the mobs, they were mean-mugging him, and some of the guys had towels around their necks, with their hands in their pockets.

"Say, anybody here know anybody from Detroit?" Sten asked, giving himself less powerful strokes.

"Yeah, you have a ball-playing ass homie, named Tario, in CD block," someone in the crowd replied.

"Man, Tario is like that with that ball, ain't he?" Sten shouted excitedly, wheeling his chair around trying to find the face of the person, who had assisted him with that little piece of information. Nobody replied to his second question, though. Sten wheeled himself backwards a few times, waiting patiently to get a response, but it never came. He wheeled back around to put some distance between him and his bus people.

As the guys came down the sidewalk, they were repeatedly running upon the same questions. "Where you from? Where'd that bus come from?" Before they reached the end of the runway, they would all have met someone from their geographical location.

"Hey Homie, come take a walk with me, I'll take you to meet the other homies," KC announced to a new arrival. KC led the guy to a blind spot, as his homies trailed them. The whole compound knew that this guy was about to get smashed. They posted up. KC's homies closed in on the new arrival. "Man, you did say you know RB off the streets, right?"

"Yeah, I know him. He's from my side of town." RB stepped forward from around the crowd. Wrapped around his right fist was his belt and dangling from it was his lock. The guy started talking fast, when he saw the lock on the belt. "RB, I used to fuck with ..." RB wasn't trying to hear anything the guy had to say, he had some words of his own.

"Yeah, nigga, I know who the fuck you are. You got Mayo a life fucking sentence."

With no time wasted, the locks began to leap out. An octopus' family didn't have as many arms. Locks landed against the new arrival's head. Chunks and chunks of flesh hit the pavement, and finally his unconscious body. The group continued to punish the motionless body with kicks as well as ice picks.

They only quit, when someone let them know the staff was heading in their direction. It was the secretary from that unit, the baddest female on the compound, petite, beautiful, slim waist, and pretty in the face. Guys would do more whistling than a flock of birds, when she stepped through. She was a dime, without question.

The mob dropped their weapons. They walked calmly, peacefully, and lustfully toward her. If their lookout man had continued trying to get him a blow off, they would have been caught red-handed. She smiled at the mob to let them know she came in peace.

"There goes that baby," someone screamed.

They were going to give you the punishment, they felt you deserved. They could be ruthless, or they could be passionate in the next breath. After it was done, they felt no need to continue punishing the informant. Especially, since their lust had kicked in from the sight of the beautiful woman that was walking up on them. They immediately switched roles from murderous devils into their lustful state. A few guys were in the windows, watching Chase and the other two guys climb the steps to their unit. The officer ran off their names and cell numbers, as they entered the unit.

"Damn, man. I hope I don't get no celly!" Mareese cried.

"I'm going to see where they from," Mustafa said, pushing off the rail. He waited, until the officer finished giving the new inmates their hygiene and three stamped envelopes. "How many people came off that bus?" he asked.

Damn, I hate when these niggas always ask that same damn shit, one of the arrivals thought, but he answered the question, "Thirty-one"

He related everything to Mu, giving him the lowdown concerning their bus crew. "Eleven checked in ASAP. Eight check-ins at the door, so only twelve hit the pound."

Now that all the information was in the open, he depended on Mustafa to relay it to everyone, hopefully cutting down on answering the same question a hundred times. Chase looked around the unit, looking for his homies or for someone he knew. He caught two guys scoping him out, but to his knowledge, he didn't know any of them. Not a face looked familiar to him.

J-Copone walked out of the laundry room to get some more washing powder. Chase's 5'6" frame and Al-B-Sure look caught his attention. *Dude look like Gangsta B lil brother*, he thought. Gangsta B used to be J-Copone's main man. He actually tried to walk in Chase's big brother's footsteps. Gangsta B was an all-around playa, a hood legend. Chase was among his bus crew, when J-Copone walked up on him.

"Say, woady, don't I know you?" he addressed Chase.

"I'm Gangsta B's lil brother," Chase revealed, thinking maybe this guy would know or had heard of his brother.

J-Copone nodded, biting down on his bottom lip, "Yeah, round, I thought so." J-Copone first used the term *woady,* because that is what they called a person, when they didn't know their name. Then he called Chase *round*, which is what they called someone that was from a *surrounding* city.

"How old were you, when GB died?"

"I was seven, when my brother got killed." Chase never tried to get credit from his brother's name. He built his own reputation.

"You just coming to jail?"

"Naw," Chase stated, with a head motion. "I been in the system for a few years."

"Where you coming from?"

"An FCI in South Carolina."

"I heard that one of them places is full of hot mothafuckas. They say cats go back to court, and when they come back, their homies fix them niggas a meal, and niggas run around braggin' about how they got real nigga's life sentences! Round, you're a better man than me. I can't feel comfortable around shit like that! Shit, woady, I been done spilt blood, ya heard me?"

"I did. That's why I'm back in the penitentiary," Chase told him.

Chase did not have his brother's size, but he definitely did have his heart and carried the same mentality. People would often take Chase's 140 pounds for granted. J-Copone and Chase were kicking it about the old days, discussing how hustlers could easily have made a dollar on the corner and didn't have to worry about getting snitched on. Once drug dealers got to talking that talk, no other issues could change the channel, but one of the guys, who had been scoping Chase out, decided to try his hand.

"Yo, Capone," the guy called out.

Chase's eyes found the mouth to the voice. J-Copone's back was turned to the two guys. "J-C, you can't save them all," the guy finished the sentence and winked at Chase.

J-Copone knew the guy's characteristics, since they had been in the unit together for a couple of years. The guy would always play homosexual games with the new arrivals, in some form or fashion. The majority of the time, he wanted to be the woman.

J-Copone worked open his three bottom buttons on his long sleeve khaki shirt and secretly removed the nine-inch razor sharp bone crusher. With the right force applied, it would sink through a concrete block.

"Here you go. You gonna need this worse than a hog needs slop, lil one. Use it, if you even feel disrespected."

J-Copone knew the hood-bred killers, and they didn't play games. They were strictly about handling their business and putting guys to sleep. The crew Chase used to run with, had grown up to kill or be killed. Chase came off the porch slanging heroin, dealing hand-to-hand combat with murderers, thieves, gangstas, and killers.

The two guys were walking away, laughing and joking. The big mouth predator didn't see the knife, but he felt all nine inches of it, as Chase drove it into his side several times. With the last and final strike, Chase twisted the knife, trying to cause internal bleeding.

"Since you want to play pussy, now you gettin' fucked," Chase growled.

J-Copone stabbed the other guy in the jaw. When he attempted to stab him again in the head, the eight-inch piece of Plexiglas broke off in the guy's head.

As the two guys went and got sewed up, there were no loose lips sinking ships and neither was revenge on their agenda. Chase and J-Copone became more than homies; they became co-defendants.

∂ - ∽

AA Unit was exceptionally quiet, unlike any other unit, as they sat there watching a movie. If something funny was said or done, there would be only a little chuckle or laugh and that would be it. On the other blocks, they would go on and on with things, and there would be loud, outright laughter.

As Zeek Bey walked into Room 349, the lockers immediately caught his attention. Both doors on both lockers were cut off. He already knew what had become of the doors. They were used to make knives. *Knives to supply an individual's car. Knives to pay off addiction bills. More knives to take lost souls with.*

"Hey, brother, you tryin' to cop a piece of steel?"

Zeek Bey turned facing the door. A guy stood there smiling at him.

"Naw, fam."

"Sometime, they're better off left, where they at," the hustler replied.

He was aware that his homie had an expensive, serious drug habit. The hustler landed a deal his homie could not refuse. He had offered fifteen books of stamps per door. Since when was a junkie going to turn down a free hundred dollars? His addiction was way stronger than his will to do right. The knives he distributed, were the same knives, that left him looking like a cheese shredder. He had sold knives outside his car, and that was a major violation.

Chapter 5

Monday Morning, 7:30 a.m.

At the announcement of general work call, Zeek Bey went outside to the rec yard. He didn't have to report to a job like Facilities. People work in the facilities department as painters, plumbers, electricians, and brick masons. They were the maintenance crew that fixed things around the prison. Other guys worked in Unicor, a slave factory, building cables, making mail bags, furniture, or clothes, for example. Unicor was a government owned business, and they paid in grades. If you did not have your GED or your high school diploma, you could only get paid at a Grade 4.

They could make anywhere from five cents to five dollars a day, depending on their grade. The BOP claimed, this private owned business was brought forth to help the inmate with paying off their court fines. There was always a long waiting list, because some people weren't fortunate to have family finances, and this was a means for them to provide for themselves. On the other hand, you had people working to save up their money. It allowed people with experience and longevity to be placed at the top of the list, disregarding the people who needed the finances, so they could meet the quarterly $25 pay requirement of their fine or restitution. If an inmate didn't have the money to make that quarterly requirement, disciplinary action would be taken. You would be placed on the FRP refusal list, meaning you would be placed on "maintenance pay." This means no matter how many hours, or where you worked, you would only earn $5.25 per month. There were other types of discrimination that went along with FRP refusal. For example, you could only spend $25 a month at the commissary, while the rest of the population could spend $290 a month. No matter what, you had to somehow get the $25 into your account each quarter, so you wouldn't miss your payment.

As the day began to unfold and take its toll, Zeek sat back on top of a white steel removable table, enjoying the fresh air and soaking in his environment. In the prison environment, you have to stay aware of your surroundings at all times, especially on the rec yard. If you see different cars, clicks, or sets huddling up, you knew it was time to head back to the unit. However, if it was your set, you would have to support your homies or your people.

Zeek's eyes scanned the two guys standing by the track, three more leaning up against the fence, and a couple more youngsters posted up over at the gate. Zeek smiled, because he knew these guy's intentions. They were all waiting on Shakur to finish his exercise, so they could pick his brain. Shakur ran five to ten miles every other day and afterwards, would do pushups around the track. Shakur stood 6'2" and weighed around 180 pounds. He had maybe two or three percent body fat.

As Shakur made his way off the track, the three different groups of brothers stumbled over each other, trying to beat the other one to Shakur. The first one to arrive would be able to get an answer to the question, that disturbed him the most.

The guys started forming a full circle around Shakur, standing heel to heel. The officer in the tower opened the window. It was not because he feared a violent event was about to take place, but rather to see what type of knowledge he could gain from the conversation and maybe apply to his own life as well. He knew Shakur did not give out misinformation and did not sugarcoat anything. He had heard Shakur say that's what was wrong with the world today; people were always trying to sugarcoat everything.

The Tower-2 officer laid his gun in the chair. He knew Shakur was among good company. There was another group of guys that all had their attention set on the female guard, as she was patrolling her area of the rec yard. This sister had Beyonce hips and Lil Kim lips. They all said they would catch her again, before shift change, and if not, then they'd catch her again tomorrow.

It wasn't too often, you would see Shakur with a group of people other than at the chess table. This activity had come into play from one of the youngest, who Shakur would counsel. Every time he asked a question, bystanders always gathered to get a piece of the conversation or just half a sentence.

New Jersey-G, a.k.a Blind Man, was good about having debates with people. He would try to repeat words and sentences of Shakur, but couldn't fully explain himself, by producing that full understanding, so he would end up bringing his opponent to Shakur. Shakur refused to let anyone walk away feeling lost, so he would take your misconception and break it down off the dribble, like Dwayne Wade.

The brothers who huddled around Shakur would be an Anthony Hamilton or a Jada Kiss. Every question that flew out of their mouths would be a Why? A brother approached Shakur and fired off a question, without even having the common courtesy to ask, if he could ask a question.

"Brother Shakur, why black folks can't come together for nothing?"

Shakur understood that every prisoner in America was in some form of gang. It came down to religion, state, where you came from. The Midwest rode together, the North rocked together, and the Dirty Dirty South ran together.

He looked at the faces of each individual. "Because we look for things to keep us separated. Some of us snorted up our nose, and say I don't like him, because he's a Blood, or I don't like him, because I'm a Muslim, and he's a Christian. When we divide ourselves, we allow ourselves to be conquered. We need to put aside those little differences. Religion was broken up into seventy-two groups."

Zeek closed in on the group, like a dangerous species tiptoeing in on its prey. He needed to hear what Shakur had to say, before he went into one of his long speech spills. Like Mr. Mack used to say, "You just can't say everything in one word."

Shakur continued, "We were born in the fetus position, and we all have different ideology, due to our differences. It could be religions ... one could be Muslim, Christian, Buddhist. When you look at the fetus, it is in the *Salat* position. The fetus does not have a religion; it is just in a total submissive position. As it grows up, it learns about different religions, and it starts deviating from its Muslim beginning. The different ideas of these religions give separation a birth in the heart of the fetus. We have to put away these silly differences, in order to secure a future of greatness for our seeds. It is our responsibility to teach them and show them, our ways were wrong, and they need not to follow our wrongs, but express themselves. Teach them to stand up and take their rightful positions. We must stop being selfish and put our differences aside, so we can overcome this hell that we are living in and give our babies the future they deserve. Each and every one of us must look inside ourselves, and change the wrong we see within ourselves. Once we make those corrections, then we will know that we will be back to getting on the right path. The path the creator put us on!

"We must teach them to respect their mother, their father, family members, all the people in their community, and even people not in their community. Like Dr. Martin Luther King, Jr. said, *It is best, we shall overcome.*"

ॐ - ॐ

9:00 a.m.

Sten decided to go outside to get some fresh air and take advantage of the beautiful sunshine, while it was available. Sten held the job title of a weekend orderly. All that was required of him was that, he dumped the trash on Friday and Saturday nights, before he went to bed or early the next morning. It was done on his call.

Sten saw the crowd around Shakur. On numerous occasions, he briefly heard bits and pieces of Shakur's conversations. He thought the brother was brilliant, so he rolled over to the group.

"It's our duty to teach the young people, because they are our future. Our youth definitely get lost like most are lost today. Generation after generation will be repeating itself. If our generation doesn't get any better, we gonna be in serious trouble. Things that take us off our duty are a lack of commitment and self-respect. The thing I fear is not the lack of care we have for our seeds, it's just we have taken our eyes off them completely due to the drugs.

"There is no way on God's green Earth, we should be afraid of our seeds... that goes against the principles God set in operation, and the original people would never accept such a thing. We need to get back to our original state of mind, in order to stop the fear cycle, due to drugs affecting our communities. Our babies see our lower self-control in our lives, and we've lost their respect. Once we get our respect back, we'll get our generation back in order. We adults, mothers, and fathers, must cease to do things of the lower nature in view of our seed, because these things cripple us, and we lose generations, due to the fact of not acknowledging our seed as important."

℮ - ℴ

8:30 p.m. After Yard Recall

Yard recall is that time, when most of the prisoners have to leave the yard, the education department, their work area, or anywhere else, and report back to their assigned housing unit.

Sten wheeled himself out of his cell. He pushed his wheel chair against the wall, so it wouldn't interfere with the guy's path, as they traveled the tier. He stood by the rail twice a day. This was his form of exercise to strengthen his legs. His legs were completely out of shape compared to his forearms and biceps. He could wheel himself all day over the large compound, but after standing at the rail for ten minutes, his legs couldn't wait to get back in the wheelchair.

Sten's unit could house a hundred and fifty people, but now, there were only a hundred twenty-five people in his unit. Most were African-Americans, and the reason wasn't by black being the dominant color. The other twenty-five people had either transferred or had been sent to the SHU for a disciplinary reason.

The unit had twelve showers. They were all located at the end of the range: six upstairs and six downstairs. There were nine phones and four TVs. The TVs were designed to entertain and hold each group hostage. The Spanish guys had their own TV, which would play nothing, but Spanish programming. You'd catch other races gathered around the Spanish TV, their eyes glued to the screen, as they drooled, craved, and lusted over the Spanish senoritas. You couldn't escape a beautiful, sexy feminine female anywhere on the Spanish TV. Even the news broadcaster was a dime. On the commercials, you were guaranteed to see nines and dimes. The soap operas were loaded with models and video honeys.

Then you had the sports TV. You'd catch nothing on that TV, but baseball, basketball, and football, because brothers don't watch soccer or hockey. Sometimes, they'd be generous and show their hospitality, by letting the white guys watch NASCAR. The white guys would trick the brothers into looking forward to watching the races. Hell, they'd been tricking them for over four hundred years, so why stop now!

Then you had the BET fans. That crew wasn't going for anything else. The only channel they would watch was BET. They were so in love with that station, they'd watch re-runs of old BET movies over and over. The only time they'd even contemplate changing the channel, was when the BET news would come on. They were BET babies, raised by the TV and rap music.

The white guys also had a TV, where they'd watch CMT every morning, John Wayne westerns, or Animal Planet all day. Sometimes, they would watch the news if something interesting was happening out in the real world.

Then you had the movie bandits. They lived to watch that TV. When the prison would show the institution movies on the weekends and holidays, you wouldn't hear a peep out of them. They'd be quieter than a church mouse. You could hear a pin drop in the unit. From when the doors unlocked at 5:30 a.m. until lockdown, you'd have these mobs posted around all four TVs, and if you changed the channel on one of them, you did so at your own risk. You could look forward to some stitches. You might get a lock slammed across your head or penetrated by a knife. Or who knows, it might be your unlucky day, and you'd get a taste of both.

The guys in the unit were an equally divided set on a triple-beam scale. If they spent twelve hours minding their

business, and the other twelve hours handling their
business, they wouldn't have time for anyone else's
business.

This was the new system, which was different from the
old system. The federal prison system had changed. There
was a new state of mind that overshadowed the prison
culture of a few years back. In this day and time, there was
a shortage of real people. You had more guys willing to be
a snake than be real. Respect had gone out the window,
and you had guys playing roles, like they didn't need to
respect anybody. You had fresh guys coming into the
system, who had messed up the dope game, now they were
messing up the chain gang.

Sten smiled, as he watched a group of inmates hugging
the steps. He knew for a fact, from experience, that two of
the individuals among the group would be telling those
federal riley-ass lies. Sten allowed his eyes to roam the
unit. He saw that the new brother, who had just come into
the fold of Islam, had his cell door open. Sten put his arms
to work. Brother Desmond was sitting in his cell watching
TV.

"As-Salaamu 'Alaikum!" Sten greeted him. This
meant, *May the peace of Allah-God be upon you.*

"Wa 'Alaikum-as-Salaam!" Brother Desmond
returned the greeting, which was wishing Allah's peace
upon Sten as well.

They greeted each other with the greeting words of "Peace," which was a prayer that Allah's peace be upon one, who was striving toward the oneness with Allah and the human family on the planet Earth. It was obligatory that all Muslim brothers greet each other, when they see one another. The Holy Qur'an says in Sarah 4:86, *And when you are greeted with a greeting, greet with one better than it or return it. Surely, Allah ever takes account to all things.*

"Brother Desmond, I see that you are off into the program. I'll come back some other time. I'll let you enjoy the movie."

"Naw, Brother Sten, that movie can wait. I'd rather have some teaching," Desmond said, making room for Sten to wheel in.

Sten pushed his glasses up the bridge of his nose and said, "Man can never know anything, unless he has been taught, and he can never be taught, unless he has a teacher. It is our responsibility for those who know, to pass on the knowledge, wisdom, and understanding that we have deep within us. Now, think about this, Brother Desmond. What if the person, who invented shoes, hadn't passed on the knowledge of how to make shoes? Would we have shoes today? Of course, the shoes we have today are better than the ones our parents and grandparents had yesterday, but it is that knowledge, and know-how from yesterday, that we build on and the knowledge of today, is for our generation to build on for a better shoe in the future."

"Why did you use the shoe for an example?" Desmond asked.

"Well, brother, the shoe is made for what?"

"The feet!" Desmond responded.

"And the feet serve what purpose, Brother?"

"To walk, to stand, and to run on," Desmond replied, excitedly.

"That's right, Desmond. However, let's look a little deeper, today. The shoe is a covering, for the protection of the feet. As you said, brother, the purpose of the feet are for walking, standing, and running, to name a few. Where are you walking or running to, that you need protection from? What are you standing on, that you need to have a covering for?"

Sten smiled, as Desmond was pondering the questions. He continued, "Listen, Blackman. For too long, the black man has been standing on the wrong principles--walking and running in the path of destruction. We need protection, as we strive to get back on the straight path of Allah. In our prayers, we say, *Oh, Allah, guide me on the straight path, the path of those, who have favor, not those whose portion is wrath, or those who go astray.* So, we need a covering that only Allah can give. Are you with me? You see, Brother Desmond, the foot has twelve inches in it. There are twelve inches on a ruler, so we have rulers called feet. A left foot and a right foot. The guide to hell and the guide to Heaven. It's all on which way you go with your feet. Okay now, when the Muslim pray, and he is in the position of *Jalsa,* the sitting position. He plants the toes of his right foot firm, as he sits up straight and pulls the left under his body, under submission. Brother Desmond, you know this is a very deep subject, and I don't have the time to break it all down at one time..."

Desmond interrupted Sten mid-sentence, "Break down some of... what we didn't finish tonight, we'll finish tomorrow, if it's God's will!"

"Hold on, little brother. We are going to get to that, but you know that the Holy Day of Atonement is coming right up!"

"A-toll-ment. What's that?" Desmond queried.

"Atonement, Brother. Not A-toll-ment. Think At-one-ment. Because the Blackman is meant to be at one with each other and with their God. The Holy Day of Atonement is a nationally recognized Holy Day, that was born October 16, 1995. You may have heard this day called the Million Man March. This day was given to us by Allah, through the voice and call of the honorable Minister Louis Farrakhan, who said that as a Blackman, we should take a day of absence from work, school, or hustling--whatever he may be doing and wherever he might be and come and bring their sons or grandsons, or sons bring their fathers and grandfathers. All males leave their wives, girlfriends, and daughters at home. The honorable Minister Louis Farrakhan called for a million black men and nearly two million showed up! During his national address, Minister Farrakhan spoke on unity among us and regaining unity with Allah, the creator of Heavens and the Earth."

"The basis of the Holy Day of Atonement and the Eight Steps of Atonement is to regain our source of power recognizing and reconnecting with the power source, Allah. This is a force that we have to recognize within self. As the first step, notice that we are talking about stepping, which takes us to what were just talking about, our feet. However, the first step is recognizing that we have been wrong and off the straight path, when the wrong has been pointed out to us by someone that Allah has brought into our circle of influence, or by the *Self-Accusing Spirit*. This is the beginning of the Resurrection and coming forth by night. Once this wrong has been pointed out, or we should acknowledge the wrong, and we should confess our wrongs to Allah and his creation."

Desmond saw Sten look at his watch. It had been twenty minutes before lockdown, when Sten arrived.

"Brother Sten, I know you have to go, but what are the other steps of atonement?" Desmond asked.

"I want to be the first to invite you out to this year's Holy Day of Atonement program on October 16, as we commemorate this great day."

"Are you going to be speaking?"

"Yes! And there will be a host of other speakers, as well from other communities and some poetry. Brother Desmond, you write poetry, don't you?"

"Not really, you know, just a little," Desmond replied.

"Come on, brother, what you have is a gift to be shared with your brothers. Don't ever bury your talents, Blackman! You see, it is written word that gives us insight into the past to prepare for the future."

"Brother Sten, let me ask you this, before you go. How come you always talk about the past and future, together?"

Sten looked at Desmond for a few seconds over the top of his glasses and took a sip of coffee. "The most honorable Elijah Muhammad taught us, that history is best suited to reward its researcher. So, it's true that what you don't know, can hurt you!"

"I thought it was *what you don't know can't hurt you*," Desmond said, thinking that Sten had made a mis-quote.

"No sir, Blackman, what you don't know can hurt. The scripture says, *The people are destroyed for the lack of knowledge.* What kind of knowledge does the Blackman lack, that keeps him in the destructive patterns of living? The same destructive patterns of living that got both of us right here at USP Petty Rock! Around people, who are still being destroyed and destroying themselves and each other. Do you feel me? You know, Brother Desmond, many black men never knew who their father was. Now, just imagine you have a son, whose father might be a great man. A rich man with power and respect, but the son, because of a separation between the father and mother, never knows him. The father is the son's link to his heritage, his history. The son has no family history, other than what he creates for himself, because his mother was made a prostitute or a junkie and gave her son to foster care to be cared for, by someone other than herself. Therefore, he lacks any knowledge of his family. This is what has happened to the Blackman, Brother Desmond."

Sten looked at his watch again. "Beloved, we only got a few more minutes, so soak this up. The most Honorable Elijah Muhammad said on page 31 in the *Message to the Blackman in America, It is knowledge of self that so-called Negroes lack, which keeps them from enjoying freedom, justice, and equality. This belongs to them divinely, as much as it does to other nations of the earth.* You see, Brother Desmond, it's pertinent that you and I study history. In particular, our black history! Then we can rid our people of misguidance and mis-education. Do you know who Carter G. Woodson was?"

"No, sir," Desmond said, looking a little embarrassed.
"Brother, never be afraid to say, *I don't know.*" Because if you act as if you know, then people usually assume that you do, and you know what they say about assume. You make an ass out of you and me!"

Desmond laughed aloud. "Brother Sten, you crazy!"
"No, sir, beloved. Crazy like a fox! Anyway, Carter G. Woodson was a black scholar, author, and educator. You may have heard of one of his most popular books titled, *The Mis-education of the Negro*, where he writes on page 84 and I quote, *Starting after the Civil War, the opponents of freedom and social justice decided to work out a*

program, which would enslave the Negroes. Mind, in as much as the freedom of his body had to be concealed. It was well understood that if by teaching of history, the Whiteman could be further assured of his superiority, and Negroes could be made to feel that he had always been a failure, and that the subjection of his will to some other race is necessary. The freed man, then, would still be a slave. Yes, brother, a slave to mental death. Easily led in the wrong direction, and hard to lead in the right.

"So, Dr. Woodson came up with Negro History Week. A week where, so-called Negroes got together and studied their ancient history, then took that knowledge back and shared it with those, who didn't know that they were more than just a slave, and that they were all descendants of illustrious kings, queens, great military men, and successful farmers. The cotton that cloth is made out of today came from Africa. The rice that many of us eat today came from Africa. The date palm, the banana, and if I had more time, I could go on and on, Brother. But Negro history week is how we now have a Black History Month! And it's so important to recognize that other people have a history month. You don't hear about a Mexican history month, a Chinese history month, or an Italian history month.

"We are a people who have been displaced and had everything taken from them: our language, our religion, our God. It is vitally important that the base of our knowledge start with who we were, because as Noble

Drew Ali said, *What your ancient forefathers were, you are today.*

"So this shows you and me who and what we can become. The Atonement process is just as important. We are drastically in need of spiritual rejuvenation. Why do black folks tear up their own neighborhoods? Why are we so divided? Why do we fight, kill, and hate one another? It's a spiritual disease that we suffer from, Brother Desmond! We have to recognize that we have lost our connection with each other and when we've lost that between each other, we've lost our connection to Almighty God Allah. When we connect with each other, we will connect with God. This has to be taught.

"Too many of us ritualize religion. We need to recognize the ritual is a painted picture of what we need to be doing. When we reconnect with the power source, we'll create a new government and totally new way of life that will include freedom, justice and equality for all people. But it starts with self-improvement, which is the basis for community development.

"As Salaam Alaikum Wa Lihub Billah, may the peace and love of Allah be with you. Brother Desmond, I have to go and don't forget to come on out to our program next Saturday. Inshaa-Allaah."

Brother Desmond greeted Sten, as he was wheeling back out of the cell, and Sten returned the greeting once more.

Chapter 6

"Chow call," the unit officer's voice echoed, through BB housing. "You're next for chow. You have exactly five minutes to exit out the door, before the sliders close."

Chase heard the CO make the announcement, as he was sitting in his room, looking out of the window at the inmates from the other units racing back and forth to the chow hall. He really didn't want to go to the mess hall, but since they had started this controlled move thing, he would go to chow every meal, just for the fresh air and to stretch his legs.

"Last call for the dining hall. Make sure you take your IDs," the CO shouted.

Chase threw his prison ID in his pocket and glided out of the door. Chase never touched the rail going or coming, when he used the stairs. Grabbing the rail was like collecting a palm full of germs. The stairs were trashy, with commissary wrappers draping over them and would remain trashy, until 7:30 in the morning. The orderly assigned to that detail cleaned them twice a day, at 7:30 a.m. and 12:30 p.m. That was it, and that was all. The institution didn't pay overtime, and the orderlies weren't trying to do community volunteer service.

An officer stood in the center of the softball field. He called himself trying to keep the guys from taking a shortcut.

"On the sidewalk, guys. No walking on the grass," said the officer.

"Man, fuck you! If a mothafucka knock ya ass down, I'll walk on your ass," someone in the crowd called out.

"Come on, you guys. Don't do me like that," the officer pleaded, as a herd of guys made their way past him, walking in the grass.

The officer knew that it was going to happen anyway. His job required him to stand out there, looking stupid, at least attempting to keep most of the guys on the sidewalk. He was only there for decoration and to keep the higher rank happy.

Two more COs were posted up like light poles, by the metal detector. They stood firm guard by the detector and would not let you enter the chow hall, unless you cleared it.

"Hats off, shirt tails in," one of the COs ordered.

Ms. Coon walked up and joined the officers. Chase pushed through the chow hall double doors and intentionally brushed the sides of the metal detector, setting it off.

"Justin Chase, get over here, so I can pat you down," Ms. Coon ordered. Chase put his arms out and spread his legs, going along with the normal process.

"What you got on you?" Ms. Coon asked, as she was giving him a thorough frisk search.

"Nothing, but my gun," Chase replied, with a lustful smile.

"Umm-huh. I thought the Feds stripped you of that pistol..."

"24/7, I'm palmin' that iron. 24/7, I'm try'na smash a dime. 24/7, I'm committing a crime," Chase sang.

"Go on about ya business now, Justin, and stay out of trouble."

"I'm from CP-3. Gangsta is the only thing I can be."

"Then you need to change that," Ms. Coon replied, as she waved at him.

"Then it wouldn't be me," Chase remarked, with a wink.

Ms. Coon watched Chase walk away and a smile crept onto her lips. She thought of the very first time she frisked Chase, because he had set the metal detector off.

"Maybe it's your watch or your glasses," she suggested.

"No watch, no glasses," Chase replied.

Ms. Coon looked down at his brown Timberland boots. "Your shoes. The steel toes will set the metal detectors off every time," she advised.

"It went off, because I'm in heat," Chase stated back to her, laughing.

Chase walked on into the chow hall and looked over to his car's tables. He noticed, that lots of the seats were vacated. Normally, their table would be packed with guys from New Orleans, Louisiana, Mississippi, Baton Rouge, and other surrounding cities. Now, the institution control system allowed them to eat with inmates from their building only. The only way Chase would be allowed to eat with guys from another block, was if he'd take in a function with a religious group. That just was not going to happen. Chase was not into religion on the street, and he sure didn't come all the way to prison to get religious. Chase wasn't trying to hear about anybody's religion. When a guy invited Chase to church, Chase replied that church was no good for him, he needed to talk to God, himself. A Muslim asked Chase if he believed in God, and Chase answered by saying is pig pork. Chase produced his prison ID for the staff and after getting it scanned, slam-dunked it back into his pocket.

"You ate already. Get out of my line," the staff said to Car Wash, who was standing in front of Chase.

"I'm a repeat offender, so I'm going to double the line every day," Car Wash replied. "I'm going to get my issues."

"And try to get the next man's issues too," the staff added.

Chase's two homies saw him at the hot bar. "Man, lil one 'bout it. He put in work. That's why they call him

Chase, cause he bring that heat and ain't got no problem with pushin' that steel," Assassyn rapped.

"Stop puttin' stars on anotha nigga chest and put 'em on your own. All that fuckin' dick ridin'," scolded Tree.

"Nigga, fuck you!" Assassyn replied.

After the last inmate in line sat down, the clocked minutes of precision took effect. Cold hardened criminals dining in the chow hall had only ten minutes to eat what they chose to eat off their tray, and then had to vacate the building. No portion of the meal was allowed to travel off the mess hall premises. A variety of staff officers patrolled the area, observing the time, as if they were counting down the seconds on New Year's Eve. They screamed out every few minutes.

"You have two minutes left!" yelled a staff member.

The inmates were usually too busy in conversation with their homies to notice, if they were receiving the full ten minutes or not.

"You now have one minute and counting," the school teacher announced.

"This is their favorite part of the day," Sife commented, to Shakur and Mr. Pete.

"Y'all ain't gotta be scared to leave. I'll protect ya," taunted a skinny, pale-faced CO, with red hair and a penguin nose.

"Man, your scary ass couldn't break up a dog fight with pepper spray," an inmate replied.

Inmates took turns bumping their gums with this CO, and the CO lived for it.

"If y'all guys continue to talk instead of eating and get locked in my kitchen, I'll have y'all asses waxing the floor," threatened the CO.

"Man, fuck you and that mothafucka kitchen floor," a guy shouted.

"Naw, don't fuck the floor, fuck y'all celly," the CO said, smiling. He was a natural shit-talker. Guys would often tell him that he wanted to be black, and he always replied with, *My ole lady say I am from the waist down.*

"You poppin' off mighty slick, cause you got your bodyguards wit'cha."

"I don't need no bodyguards. I'm their bodyguard."

"The door is beginning to lock," the lieutenant shouted.

"The same way they lock the mothafuckin' door is the same way they'll unlock the mothafucka," someone shouted back.

The lieutenant chuckled and spoke into his walkie-talkie, before securing it back to his hip. The intercom erupted, "Beginning of the ten-minute move."

The inmates fell for the trick every time. They were the last unit to eat. They immediately deserted the chow hall and headed out the doors. They had places to go and people to see. The minority raced for the law library, while the majority flew like a bat out of hell to get a handball court, to the basketball court, the softball field, or the gambling games.

❮❯ - ❯❮

A group of Muslims was walking down the walkway in front of AA building. This unit was the capital of mischief. The guys pad-rolled from sunup to sunset.

"Popper Charlie, I'm going to beat you today," Tate promised, as he rolled the dice underhanded. The dice marched down the green blanket side by side, like a groom and bride walking down the aisle to the altar.

Popper Charlie caught the dice, before they could stop on the seven. "Not today, Tate. You might beat me, but it ain't gonna be none this year," he replied, while rattling the dice. He was called Popper Charlie, but the hustlas and playas called him Charging Charlie, because there was always a fee for everything, whether he just did something for you, shared the 411, or fed them a propaganda conversation.

Main's Girlie Girl magazines laid scattered on top of the red raincoat. He spotted Shakur among the group of Muslims and immediately put the sister books underneath some other magazines he had on display. Main wanted to show Shakur a little respect. He recalled Shakur's speech, the time he had seen his homie trying to rent out some magazines.

"Come holla at a pimp. I got these paperback ho's. Rent 'em by the hour, money back guarantee, if the magazine don't perform like kryptonite and leave ya feeling like superman with no power."

Shakur zoomed in on his homie, "Is that what you think about the sister, someone's mother, daughter, or wife? Our sisters have been disrespected for over four hundred years. When is enough going to be enough? We destroy our own queens, our own sisters, our own bloodline. When you kill one woman, it's like killing a whole nation. She produced two lives, two lives bring forth three consecutive lives and then the vine will multiply and bear the fruits for generations and generations to come," Shakur announced, with a strong voice. He peaked his fingers together in the form of a pyramid "So why feed our sisters crack? We don't need them at their lower self, but at their highest self. Our women have to raise, guide, and teach our babies! She nourished the infant, you and me! Now ask yourself, do you want a weak woman to have a weak baby? The weak-minded come from other weak minds. You have some mothers, who are powerful teachers and powerful leaders. You didn't want to have a weak mother, a weak grandmother, now did you? There will come a time, when all the drug dealers, the so-called pimps, and other people, who have mishandled and misguided the Earth, will have to answer for their inappropriate behavior. They call the woman Earth, because only she can shower the land with seeds.

Sometimes, you'll hear a guy say, I don't need no woman, I can take care of myself. That's one of the most foolish things a man can say. He's speaking through emotion, ignorance, bitterness, or hurt. A person with a rational mind should make clear thoughts. An irrational person is going to have cloudy thoughts and going to speak out through their hurt and pain of those ignorant thoughts. Man can't have sex with himself. He was put on earth to bear fruit. If he goes against that form of nature, he's breaking one of the wills of Allah, he's going against God"

"I see you're back at it again," Shakur said, bringing Main back to reality.

"I can't lay down, Akh, I gotta get down. You don't see no sister layin' down here," Main responded, pointing down to the magazine, as if Shakur's eye would follow his finger.

"When will I see you at Jumu'ah?"

"Friday."

"You said you'd be there last Friday and the Friday before that."

"Ice Cube got three movies called Friday," Main joked. "I'll be there this Friday."

"Inshaa-Allaah," Shakur replied.

"Inshaa-Allaah," Main repeated. *Yeah, if it's the will of Allah.*

After Shakur circled the block a couple more times with his brothers, he branched off to join Dirty.

102

In the Qur'an, they call the creator Allah. In the Bible, they call the creator God. The creator says a man should travel the Earth and make friendships all over the land with people of all walks of life.

Shakur and Dirty's communication had developed, the day he saw Dirty looking through a gun magazine. Shakur tested Dirty, to see if he really did possess any knowledge about weapons. Dirty passed with an A-plus, he actually knew more about guns then Shakur.

Dirty had gotten locked up for a petty white-collar crime, credit card scam. It would only be thirteen more months, before he would reach society once again. This was his first time getting locked up. He looked at his prison term as a vacation. He'd been giving a great deal of thought to selling guns. He mentioned it to Shakur, Shakur had made it his obligation to spend time and walk the track with Dirty. Shakur would put Dirty at the top of his agenda upon sight.

"As-Salaamu 'Alaikum, Shakur."

"Wa 'Alaikum-As-Salaam," Shakur greeted Dirty back.

"Akh, I saw a bad magazine today. They got some new handguns coming out," Dirty said, trying to bring up their daily topic and discussion about guns.

He liked to talk to Shakur about guns, because Shakur would fill in the gaps, where he wasn't too knowledgeable. Dirty knew that, once he got Shakur on the track of backsliding, Shakur would take him for a ride talking about the guns.

Five gang-bangers were walking ahead of Shakur and Dirty, all of them sagging. A couple of them wore shorts underneath shorts, to triplelize their sagging. They took turns hitting a blunt, passing it back and forth. The smell of weed was slamming into Shakur's face. The guys were discussing how they would smash the other gang-bangers, when they caught them off their territory.

Shakur's mind went to wandering, until his conscience cup spilled over. "You know, Dirty, in this day and time you see young guys, I'm talking about guys in their thirties, walking around sagging and acting out all kinds of other foolishness. They all are basically lost right now, and they're looking for something to follow. Take for instance, you hear rappers, NFL and NBA players are getting more money in this day and age than any other time in our history here in America. It's a good thing in one sense, and it's a bad thing in another, because now it gives them more money to put more guns on the streets. It's worse now than ever before, and when you look at that, you see that we have become the number one killers of ourselves. Killings of our people, with these guns, are at an all-time high. We need to go back and reteach our people, what to do with their money and their lives. We have to let them know how to respect each other and to come together, as civilized people, to change the condition of the younger generation, to give them better options to choose from. We have to let the people in this day and time know to stop leading our families down this path of destruction. We have to build more unity with our families, our loved ones, and our communities. It's our duty to take the guns out of our youth's hands and put something productive in their minds. You can't take something from people, without replacing it with something, so we have to step up and be the real role-models for our younger generation. We have to look in the mirror and clean ourselves up, pull our damn pants up and guide our youth into a brighter future, so our future generation will have no ignorance trying to lead them down the path of self-destruction."

"Brother, wasn't you out there sellin' guns to young people?" Dirty asked.

"Yeah, I got 95 years from slangin' that poison, killin' off our people. That is why I'm telling you to learn from my mistakes, so that yours will not cost you the price that I am already paying. My ignorance led me down this path that I'm traveling down now, but I could look at it as being a good thing, because I have become awakened to my ignorance, and now I'm trying to give something back to my community, to my people, as well as the world. If you put that destruction in the younger generation's hands, it will come back to slap you in the damn face. There are 30,000, who die annually from gun violence," Shakur manifested.

Chapter 7

On Friday at 12:30 p.m., Shakur made his way to the chapel for Jumu'ah. All of the prison's religious groups held their meetings in the chapel. Each belief had their day and time in one of the two rooms.

The Native-Americans had their own personal private piece of land for services. They had a quarter of an acre. No white man could walk on their worship grounds. It was off-limits to everyone except the Indians. They would get in their smoke lodge and burn wood, polluting the whole compound. That's how you knew it was their day of worship. That Friday, Dro became a Muslim by taking his Shahadah. He recited the first part of the Shahadah with sincerity:

Ash-hadu Anlaa Ilaha Illallaahu Wa Ash-hadu

Anna Muhammadan 'abduhu Wa Rasuuluh.

"I declare that there is no God but Allah, and I declare that Muhammad is his slave and the last messenger of Allah!"

Dro took on the name of Luqman. Ali always stayed in Dro's ear trying to bring him into the folds of Islam, but men don't make Muslims, only Allah does. Now, Luqman and Ali were more than homies, more than hustling partners. They had much more in common. They were brothers, strivers, and believers in Allah. They were Mississippi Muslims.

As soon as Shakur stepped his right foot in the room, where Jumu'ah was being held, he said, "A'udhu Billaahi mi-nash-shaytan-nir-rajeem," which meant, *I seek Allah's protection from the rejected devil.*

Mubeen was signing the Jamu'ah list, and Na'im stood beside him. Shakur Salaamed them and followed it up with a firm handshake.

"People are living in darkness and have no sense of direction. Brother Luqman, the people's minds, ears, and eyes need to be opened, they need to come out of their la-la land and come face to face with their reality," Shakur stated.

"Some people are mentally disturbed and emotionally blind. All they do is let their minds rumble. They can't get their feelings in perspective," Mubeen elaborated.

A brother called the adhan. He faced Mecca, with a finger plugged in each ear, to block out the other people's activities.

He chanted very clearly in moderation:

"Allaahu-Akbar, Allaahu-Akbar, Allaahu-Akbar, Allaahu-Akbar."

"Allah is the greatest."

"Ash-hadu An-laa Ilaha Illallaah, Ash-hadu An-laa Ilaha Illallaah."

"I declare there is no God but Allah."

"Ash-hadu Anna Muhammadan Rasuu-lullah, Ash-hadu Anna Muhammadan Rasuu-lullah."

"I declare Muhammad is the messenger of Allah."
"Hayya 'alas-salaah."

"Hayya 'alas salaah," (Come to prayer) he said twice, as he slowly turned his face to the right. "Hayya 'alal-falaah," (Prayer is ready) he repeated twice more, as he slowly rotated his face back towards the left. "Allaahu-Akbar, Allaahu-Akbar, La Ilaha Illallah," he said, facing straight ahead.

Brother Saleem gave the Khutbah. Saleem was a good brother, who talked the talk and walked the walk. People always observe a Muslim's character, and Shakur observed that Saleem was a good role model.

There were the three categories, Muslim (submitted to the will of Allah), Mu'min (believer), and Muhsin (a good doer.) Saleem was a muhsin, one who is afraid to commit even the smallest sin, as if Allah was going to drop a mountain on his head. Saleem led the brothers in congregation Salah, an Arabic word meaning connection. A Muslim performed the five daily prayers, because of their beliefs. They were promised paradise in the hereafter. The five Salah would keep them away from mischief and put them in remembrance of Allah.

"As-Salaamu 'Alaikum, Akhie," Shakur greeted Bucky Fields.

"Wa 'Alaikum-As-Salaam, Shakur," Bucky returned the greeting, with a firm handshake and higher blessing.

"You still pushing your pen?"

"Without a doubt," Buck smiled. "Another day, another dollar."

"Get your papers, Akh, and may Allah be pleased with you and continue blessing you."

"So, Shakur, what's on your agenda today?"

"I'm going to the class Leo Sullivan has twice a week, so I can support the brother with his cause. He's trying to give the young brothers a better outlook for the future. Trying to get them to come into the light and get them back on the right track. Hopefully, we can look forward to our next Obama or Michael Jordan, and make the world more peaceful."

"Anything's possible, if there's a will, there's a way. But Beloved, only Allah knows what's best."

After their conversation, Shakur went over to greet Ali and place his order, before it was too late. Their unit only had one microwave and being part of the long line wasn't his plan.

"As-Salaamu 'Alaikum, Ali."

"Wa 'Alaikum-As-Salaam, Shakur."

"What's on the menu for today?"

"I'm making some beef and fish corazon."

"Put me down for a fish one."

"Inshaa-Allaah," Ali replied.

Zayd walked over, "As-Salaamu 'Alaikum."

Ali and Shakur returned the greeting.

"What y'all two good brothers up to?" Zayd asked.

"Before recall, I'm running down to Ali's unit to get me a fish Corazon," Shakur stated.

"That sounds like a plan," Zayd replied.

"All the fish ones are gone. All I got left are three beef," Ali notified Zayd.

Zayd adjusted his glasses. "I'm cool. I'm trying to stop eating beef, and I need to lay off that grease for a while."

Mubeen's celly, Muhammad, joined the couple brother's small circle. "Ali, I heard y'all over here talking about them corazons. You still have me down for two, ain't ya?"

Ali looked around the entire room, like he was lost. Shakur started to smile, because he knew why Ali was looking crazy. Ali had pulled the same move with him before. He bumped Ali, "Akh, don't you hear Muhammad talking to you?"

"Muhammad can't be talking to me, because he didn't give me my rights. He knows he gotta give a brother his rights first," Ali counseled.

Saleem and Ali had both gotten Shakur with the same move before, and it had taught him to always greet, before he spoke.

"Yeah, you right, Akh. I apologize, and I promise it will never happen again. Inshaa-Allaah," Muhammad corrected. Ali returned the brother's greeting and assured him that the food would be waiting on him to pick up and in the same breath, promised him that, if he did not show up to pick them up, they would be sold.

"As-Salaamu 'Alaikum, Ali still gets his papers," a Muslim brother said, walking by, while doing the Shorty-Lo dance. He continued over to where his other young Muslim brothers were seated and continued his rap session, as Muhammad followed.

"If I can change, you can change. We can change, brothers on the compound will be chanting my name," he rapped off.

"Nobody beats the IBN," Muhammad joined in. Then he repeated the sentence in a deep talking voice, "Nobody beats the IBN."

Attending Jumu'ah, everyone was wearing their best linen. Some brothers even had an outfit, just for Jumu'ah purposes only. Most wore a gray sweat suit or a pair of khaki pants, with a long sleeve white t-shirt. Short sleeve shirts were allowed, but the majority of brothers wore long sleeves to cover their tattoos.

On Jumu'ah day, with the Sunni Muslims, the community was going to make sure that every bottle of fragrance the commissary had to sell would be advertised. You'd have brothers walking around with a bottle of prayer oil, giving out samples. Some of them would get an attitude, if another brother did not accept the oil.

"Come on, Akh. Help me get some Barakats. You are going to deny a brother his blessing?"

They would feel like you were trying to stop them from getting all the blessings, that they might have

111

coming. The more oil they gave out, the bigger their blessing would be. They tried to give everybody some of the prayer oil.

If you tried to tell them that for whatever reason, you didn't want any, some brothers would become aggressive and get an attitude. All they were thinking about were their own self-rewards, and not always being considerate of what you were saying. They would see you as standing in their way of receiving their full blessing. As they were trying to reach their goal, their quarter was to give away this bottle of prayer oil, so brothers were guaranteed to be leaving the chapel, wearing a variety of fragrances from the multiple applications of prayer oil and cologne.

Zeek Bey had come into the fold of the Moorish-science Temple of America, because he had wanted a nationality. He wanted to escape being called a nigger, black, or colored, because these terms failed to link an individual to the human family.

Zeek had grown up hearing every day about the devil, who lived beneath his feet, and the God, who lived up above the clouds. As he grew older, he had become confused and considered the idea of a God in the sky, as ludicrous. Moorish-science had taught Zeek that these were actually beings, that lived within each and every one of us.

Zeek Bey wanted to know himself. He had been at his lower self, for Allah only knows how long. Islam had been broken into seventy-two different groups, and Noble Drew Ali was not counted in these groups. They were known and counted, as a brotherhood.

The teachings upraising the dead, the hollow, and the ignorant. It brought forth light, love, peace, equality, freedom, and justice, as well as put people back on the plane to their higher self. The Moorish American was about unity and the uplifting of the condition of the people.

During Zeek Bey's 6:30 p.m. service, everyone faced east. Jones Bey opened with, "Allah, the father of the universe, the father of love, truth, peace, freedom, and justice. Allah is my protector. My guide and my salvation by night and by day through his holy prophet, Noble Drew Ali, Amen."

After everyone sat down, he went on to explain why Friday was their holy day.

"Friday is our holy day of rest, because on Friday, the first man departed out of flesh."

Jones Bey shared the pulpit with his brothers; he let them spread, spit, and share the truth.

Zeek Bey spoke second, by the guiding of his father, God, Allah, the great God of the universe, to redeem man from his sinful and fallen stage of humanity, back to the highest plain of life with his father God, Allah. If it was the will of Allah, each one could and would be the grand sheik of their family, community, and continue to carry on the will of Allah.

After the service, Zeek Bey called his son. The child was a spitting image of him. Their youth formulated each other. His son was being brought up by two parents, his mother, and his mother's husband. Zeek Bey grew up with only a single mother, and made bad grades in school, but his son was on the A and B Honor Roll, for his first seven years of school.

"Daddy, I got my report card, today," Zeek's son reported.

"What kinds of grades you make?"

"All A's and B's."

The previous report card, his son made a B in history, and Zeek gave him a little lecture about how as the darker people here in North America, they could not always just look at their past in the eyes of American history, since it was one of the youngest ones in the whole world. To really see where they came from, he needed to go back about 400 years and look at the history in its totality.

"What'd you make in history, this time?"

"An A!"

"Good," Zeek Bey mumbled, and did not delay the issue on his tongue. "Son, I hope you're not running with any of those idiot gangs out there, destroying your community. Let your actions speak louder than your words. Son, it's important to me, that you don't grow up in my footsteps. I made a lot of poor choices and decisions. I do not want my path to be your future!"

Zeek's son interrupted, "Daddy, you sound like a Tookie Williams."

"In that case, son, all these fathers and incarcerated men should do the same. It will better our society, better our family, and better our race, as a whole. Then maybe we can all come together, as a whole. I have no problem with sounding like Tookie Williams. You and I can start this as a tradition throughout our generation," Zeek Bey encouraged.

He didn't get a chance to say anymore, because the phone line went dead. He'd only had two dollars on his pre-paid phone account.

After the 2:00 p.m. Nation of Islam service, Sten went to the rec yard to watch the best of the best play chess. A double match was taking place on the same permanent concrete picnic table. Baltimore Rick was playing Mr. Pete, and the Chinese finest, Lyn, a.k.a., The Hardest Man to Beat in the BOP, was playing Willie Carter.

Mr. Carter talked that Jesus talk and was literally trying to walk that Jesus walk. He would have Bible studies with the young brothers every night, and armor them with Jesus' word as needed. Mr. Carter said the devil had given him the street name, "BIP." Now the Lord showed him the blessing in his alias. *Big. In. Praying.*

In the book of Genesis, God told Abraham to leave his country, and he would show him where to go, and he would make his name great. Mr. Carter felt that God had spoken to him no differently. Mr. Pete and Brother Omar were slowly welcoming Sten into the fold of their knowledgeable circle.

Sten spun a few laps with Brother Omar from time to time, whenever he caught him walking the track. Brother Omar was deep with knowledge. They would universally build, when they came together. For some strange reason, Sten wanted to talk about what his mother had advised him.

Sten said, "*My mother told me at a young age. Son, be a leader and not a follower. I lived by that code, but now I have awakened. I have to learn how to be a good follower. The blind can only lead the blind, but mark my words, the follower's third eye will eventually open, and they'll realize they have a drunk sitting behind the wheel. Some people don't get on this reality, until they get knee deep in booboo.*

A rising force tears and pulls apart a falling force. That's why Black men must be kept blind, deaf, and dumb, because our rise would mean their fall. Soloman seeks knowledge, wisdom, and above all, understanding. Mind perceptions taught sight is not just observed with the eye, but the mind interrelating with reality. God breathes into the body of live souls, physical life, but when God breathes in man's ear, his knowledge, wisdom, and understanding, man becomes mentally and spiritually alive. We've been dead for too long, mentally. Now it's time for us to rise physically."

Mr. Pete wanted to touch up on the subject and to give Sten the harsh, cold reality. He refused to let this conversation dwindle. He embellished the issue, "All the knowledge around is right there for us to see it, but we don't see it, some of us, because of our differences. Our differences keep us separated. For instance, one may believe in the Buddhism teaching, or one may believe in the Judaism teaching, or one may believe in the Nation's teachings. With these differences, these knowledgeable people will not come together to bring about a change to their condition. It is not only them. It goes beyond that and them. You have the gang-bangers, Bloods, Crips. You have the other organizations... the GD's, the Vice Lords, etc. With all these differences, we will not overcome this oppression. We have to reach out to the condition of our lives as a people. Without unity and coming together, our condition will not change. People will hear the one man or few individuals that may speak the wisdom, the knowledge, and the understanding, but they will not take heed, because their differences will not allow it!"

Mr. Pete lost his train of thought, as he snapped back to reality to focus on the table. His powerful words had become too harsh for an unconscious individual to digest, and he had not been concentrating on his chess game. You snooze, you lose!

Slick Rick had used it to his full advantage. He had attacked Mr. Pete and was applying pressure. Mr. Pete fought back, trying to calm the attack.

Rick tightened up even more. He had Mr. Pete's king hoping for a helicopter to fly over the board and drop an escape ladder.

"Is there any reason we're still playing this game?" Slick Rick boasted. "Get you sixteen more!"

Mr. Pete focused, but it was too late. He realized that Slick Rick would have him checkmated in the next move.

"You don't know what to do?" Larry True X addressed Mr. Pete. "There's a way out." He reached out and pushed up Mr. Pete's rook, thinking it would give his king a way of escape.

Slick Rick made his move, and put the checkmate on Mr. Pete anyway, Larry True X hadn't realized that Slick Rick had three different ways, he could have played it.

"You know how to play this?" Slick Rick questioned Sten.

"I know how to play everything in prison... Mr. Pete went to sleep behind the wheel," Sten answered.

Mr. Pete's 20/20 hindsight was in perfect working order, and he could see exactly where the game had gone wrong, but after it had happened.

A bystander at the table had a question for the wise chess players. "Why are the Feds so crowded?"

"Because the Feds have changed," Slick Rick broadcasted. "Nowadays, they snatch anybody and everybody. Most these people don't belong here in the Feds! He didn't have a dollar over the rent money. State crimes, the mentality of the people, the low-level crack dealers, and the low-level drug dealers."

"The Feds knew what was going to happen. They planned this. They know the mentality. They thought they could control it, but it's backfiring on them," Mr. Pete explained.

"Dissatisfaction brings about change," Brother Larry True X pointed out.

"How's the good brothers?" Shakur asked, as he walked up to the table.

"Ain't too much of nothing, slow motion," Sten replied.

"Who's the best of the best?" Shakur asked, while rubbing his hands together.

"I ain't the best, but I'll do, until he gets here," Slick Rick taunted.

"Mr. Pete's chess game's colder than a polar bear's toenail," a bystander stated. He had watched Mr. Pete destroy most of his opponents for the last three years straight.

Simultaneously, Mr. Pete and Slick Rick answered Shakur's question, by pointing to the other and saying, "He is." Lyn and Christian Brother Mr. Carter did not answer. They were too engrossed in their game to pay any attention to an outside distraction.

Lyn made a powerful move, leaving Mr. Carter with few options. Mr. Willis Carter could see it coming; he would soon be in checkmate. He applied volume to his Walkman jamming to a Lionel Richie song. He knew the game was over. A stalemate was not in his future. He helped Lionel Richie sing the beautiful song. *"Jesus is love and that's forever in my heart. Teach your children to love one another. Help 'em to walk through temptation. Who can bring you joy? Jesus. Who can turn your life around? Jesus. I wanna walk with you. I wanna talk with you. Who has the glory? The power? It's Jesus,"* Mr. Carter chanted, throwing a fist in the air with each verse. In the process of stalling, an escape route had appeared. Mr. Carter confiscated Lyn's rook, freeing himself from the oppressor.

"I had him checkmated, until he started singing," shrugged Lyn.

"Mr. Willie Carter, continue to stay you," Shakur encouraged.

"Some migrating Muslims, who proved that Prophet Muhammad was the last and final messenger, found refuge under a Christian king, who truly acknowledged Muhammad, as a man of God," Mr. Carter said to Shakur, with a smile that showed no disrespect.

Larry (Neo) Williams was still laughing at what Lyn had said. He had tears rolling down his face. "Mr. Carter, Lyn said, he had you checkmated, until you started singing."

"Jesus is all I got. Jesus can pull me through anything," Mr. Carter smiled. "Jesus can turn anyone's life around."

"I can Amen to that," stated Larry.

રે - ન્જ

A 2:00 p.m. bus came in Friday afternoon. The inmates reached the compound five hours later. Killer was among the group. Chase welcomed him into the system, by getting him high.

Chase put Killer on the highways and byways of prison life, as they sat in his room smoking weed and trying to drink two gallons of prison wine, with the main ingredients of water and spoiled fruit. Their faces puckered with each swallow. The wine was good, but smelled like athlete's foot. Prison wine would get more potent the more days it sat. It was a true saying that the wine would get better with time.

Before a purchase, everyone would get a tester. They'd slurp a mouthful and treat it like mouthwash. The alcohol in the wine would function like water and oil. Small portions of alcohol would drain down their throats, like the bite, similar to a cough drop.

"Damn, round. I took the case for you, and you just couldn't rest, until you came to jail, ya heard me?" Chase told Killer, between swallows.

"Ya know, Chase... I gotta keep that heat. I feel naked without it. My body doesn't function properly without that iron."

Chase pulled an eight-inch knife from his front pocket, and then removed a twelve-inch murder weapon from his waist. Both weapons had a rip-braided sheet handle and a loop to keep the knife from being snatched out his hand.

"These pretty babies are like my toys... they are my life. They like my ID, I don't leave the unit without them. I shower with them. I sleep with them. I take a shit with them."

"I need me some too, like right now. I can feel my body trying to do the Harlem shake, ya heard me?" Killer said.

"Killer, be easy, round. I have a twin to this pretty baby," Chase informed him, giving the murder weapon a kiss. "I'll give her to you, ya heard me?"

"Say, round, you say you made this all by your lonesome?" Killer asked, looking down into his cup. The fungus was doing the backstroke. "This some firewater. You need to make us a batch every week, ya heard me?"

"All you got to do is say the word. I'll put five gallons in ya locker. We'll come down every three days."

"What my bunky gonna say?"

"Shit, 'cause I'm gonna teach ya how to arrest the smell, and how to keep ya room clean. Round, all ya gotta do is be twenty-one, when the man comes, ya heard me?"

"Chase, I just took a fresh baby life sentence, and the hole don't bother me. It just makes me stronger. Ya heard me?"

"That's right, round, cause if the man walk in my room and catch us with this shit, don't be afraid to stand up, raise your right hand, and tell him it's ya' shit," Chase joked.

Four knocks rapped on the door. "See, there's the CO, ya heard me?" Chase joked again. "Come in, ya heard me?"

Killer hopped to his feet, with his right-hand level with his head, "It's my shit. It's all my shit!"

As Playa walked in, the weed smell attached his nostrils, and the sight of wine made his mouth water.

"You came down today, Chase?" he asked.

"Say, woady, didn't I see ya mopping the floor up front?" Killer asked.

"Shit, round, down the rest of that shit in the jug. Sit down and let's get fucked up. You know how we do it every Friday," confirmed Chase.

"No need for the cups, let's get F-up, fire the weed up," Playa said, because even though he smoked the weed and drank the liquor, he didn't cuss or carry knives.

Chapter 8

Mr. Camel's whole life had been a downhill struggle. He didn't look at his life as being about uplifting someone else, which was the problem. There was no way for him to uplift anyone, when he always looked at his life in such a negative way. There was no way for him to lead someone to a positive result, when he couldn't even be positive about his own life.

Mr. Camel's incarceration had been brought about, by his son finding his gun underneath the couch and accidentally killing himself with it. The bullet had struck a toy and ricocheted off a metal clock bell on the wall, and then hit the kid in the eye. It was a complete freak accident, but Mr. Camel did not see it like that, because he knew that the gun should have never been within reach of the child. This thing should never have happened. Now, all he could do is sit back and think about what went wrong. Mr. Camel was a dope boy. He had kept the gun underneath the couch, because he thought it would be a good place to have it, when the stickup boys came around. Little did he know, how tragically the easy access would work against him.

The terrible tragedy had awakened all the neighbors to remove their firearms, or other life-threatening objects, that they had not thought anything about keeping in easy reach of their children. They had secured these things, so they would not have to grieve the loss of a child, like Mr. Camel was having to do.

All Mr. Camel could do these days was sit around and blame himself. He did not allow, but a few people, to come into his close circle. He wouldn't even talk to most people. If they were lucky enough to get anything out of him, it would likely be just a grouchy grumble. There was one person that he allowed himself to open up to, and that was how his message was able to get out.

Mr. Camel always put his chair in the grass and sat with a towel over his head. This was a normal routine of his, to shut out the rest of the world. He would be in his own little world.

Zeek Bey walked up, "Is-lam Mol."

Mr. Camel lifted up a corner of the towel draped over his head and peeked out with a smile. He already knew who the familiar voice belonged to. Zeek Bey always brought a smile to his face.

"Peace, Moor," Mr. Camel returned the greeting.

"Mr. Camel, what are you doing out here on this glorious day?"

Mr. Camel looked up from underneath the towel. "Just another miserable day for me in this land of misery."

"Mr. Camel, I don't want to hear about the misery days. I want to hear about the glory days," Zeek said. To keep him from continuing to live in his misery, Zeek would switch it up and get him talking about his days of glory.

Mr. Camel smiled once again, "If you're talking like that, I did have some glory days, but when I look at it, now I see that I made a lot of errors in my glory," Mr. Camel admitted, looking back into time. He regretted the slinging of that poison to his people.

In living that lifestyle, he knew that not only had he hurt the people, who were actual users of the poison he sold, but their loved ones as well. He had put his whole family in danger of the stick-up boys and the DEA raids. His wife and two children could have been killed by either group.

"If we could turn back the hands of time, my life would go down a different road. I would make better choices, even from the very little that I had to choose from. Providing for my family and securing their safety would be my first priority. I jumped into the game with just a half of thought, looking to get ghetto rich, not looking at the danger that I was putting myself in, as well as my family. I would give anything to be able to bring my baby back and take this pain away. All I have now is nightmares of the past! Some days, I don't know if I truly want to live and see another day!"

"Mr. Camel, you know these days, your living can be a message to the people, if you choose to tell the people about your life, and what has caused you so much hurt and pain."

"I'm no role model. I'm not a good example of a father figure. Talking about misery and pain never helped anyone."

"Mr. Camel, you can let the people know, that they do not have to face the hurt and pain that you may be facing."

"There's no way I can stop anyone else's pain, when I can't even stop my own!"

"Ole Mr. Camel, the message in your life can help and save a lot of people, if they stop and listen to the message."

"What is the message in my life that would help people so much?"

"You could let them know what they should avoid, so they would not have to pay the price that you are paying now."

"You may be right, young Zeek. I am paying one helluva price," Mr. Camel agreed. He started relating to Zeek what led up to his pain.

Zeek did what every young individual is supposed to do in the presence of an older, wiser person. He shut up and listened.

"It's the penalties in life... people jump into the drug game blind. They're blind to the penalties that come with the game. They only look at the superficial rewards that come with the game, overlooking the cold reality of the penalties. They don't know that when they pick up one or two possession charges, or even the little sales, that they no longer appear little, when the Feds come in and convict them of another crime. They use all them little ole possession charges, that you thought wasn't nothing, to enhance your sentence and sometimes give you a life sentence for dope."

"In your travels in life, you'll run into different people. You'll have some blindly led by the blind. Then you have another type of people, who are the guiders, then another type, the mentors. These are the people you run into, when you're dealing in and living the street life. Your guider, is the one that will guide you through the things in life, you are dealing with. Your guider will give you the direction in which way to go, so that you will be able to do whatever it is that you do."

"The mentor plays a more significant role in your life. Your mentor will nurture you and make sure that you know the ins and outs of whatever it is that you are doing. Your mentor will know you have grown into the role that is necessary for you to become successful. Your mentor truly has your best interest at heart. There will be no doubt that when your mentor is finished, you'll be able to pass the test."

"We have to let you know what comes with the penalty in the game. I know people do not like to talk about the flip side of the game, but it's too real not to warn you of the traps that are already set for you out there. For instance, do you know about the 100 to 1 ratio? If you don't, listen up or you'll miss out, 'cause I'm about to school you on that one ounce of crack, you just got busted with... it's no longer one ounce. It becomes a hundred ounces. I know you say, *I never had that much*, but if you had one gram, it becomes one hundred grams. Now, you know how you became a king-pin overnight. When you woke up, I know you thought it was a nightmare, but it's the truth, brothers and sisters. It's the trap that the federal government has laid out for you. Believe it or not, take heed or not, this is what they have waiting for you out there. Listen to my warning, do not get caught in that vicious trap!"

Once Mr. Camel had opened up, he gave Zeek even more than he was looking for. Zeek Bey was one of the positive brothers, who could get into those closed circles and break through the barrier of these closed down individuals. The people would respond to Zeek's positive energy, and before they knew it, they would be speaking about their trials and tribulations.

Positive energy draws out positive results, and that is how Zeek would get these individuals to deliver a positive message.

⤛ - ⤜

It was Juke and G-Money's turn to play the rec yard, while Jerry sat in the gym watching Hard to Guard fight against the clock and scoreboard, trying to outdo Tario's three-pointers. Every time Tario shot a jumper, the ball would go clean through the net, without touching the ring.

When he did miss one, Baby June would catch it off the rim and dunk it. Catmouche and Hard to Guard played their hearts out, but they had lost the championship. They had won it last year though, and it was impossible to achieve two times straight. They probably would have won it again, if Toot wouldn't have sprained his ankle in the first quarter of the season. Toot's ankle would not properly heal. He would attempt to play, before it was ready, and injure it again. Toot's double digits were well missed.

Three prison guards patrolled the gate, as the sweating gym guys bum-rushed out of rec, trying to beat each other back to the unit and shower. The correctional offers could be misidentified as security guards, as they frisked and thoroughly searched inmates like robo-cops.

Juke strolled his usual normal pace with the crowd, and the CO did not single him out; it was just a random search. Juke stood before the staff, in a lazy jumping jack position. The pat-down was halfway complete, when the guard's hand landed in the off-limit zone.

Juke broke camp, racing toward his unit. Even though he had a head start, the officers set out to run him down. Juke's head start could not outrun the officer's walkie-talkie and a quick call shut all the sliders.

He witnessed and heard the doors shut, but he continued running up the steps. Juke deliberately dropped his weapon on the stairs. He didn't care if the COs got it, he just couldn't afford to let them get it directly from his person. He'd have a good argument that it wasn't his, because the institution wasn't going to go through the trouble to get the knife fingerprinted to see if it was his.

Zeek Bey walked out of Mr. Camel's unit, just in time to hear the metal connect with the concrete steps. He watched the bone crusher bounce from one step to another. Out of the corner of his eye, he could see the out of shape COs, running their hearts out.

Zeek Bey's criminal instinct kicked in, and before he could think rationally about it, he scooped up the knife and secured it between his legs. Zeek Bey was cut from that cloth, he had to help a fellow inmate.

The officers cuffed Juke and marched him straight to the Lieutenant's Office. Since he had nothing that violated institution policy on his person, they would let him go after asking him a hundred questions about why he ran from the rec area.

These four Christian brothers were in the world but not of the world. Their old ways were washed away. They were not only into cleaning their outside, but also their inside. This meant, they not only talked that talk, but most definitely walked that walk. Seven days a week, they were

131

on the rec yard, which was known as the danger ground. They were in harm's way, doing the will of God.

"Let's be like Christ, walk like Christ, and talk like Christ," Mr. Billie would always encourage. Their Mexican Christian brother, Rufino, repeated the sentence in Spanish for the Hispanic guys, who could not understand English. They both passed out slips of paper that had the following invitation for a church service printed on it.

When: Sunday 5:30 p.m. -7:30 p.m.
Where: Large Chapel

Brothers, God is establishing himself greatly on
this compound. His Holy Spirit is definitely moving
amongst this place, comforting ailing hearts and
establishing new paths for those who love him. He
has prepared a new worship service for all who are
interested in experiencing the power of His
presence.
Come and join us, as we give His due glory, with
our highest praise.

Proverbs 3:5-6- Trust in the Lord with all your
heart and lean not on your own understanding. In all
your ways, submit to him, and he will make your
path straight.

Ephesians 6:12 - For our struggle is not against flesh and blood, but against the rulers, against the authorities, against the powers of this dark world, and against the spiritual forces of evil in the heavenly realms.

Lord, I know I'm not the man that I ought to be, but I thank you, that I'm not the person that I used to be, the brother thought, as he watched the COs race across the compound, as another one of his Christian brothers walked through the gate. He was internationally well-known. *What good does it do, one to gain the world and lose his soul?* danced around in his mind. *Now, you have to get rich in spirit, brother, and have to get right with God. God created us, as well as God can destroy us.*

A group of youngsters walked by, and one of them yelled out, "Good brother, be careful not to cast your pearls before the swine." He and his homies laughed, like it was the funniest thing they had heard all year.

"Lord, keep them in your good grace, because they know not what they say or do," Ray mumbled.

"Brother, brother, let's say a prayer for them," Rufino suggested. "Jesus is not finished working with them, yet."

"You couldn't come up with a better idea," said Mike.

"You know all my ideas used to be bad ideas," Rufino smiled. "This is God speaking through my sinful body."

"Amen, brother, amen. God works through the people, who he chooses," Jay pointed out.

Chapter 9

The staff meeting took place in the officer's dining halls. The staffers that arrived first, did their best to get comfortable. There were some tables with two seats and other with four. Some of them pushed the smaller and larger tables together to make six seats. The room could hold around fifty people, and that would be pushing it. Forty-eight people had arrived, and the room was getting crowded, with still more arriving. The P.A. lady and the X-ray lady decided to attend the meeting. It wasn't compulsory upon them, like it was for the officers. The door was wide open to any staff.

The warden was a 47-year-old Mexican-American. He had twenty years experience in the system. Though he had four years in the state and sixteen more terrible life-threatening years in the feds, he had only three years in a medium security facility. All the rest had been at maxes-penitentiaries. The warden knew how to deal with the mentality of the people. He was sent to USP Petty Rock to clean the place up, like he had done in numerous other penitentiaries. He had his own personal crew. The assistant warden was his uncle's oldest son. He had personally trained him how to be a professional.

Many of the upper level managers in the BOP thought the situation was strange, but they had proven themselves and shown they could get the job done.

The warden leaned over to his personal lieutenant, who he had also brought on board for this project. "This room is getting too crowded," he whispered.

Several of the male officers were standing, leaning against the wall. They were acting the perfect gentlemen, giving up their seats to the female staff, who had arrived too late to claim their own seats.

"People, before this meeting takes place, I need you all to cooperate with me once again. It would be in our best interest, if we all went over to the visiting room, where we would all be a little more comfortable, please," the lieutenant announced.

He was glad, himself, to be moving into the visiting room. He had already given up his seat in the dining area. The staff thought, they could not have come up with a better idea. Sitting at the small tables had their legs all bunched up. The X-ray lady had long legs, and she needed her stretching room. She already had a cramp in her calf, from sitting with her legs crossed in an uncomfortable position.

After everyone was seating in the visiting room and finished shopping at the vending machines, the warden laid out his plan, giving his staff the solution--the law of the land. The warden had heard so much about this place, that his anticipation was already sitting mountain high.

"For a month and ten days straight, we've had an incident per day, where an inmate or more has been treated for stabbing injuries or from getting beat half to death by a lock," the warden updated his staff. He looked over the employees. He wasn't looking to see if they were showing any sympathy for the victims, but he was watching to see who of his staff was paying attention, and who wasn't. He might occasionally forget a name, but he did not forget faces, and if he caught them not paying attention, you could bet they would be getting reassigned and riding around the perimeter of the fence, for eight boring hours in a vehicle.

The PA that released the documented injury report nodded and locked eyes with the warden briefly. The warden's eyes began to travel, as he continued to speak, "The next time the deuces go off, I'm going to make these inmate's time hard. Assistant Warden, would you please pass me the list."

The assistant warden removed his personally handwritten list from his breast pocket. The warden did not rush to unfold the long yellow piece of paper. He collected his thoughts and cleared his throat. "I say, once again. The next time the deuces go off, I'm locking the place down. We're going on lockdown. Since they want to make my job and your jobs hard, I'm going to make their time hard," the warden promised and threatened. Then he went about reading the sanctions his cousin had put together. "Lock down time will go from 10 p.m. to 8 p.m. Commissary weekly spending limit will be only fifty-two dollars a week, no exceptions. We'll feed only the two connected buildings at a time. E-A will eat with E-B. C-C will eat with C-B and so forth. By the time we finish feeding after four o'clock count, it will be close to 7 p.m. We will then open the yard. They'll have only one hour of recreation. No more ten-minute moves. We are going to cut back on every little thing they have. It's going to be five-minute moves. Once they start acting like humans, we'll start giving some things back, but they'll have to earn it."

"Are we going to leave any room for subjection?" the lieutenant whispered, to the warden and the assistant warden.

"No! There will be no grounds for subjection," the assistant warden stated, reminding the lieutenant that he was his direct superior, and had first say-so on questions from his lieutenant.

"Right now, there is no need for suggestions," the warden noted. "But for future reference, Lieutenant, any suggestions you do have, just run them by the assistant warden. I'm sure he'll accommodate you. I have full faith in him to make the right decision."

The staff was taking turns shaking the warden's hand and welcoming him aboard their sinking ship. When they heard the tower bomb go off, each staff member's walkie-talkie made a loud crazy siren noise. A staff member somewhere hit their body alarm--had hit the deuces.

"There's a group war on the basketball court," the tower's strong voice sped through every walkie-talkie. Every staff member in the meeting raced out of the visiting room, running for the designated areas, as if they were trying to save their one and only son's life.

"All unit officers, lock down your units. I repeat, all unit officers, lock down your units," the assistant warden yelled, into his walkie-talkie. The unit officers did not recognize the voice, but they did not hesitate to fulfill the order.

๛ - ๛

Earlier, Chase had been standing in front of BB unit, looking for the soda man. He needed a cold drink, before he went to play softball. As the guys came and went from the unit, Chase did not know any of them. The sun was pushing him towards dehydration.

"Man, tell the soda man to bring me out a soda... any kind, it doesn't matter. I just need a soda, bad," Chase said, to the next guy headed into the unit.

"What cell he in?" the innocent by stander stopped in his tracks to respond.

"Old Man Cash in cell two or three," the CO furnished. "No, he's in cell two," he corrected.

"Man, what the fuck you doing in my business?" Chase barked on the CO.

"Just tryin' to help you out, man," replied the CO.

Some COs were aware of their surroundings and knew exactly what type of move or power, everyone was capable of. People couldn't say that many of the COs were not doing their jobs.

Another guy was getting ready to go into the unit, so Chase decided to speak to the brother, before he inquired about the soda man. "Brother, how you doing?"

The man stopped and looked at Chase, as if he had said something wrong or disrespectful. "Bro, as long as I'm breathing, I'm gonna be alright. My mother died, my father died, and my son died... all while I was right here!"

It was like he said. It was not a good question to be asking. *I should have used a simple hello. It would have been better*, Chase thought.

As Zeek Bey walked out of the unit, Chase's interest was no longer on the soda. "Say, woady, you came on the bus with me, ya heard me?" Zeek Bey said, smiling. How could he forget about Chase and his homie? They would end every sentence with, Ya heard me?

"My name's Zeek Bey, JC," Zeek Bey introduced himself, using Chase's initials. Zeek looked Chase's team jersey over, "So you play with the Bangers, huh?"

"Yeah, I play a little softball, ya heard me? Old Man Corn Bread needed a player."

"I'm on my way to play chess on the rec yard. You going that way? Let's walk," said Zeek Bey.

"Man, let me tell you some crazy shit. A crackhead sent me ten dollars, woady, ya heard me?" Chase said, making a joke out of the situation.

But Zeek Bey did not look at the situation the same way. He explained, "You see how we just get titles and throw them around loosely? You didn't say, I have a friend with a problem with addiction, or who's messed up on drugs or something. You just went straight to the term to describe one with that problem, using the most degrading term to describe one in that condition."

Chase couldn't wait to get to the softball field, so he could separate himself from Zeek Bey. Zeek was a little too serious for him. Chase was hoping they could enjoy and share some laughter.

 જ - ૭

The pitcher stood on the mound, looking at the back-catcher for a signal or some type of direction. Chase had one strike and a foul ball against him, which totaled up to two strikes. The catcher punched his mitt a few times. "Let's go, homie. All we need is one more strike," the catcher announced, as he rocked from side to side, in the squatting position.

The pitcher nodded at his catcher's guides. He wrapped his fingers around the softball and delivered the pitch. The ball looked like it would be a strike, then abandoned its path, striking Chase on the temple and drawing blood.

Chase's hand immediately shot up to his temple and felt the warm blood. The sight and feel of his blood sent Chase on a mission of blood for blood. He ran after the pitcher, pursuing him around the field, while trying to beat him down with the aluminum bat.

The pitcher ran to where some of the members of his team had huddled up. They scattered, wanting no part of the aluminum bat. The pitcher grabbed one of his players, Norwood, and used him to block Chase.

"Man, how you gonna just get behind me and use me for a shield," Norwood snapped.

"Man, that lil nigga your friend? Not mine! You better talk some sense into him," the pitcher croaked.

"He after you, not me," Norwood reminded him.

Everybody knew that Norwood and Chase were cool, since they would always go to chow together. What they did not know, that Norwood had often tried to counsel Chase about how trouble was easy to get into and very hard to get out of. Norwood was constantly reminding Chase, that he was two months from going home. Chase was a complete hothead though, and believed that all problems had to be solved with violence. The fact that his release was sixty days away still didn't make him duck rec.

If someone wanted to fight or have some knife play, count Chase in. Norwood did his duty by letting Chase know that their surroundings included brothers, who would never be able to see or smell the streets again. There were people here, who would be willing to give up both arms or both legs to be able to have Chase's release date.

"Norwood, get the fuck outta my way. I'm gonna beat this nigga to death, ya heard me!"

"Gotdamn, Mr. Norwood. Tell 'em I didn't try to hit him with the damn ball. That shit was an accident," the pitcher pleaded.

"Chase, what was we talking about earlier?" Norwood cautioned. A couple of days before, while they were on the handball court. Norwood had made Chase aware, that people with life sentences could only travel in circles around the compound and around the track.

"Norwood, get outta my way," Chase shouted.

"Chase, you try'na walk around in a circle for the rest of your life? If that's what you're after, just tell me. You might as well take my time, and let me have your time, so I can go home and raise my two daughters and take'em fishing."

Every time Norwood mentioned his daughters it made Chase come to his senses. Chase did not have a daughter or a son and had never been fishing in his life.

"Chase, I'd see if the man tried to hit you with the ball. I'd want my lick too, but it didn't happen like that..."

The pitcher cut in on Norwood, "Playa, I didn't try to hit you with that ball. I don't have no reason to do some bullshit like that."

"Yeah, Chase, man, dude a good dude. He don't get down like that," one of Chase's teammates added, on the pitcher's behalf. Corn Bread didn't want to see the youngest throw his future life away.

"It was an honest mistake." Norwood walked up to Chase with his hand out. "Do the right thing, and give me the bat?"

Chase handed the bat to Norwood, however it would not have gone to anyone else besides Norwood. The crowd spread apart, leaving Chase and the pitcher to their privacy. The pitcher tried to apologize again, as Chase made an exit off the rec yard with Norwood.

"Chase, I know you're a hothead, but man, don't fuck around and trap yourself behind these walls. You already done your time. Leave here, man. This place isn't even for the birds. If I was home right now, I'd be on a lake somewhere with my daughters."

Chase and Norwood split up at the gates, and Chase headed over to Killer's unit. A female officer guarded the front of her unit, armed with a clipboard. If your name and number were not on her roster sheet, you were not going to get in her unit. As Chase tried to slip pass the female guard, she blocked him with an outstretched arm.

"Do you live in my unit?" she asked.

Chase looked at her like she was crazy. "Yeah, I live in here."

"Name and number?" the sister requested.

"Damn, woman. Why you always be askin' everybody this crazy-ass bullshit?"

"Yeah, you don't live in here. I thought so. Now bye sir, and have a nice day," she said sweetly, giving Chase a good-bye wave.

"Woman, you sit around here playin' games. Don't you know you're around hardcore criminals from all over the world? We are America's backbone. This is a privilege for you to be around guys like us. You ain't never stood this close to a nigga like me before, have you?"

"Who you came to see?" she asked, thinking, *Lord Jesus, please help me, before I tell this lil' boy a dang thing or two.*

"Woman, you don't know him."

"What's his name?"

"Shit, I don't know. I call him Bro, Bro."

"I don't like letting people in my unit, because the deuces go off too much. You got two minutes to holla at your guy, and if you get caught in my unit within the two minutes, you going to the SHU."

"Woman, I don't give a fuck about the SHU. The hole ain't shit but another part of the jail," Chase barked, walking past her. All he was focusing on now was getting high.

"Okay, Mr. Tough Guy. Let them two minutes catch up with ya, or let the deuces go off, and I promise you will be seeing the inside of the Special Housing today, Mister."

Chase gritted his teeth at her threating promise and hurried into the unit.

ôô – ôô

One of the four courts had been preserved by the Alabama white boys. They all thought they were Larry Birds and they already knew that going up against a group of brothers was like challenging Kareem Abdul Jabbar, Vince Carter, Tracy McGrady and a host of Michael Jordans. The summer leagues were mixed with no segregation. The rec officer banned all "car" teams. You either played against your homies and other guys in your car, or you didn't play sports at all.

This event had come about by cars calling out another car. The Muslims took on Philly--best out of three. Moorish America went up against Detroit. The Nation of Islam challenged the Oklahoma car.

This was how they were secretly making alliances and bringing about a beautiful unification, but the white guys didn't look at it like that. They saw this picture as discrimination. Their game was in the third quarter.

One of them scored a magnificent three-pointer from the top of the key. "Bird, Baby!" he screamed. He was only going to need to produce twelve more of those to catch up. Mario took the ball coast to coast and matched the three-pointer. "Ray Ray!" he cheered. Speaking of his favorite NBA player in the lead.

"Damn, I wanted to be Ray Allen," Sponk said to Mario "but that's ok, I'll be Kevin Durant."

"Alright." The guy held up his hand, "Carter."

One of the white guys brought the ball inbound faster than expected, and threw the ball like a spear down the court. His teammate went up for a reverse lay-up. Zay pinned the ball to the backboard.

"Get that shit outta here." He slung the ball back down-court, Jody caught the ball and glided from the free-throw line, palming the ball with one hand. The ball slammed onto the back of rim, bouncing back out. The crowd lost their enthusiasm, and someone shouted, "How the fuck you mess a pretty dunk up like that?"

B-T got the rebound and threw the ball against the backboard, caught it and demonstrated a nasty dunk. The four white guys standing under the goal could do nothing but watch. They could put their hips together and still wouldn't match B-T's hoops.

"I had him beat. He fouled the shit outta me, damn near broke my neck." the guy said, whose lay-up had gotten pinned on the backboard. He looked for Georgia Boy, Dre or Nard to call the foul.

"I should've listen. I shouldn't play with these ignorant ass guys."

"You called me ignorant?" Toby asked, pointing as himself, ready to start some trouble.

"Fuck yeah, you ignorant!" He stood on his word. Toby threw a six-piece combination, all the punches landing in the white guy's face when his body hit the concrete. He had more than a pair of Nikes to read because the whole sideline was trying to kick and stomp his brains out.

Around the basketball court and around the football field, there were always going to be Shaka Zulu Warriors. It was their territory, their land.

The white guys were outnumbered twenty to one. The war broke out in the Tower One officer's binoculars, giving him a ring-side seat making him feel like he was only a couple feet away from the live event. The tower officer felt his people's pain. He could not stop the world from spinning on its axis, but he could stop this.

"I knew them damn boys were looking for trouble! They were taught as babies not to have a damn thing to do with blacks," the officer said as he let a bomb sail out of the window. They didn't set the bombs off to blow anyone up, but to temporarily freeze them with the noise and concussion, giving the victim or victims a chance to get away and buying the staff some time to arrive on the violent scene. When the people from the staff meeting and the other COs arrived, the punishment was still being carried out. As they dove into the fight, trying to get everyone separated, some of the COs were injured as well.

Chase and Killer were in the middle of smoking up a storm when the deuces went off. They were smoking big-boy blunts and drinking the homemade liquor. The tower bomb drowned out Kill's hand sized radio. The female guard's voice could be heard loud and clear. "Lockdown, everyone catch ya cells. Y'all get off the phones!"

One guy raced toward the ice machine in his shower shoes. This was not a smart thing to do, because shower shoes were made only for wearing in the shower. If a war broke out in the unit, he would be an easy target.

"Inmate, where you think you running off to? I said lockdown. I ain't said nothing about ice call," the guard berated, trying to play her boss role.

"Lady, shut up before I knock your ass out," the guy barked. The female officer rolled her eyes at him and began to carry out her order by locking cell doors, whether both cellies were in them or not.

"Man, you heard the broad hollering lockdown. What ya going to do?" Killer asked Chase.

"Shit, I'm stuck, and I'm going to the hole fucked up," Chase answered.

Killer's cell window had a black cover over it. The female guard snatched the door open without even knocking. Chase was sitting on Killer's desk with the blunt between his fingers. The officer did not put a mustard seed of fear into Chase's heart when she snatched open the door.

"Man, you out of bounds and you smokin' something they don't sell. That's contraband. You goin' to jail."

"I'm already in jail... woman, my time is going to go on regardless whether I'm in the SHU or on the compound. The hole ain't nothin' but another part of the jail," Chase snapped. "Fuck you, and fuck the SHU. I'm a grown-ass man and I'mma do what the fuck I wanna do."

Chapter 10

Shakur's 45-year-old mother, Annie, always made his 13-year-old brother ShaBazz's bed every morning. She had been making the bed for so long, why stop now?

As ShaBazz was getting older, it gave his mother even more reason to make his bed. Annie would know if ShaBazz had brought a girl into her house. She would also know if ShaBazz had been in bed while she was at work. Five days a week ShaBazz would get on the school bus at 7:15 in the morning and Annie would leave for work about thirty minutes later. She would complete her full eight hours and be back home by 3:45 in the afternoon.

Annie stripped ShaBazz's bed and put on the clean sheets. She replaced the pillowcases on both of his pillows.

ShaBazz had been going down the street lately to play sports with a few of the neighborhood teenagers. Annie thought it would be nice if her son could get into the pros one day and play professional ball. ShaBazz didn't need to become the next Rasheed Wallace, Deion Sanders or Sammy Sosa. Just his name on a roster would have been enough for Shakur's mother.

As Annie finished playing maid in ShaBazz's room, her mother's instinct was working and she felt around between his mattress and box springs to see what he might be hiding there. To her surprise, she felt something and a second later came face to face with a .25 automatic pistol.

Annie's body became hostage to rage. She refused to go into work and called in sick. Annie sat down on the couch and faced the front door, waiting for Shabazz to walk through it. She didn't eat, she didn't sleep, and she did not watch TV. All she watched was her wristwatch.

Eight hours before, Shabazz and his homies had gotten in a couple good hours of basketball before daylight savings blew out the candle. They were walking home from the park and when they came under a streetlight. Bo said, "Y'all hold up a minute. Hold my ball," throwing it to Fado, his next-door neighbor. He pulled the pistol out of his waistband. "ShaBazz, look at this baby... homie, you gotta get you one of these babies."

ShaBazz embraced the gun and was excited. It was his first time holding a gun and it made him feel powerful.

"What would I need one of these for?" he fished, with a notion that it would be a bad idea. He knew that weapons were his big brother's downfall.

The other two guys pulled out their guns as well.

ShaBazz's eyes traveled from one of their palms to the next. Bo's brother, Lil E started off, answering why he had gotten a gun. "I got this little baby 'cause I plan on murderin' a fool soon as he get outta line. Shit, who knows? I might rob the Korean store with it. If ya want to, I know a weed man we can all rob."

"I got mines just in case somebody breaks into our house. My daddy won't be the only one with a pistol. I wanna shoot somebody too," said Fado.

ShaBazz frowned when Lil E was talking, but liked what Fado said.

"I got my gun 'cause I'm tired of them men on the corner whistling at my momma. I ain't gonna let nobody disrespect my momma. I told my momma's boyfriend he better not try to hit on my momma 'cause if he do, I'm gonna shoot him until my bullets run out. He know I got a gun, too," said Bo.

"You wanna shoot ma's boyfriend tonight, Bo?" his brother asked. Lil E was pugnacious and was always aggressive and eager to fight.

"All y'all got one, huh?" ShaBazz asked as he admired their weapons.

"Everybody, 'cept you," responded Lil E.

"Brother ShaBazz, every man needs that iron as his protection,"
encouraged Bo.

"Allah is my protector," ShaBazz told them.

"I ain't tryin' to knock that, but that tiny piece of

steel you're holding can take a life, just like God, in the blink of an eye and faster than you can snap your fingers. When I got a gun on me, I feel powerful. If somebody look at me crazy, it must mean they ready to die," stated Bo.

"We got one here you can have," Fado told him, pulling out a second gun. "I stole it from my dad's friend's car a while back."

"Fado, you said you got one just in case someone break in your house? I guess I need one for that too," ShaBazz said. Really, he was just using that for an excuse, taking the gun because he didn't want to be looked upon as a square, as a sucka, as the odd ball. He accepted the pistol, joining their .25 automatic club.

When they got closer to ShaBazz's house, he ran in and put the gun under his mattress. He didn't want to try to bring it in later when his mom was home. He went back out to hang with his homies until his 8:30 p.m. curfew.

Annie heard ShaBazz trying to unlock the already unlocked front door. She sprang into action. As ShaBazz stepped into the house, his mother's attack began. Annie slapped him twice across the face. ShaBazz was three inches taller than her and he outweighed Annie by twenty pounds, but she handled him like a little guy. She shook him by the shoulders. "Momma, what's wrong with you? Why you hit me?" Annie broke down and started crying like a baby. It shook ShaBazz up so bad, he felt tears coming into his eyes, too. "Momma, what I do?"

"Oh, Allah, tell me... what did I do?" Annie moaned. "All I ever did was be your servant. Why my sons always got to have these guns? Allah, pick them back up and put my baby back on the right track, back on your righteous track."

Shakur's mother's words shook his little brother to his core and awakened him. "Momma, I will not touch a gun again, by Allah."

"You trying to go away to prison for a long, long time with Shakur?" Annie had to ask; the question had been boiling inside her.

"No, ma'am," ShaBazz said as he hugged his mother tightly. He kissed Annie on the top of her head as she continued weeping out all of her fears and frustration.

Annie was determined not to lose ShaBazz to the system, to the streets or to the graveyard. She knew that she had been unable to tie Shakur down and she was trying to keep from making the same mistakes with ShaBazz. She was trying to keep a close grip on him, because she knew how easy it would be to lose him. She had already lost one son.

⁊ - ⳗ

Big Ro dialed Sten's mother's number as he sat in traffic. The phone rang several times without being answered. Sten's mother sat in the chair, staring at the phone as it was ringing. Sometimes she did not answer it, reminded of when Sten had been on the streets. He had always stayed in trouble with somebody. When Sten's mother's phone would ring late at night, she had always been afraid to answer the phone, afraid that it was someone calling to inform her that Sten had killed someone, or someone had killed Sten. She always knew it was going to be bad news. Once Sten had gotten locked up, she was more at ease and at peace because she knew Sten was safer than he had been on the streets. She knew where he was.

The sound of a car door slamming drew her out of her seat, and she met Big Ro at the door. He was carrying a white envelope, just like the one he had been delivering to her every month of the four years Sten had been gone.

Sten would call his mother every Wednesday night at 7:00PM. They always looked forward to their weekly session. The only way Sten wouldn't keep the appointment was if they were on lockdown and his mother always knew that was probably the case if he didn't call. Sten would get in line for the phone at 6:00PM, and then let the next four guys behind him go next. A person could only use 15 minutes, and most guys would use the full amount once they got on the phone, so that would put him getting his turn right around 7:00PM. Once the person on the other side of the line pressed '5' to accept your call, you were unable to use the phone again until thirty minutes past the time you hung up.

"How's Sten doing?" Big Ro asked as he tried to hand Sten's mother the money envelope.

"Please, come in," Sten's mother invited him, unlocking the screen door.

Big Ro felt strange because this was the first time she had invited him into the house in all the months of his coming there. He was accustomed to her accepting the envelope and mumbling a polite *thank you*. Sten's mother led Big Ro to the kitchen table. A writing tablet, pen, and a stamped envelope lay there, looking peaceful. "You always ask me how my son is doing. You sit down and write him to see how he's doing."

Big Ro pulled the chair away from the table, sat down, and picked up the pen. He didn't even know how to begin the letter or how he would end the letter. Big Ro did not know what to say to Sten so he started off with the same question that he would always ask his mother. Once Big Ro began to put the pen in the wind, Sten's mother felt there was no longer any use in standing over him, and she recollected her seat. She sat and thought about how much Sten had changed and had grown into an intelligent and knowledgeable young man. "Thank you, Lord," his mother mumbled as tears cascaded down her face. "Prison saved my child and converted him back into a complete human being."

Chapter 11

Sten awakened a little bit after 2:00 in the afternoon. The sun had been standing at attention on his side of the earth, but he hadn't acknowledged it because the blanket he had over his cell window made the room more pitch black. The cool air blew out of the vent like crazy. It dancedaround his cell at a hospital temperature.

Sten had gotten a good three hours of afternoon rest. His butt and back ached from spending so much time cooped up in the cell. Sitting on the hard plastic chairs and lying in the bed were beginning to take its toll on his body.

Sten had lost track of what day of the week it was. The institution had been on lockdown now for ninety-three days and counting. It didn't look like they'd be coming off of it any time soon, either. He was glad, however, that he was not in the standard 6'x12' cell. He lived in a penitentiary mansion--a handicapped cell, which was twice as large as the normal cell. There were two of these cells in each unit--the first and the last cell on the bottom range.

Sten crept over to his window and peeled aside the blanket. The hot sun sprinted past him, bathing the cell and chasing the darkness away. "Let there be light," he mumbled.

The campers in their yellow suits were pushing the food carts across the compound. These were the inmates from the nearby minimum security "camp" who did most of the work on the compound when the institution was locked down.

Sten talked to them, even though they could not hear him. "My dear brothers, we're tired of cold cuts and peanut butter and jelly sandwiches. They done fed me turkey so much I don't even like it anymore. Today should be a hot meal... where's the hot meals at?"

By policy, when on lockdown the inmates had a right to have a shower and a hot meal every three days, but the inmates considered themselves lucky if those events happened every seven days.

Sten knew that other inmates had seen the campers pushing the carts of bag lunches on his side of the building because he started hearing turkey noises, letting the whole unit know it was time to eat.

Sten sadly shook his head at his celly, who was sitting by the door smoking a cigarette and enjoying a lukewarm cup of coffee. Trey saw the look in Sten's eyes. He knew a lecture was about to begin, and Sten did not prove his instincts to be wrong. "My momma was sitting there drinking a cup of coffee, and she told me *Look son... I don't even want you to start drinking this,* and I said, *Why, momma, you drinking it.* She told me that if I started drinking it, I would become dependent on it, and think I had to have it to get me started in the morning. Then she went on to tell me about the cigarettes and how they would control me as well if I ever got into smoking them. Man, you don't want anything to control you or to have to depend on anything but the Lord."

"Brother Sten, you got, something for everything. What you ain't got somethin' for?"

"The things I haven't been through already."

The mail sliding underneath their door caught their attention. Trey shouted, "CO, I told you about sliding our mail under the door. That's some shit you do to animals. We human beings, so give us our human rights and start popping that slot with your lazy tail."

The unit officer had been getting ready to open the food slot, because that is how he usually gave Sten his mail, but had intentionally thrown it under the door because Trey was sitting there. The officer got a kick out of doing little things to push Trey's buttons. He could trigger Trey easily just by saying a simple *good morning* to him.

Trey picked up the newspaper and the letter. Sten had an annual subscription to his hometown newspaper, so they knew the newspaper was his. Trey checked the name on the letter, hoping it was his. He hadn't received one letter yet this week, but he had written four--two to his oldest brother, one to his niece, and one to his sister.

"Here's your letter from your momma, momma's boy. Hurry up and read our newspaper."

"Yes, sir, brother man, yes sir," Sten replied, collecting the mail. His intention was to lay the newspaper on their desk, so Trey could read it first. Sten was going to try to get some studying done, and if Trey did not have something to read, he would sing out loud or do other annoying things that would get on Sten's nerves.

Trey did not read anything but urban novels and rap magazines. When he did look at the newspaper, he'd go straight to the sports section. He usually saved the crime section for last and did not realize that it sickened Sten how he always highlighted the crime.

The headlines on the paper caught Sten's attention, and drew his eyes to a small article. Sten re-read it three times before addressing Trey. "Celly, the world is asking America to give them a helping hand, because the youth are getting out of hand."

"In that case, America needs to give me a hand," Trey said.

"They're asking people to share some jewels with the youth to bring them out of their darkness and into the light. What would you say to the youth?"

"Brother Sten, you know I don't know nothing," Trey breathed out with a nose full of smoke. "Blackman, the only message I can relay to the people is your mother's lesson. Don't smoke cigarettes and don't drink coffee, cause now I'm hooked. I depend on it like you depend on air to breath," Trey chuckled. "Blackman, I'm sure you have something positive for the people. Put some of that on them that you always be trying to put on me. All I can say to the people is do as I say and not as I do."

Sten nodded. He was content with the little bit his celly had provided. He watched as Trey chain smoked and refilled the coffee cup. Trey was an extremist in everything that he did. He would gamble until he lost everything in his locker and his commissary validation. He would drink until he passed out.

Sten collected his pen and tablet. As he pondered the question he began to let a small portion flow, and gave them what he was about to put on his celly.

WHAT WOULD I SAY TO OUR YOUTH?

"I would tell them that first, contrary to popular belief and what they have been *taught,* they are not any of the derogatory terms and images that the various forms of the media portray them to be.

"I placed emphasis on the word "taught" because the things that we have been associated with, the way we view ourselves, our true history, our women, our brothers, our children and our life, as our relationship with and to these things and a multitude of others like the creator were all learned behaviors. They taught us to think and feel that way and this way about these subjects.

"They taught us that our history that predated the Trans-Atlantic Slave Trade and the atrocities we endured during that era were not important--no big thing--and that we did not contribute anything of importance, because we were heathens, savages and uncultivated when in reality EVERY culture that exists, or has existed, thrived and benefited because of our contributions.

Khemi is the name of the people of Khemet. It literally means "Black people." They are Black not African. "Africa" came from the name Africanus. Leo Africanus was a European that was one of the first to map the continent called Alkebu-Lan.

"The Kemitians (Egyptians) were not Caucasian or Caucasoid featured people. They were very much African. Just look at the way they portrayed themselves. Ask yourself, why would these people go to such lengths to make you and us feel worthless? Africans are not a polytheistic people. They taught you that so you would not react the way you were supposed to when you read your history.

"They portray us the way they do so that when they shoot us forty-one times, beat us in plain view, tie us to the back of a truck and drag us, rape our women and commit a host of other atrocities, we would not react instead ask "What did we do?"

"They have made us callouse and dumbed us down to the point we are unconcerned and ambivalent. But the thing that I really wants to grab you is when you begin to read books by Cheikh Anta Diop, Marimba Ani, Anthony Browder, Babashango, Joseph AA Ben-jochannan, Chancellor Williams, Ra Un Nefer Amen, and a host of others. You will begin to acknowledge that not only did they do these things, they planned them and we are so caught up in this fascist, imperialistic, colonialistic, Eurasian and patriarchal culture and society that we no longer need to be monitored. We commit these atrocities and more against ourselves, because we have been "taught" to hate what we see in the mirror, what we see when we look at our mothers, sisters, brothers, and so forth.

"History is very important because it gives you a foundation from which to deal with the time frames of the past, present and future.

"Read and learn our true history, culture, spirituality, language, innate yearnings, and our true voice. Then we begin to break the cycle."

જ - ન્જ

"Excuse me, Akh. Let me look out the window?" Hafidh asked.

"Celly, what you be looking at when you look out the window? Ain't nothing out there," Shakur said.

Shakur walked over by the door. The tiny cell was only yay-big, and normally on lockdowns they would take turns on the floor. One stayed in the bed until the other one finished pacing the floor. If not, they would constantly be bumping into one another.

Hafidh did two sets of head stand push-ups on the window bars. "When I look out the window, I see freedom," Hafidh said in a mild voice as he tried to control his breathing. Shakur watched the shakedown crew take the first ten people out of their cells to the day-room. The shakedown crew wasn't any special crew. It was just staff who happened to be available. The BOP worked the employees in positions that were needed during lockdowns. They basically disposed of their professional or job title during the time of lockdowns. When the employees came to work, they knew they were coming to a job and they would be earning their money during those days of crises. They'd do the same job as officers and sometimes a lot more. Schoolteachers, rec officers, medical personnel and business office people were a part of the shakedown crew.

They strip-searched each inmate before they took them out of their cell. They went through all institutional-issued laundry, personal clothes and personal property. They'd confiscate anything they felt was not needed. They'd take extra linen and personal property.

If there were over five novels in the cell, consider the extras a donation. If there were more than sixty stamps they would be confiscated too, and the extra books of stamps would be paid to the snitches.

All the stamps and commissary items that were confiscated were used to obtain information. Some people give up the information to keep their property from being confiscated. On the street, people have the police on their payroll, but when they came to jail, some of them get on the police payroll. The majority of the authorities had their own personal snitch. The warden had his snitches, and the same went for the captain, lieutenants and even some of the COs. They had eyes and ears everywhere. The captain would even say out of his own mouth, *If you see five guys walking together, one of them is mine.*

Shakur watched the schoolteacher female run the hand metal detector wand over both inmates pillows and mattress. The facility officers removed the cell lights, checking to see if the cellies had anything hidden up in them. They took the toilets up, checking the pipes. They took the sink off the wall as well. They looked behind the mounted locker with a small mirror. They also used the small mirror to look under and on top of the cell door. They searched thoroughly for weapons. All the knives they didn't find by the inmates sliding underneath their doors the staff were determined to find on their own.

Shakur turned away from the shakedown crew. Hafidh was still looking out of the window.

"Hafidh, a lot of time we use words that have a lot of different meanings. You said sometimes you look out the window and see freedom. There are very different meanings of words. Sometimes it's good to narrow down the difference and the meaning of the word to one particular thing. When we do that we rob it of its true meaning and beauty, most things cannot be defined with one word or with one meaning. They're broader than that. I went on to say that because you said when you look out the window, you see freedom. What is freedom to you that you see?"

Hafidh continued doing his set of Jane Fonda half-correct push-ups. "When I look out that window, I see freedom. I don't see this place, Akh. It may sound crazy but that's how I escape the prison life a lot of times. Sometimes I'll come in the room at night, I'll sit on table and look out of the window. I won't even cut the lights on--sittin' in the dark makes it even better!"

"Basically what you are telling me, right, that you look beyond this, you look into the trees and into the sky. And you escape from here and from this environment? And your mind travels beyond this wall. You are looking and seeing with your physical eyes, as well as your mental eyes, and you tell me that you broke free, you see freedom. You only see it because a physical hold that you are allowed to break from but that is not true freedom. In a way it is, but it's not a complete freedom. Freedom is when you break completely away from something that has a physical or mental hold on you. That's what complete freedom is- when you can speak your mind and not allow anything to stop or limit you from believing in yourself. See what the dictionary has to say about freedom. See what they did in the slavery days. They took the physical chains off us and put us on the plantations into another form of slavery, and when they so-called freed us physically from them plantations; they kept us in slavery in another form through our minds. We never were really free because they didn't allow us to think for ourselves with true freedom of being independent of them. They kept us in a minor state of dependency. You cannot have complete freedom until you are physically free as well as mentally free. When you look out the window, it could be complete mental freedom you have to free your mind. Don't allow them to stop your broad manner of thinking. They say things to make you think your thinking is unrealistic. You can't be a movie star, you can't do this, you can't do that. Don't let anyone stagnate you. Don't stay on the narrow road. Grow and continue to develop."

"Kick, kick, kick, kick," a CO kicked on the door.

"Yeah!" Hafidh shouted. "Man, what you kickin' on that door for like you crazy. Man, some of y'all COs dumber then a box of rocks."

"Calm down, Akh. He just don't know any better," Shakur said. "Yeah, yeah. What do you want, big boy?" Hafidh asked the CO. "Get dressed," the CO commanded more calmly.

"We already dressed," Shakur stepped up to the door, looking out to see a psychologist and Unicor staff member waiting to shake down their cell.

"You're a Muslim, right?" the CO asked as he popped the food slot.

Shakur didn't respond. He just put his hands through the slot. The CO cuffed him from behind. Shakur walked over by the sink giving his celly space so he could get cuffed up from the back as well.

The CO unlocked the door. "Yeah, you come with me. I'm going to be your escort, so I can watch you," he directed Hafidh.

"I don't know what you are trying to watch me for, 'cause I'm not gonna teach you nothing," Hafidh said, over-aggressively.

"Ain't you a Muslim?" the CO asked with a small chuckle.

"I ain't nobody's child, I bet'cha that," Hafidh replied.

"Good brother, we are all God's children," the CO stated as he was leading Hafidh down the range. "You know, good brother, when I was growing up my best friend was a Muslim."

"What's his name?" Hafidh immediately asked.

"You know, I done forgot."

"Yeah, CO, right," Hafidh replied, knowing the CO was trying to feed him propaganda and make small talk.

When they reached their destination, Hafidh was interviewed by one of the kitchen supervisors and Shakur was getting interviewed by one of the chaplains.

"Where were you during the riot?"

"I didn't know there was a riot," Shakur answered.

"Do you know anyone who was a part of the riot?"

"Say, chaplain, when we going to come offa this lockdown?" Shakur asked, reversing the interrogation.

"If not by tonight, then we'll be back on normal routine by 6 a.m. when the doors open."

"Chaplain, what's up with the hot meals? We were supposed to have had them two days ago."

"Don't worry. You'll get all three of them every day starting tomorrow."

"If it's the will of Allah," Shakur corrected.

"Chaplain, you finished?" Shakur's escort walked into the room and asked.

"Yeah, I guess so," the chaplain answered. He finished Shakur's question sheet by writing "No cooperation" beside his name. Shakur never allowed them to pump him for information.

☙ – ❧

One victim left dead, one detained into custody, facing life imprisonment. Prosecutors are pushing for nothing but the death penalty.

The news lady's words still haunted Zeek Bey's celly from fifteen winters ago.

Zeek Bey's celly perceived the misconception that he could get ahead in life by pulling off a robbery, but things went clearly against the grain. It did not work out according to his plan. He was forced to go all the way and going hard that day cost him his social privileges, but rewarded him with a lifetime of prison supplies. The warranty for his shoes, clothing, and hygiene items would never ever expire.

"Blackman, wake up. The bags are here. It's turkey time. You sleep late, you lose weight."

"Zeek Bey, what time is it?"

"Turkey sandwich time," Zeek Bey answered in a monster's voice. Zeek Bey was aware that his celly had awakened from a bad dream. He'd had them himself last night. He'd dreamed about his trial. His flesh underneath Vakeita's nails alone convicted him. The courts did not need to use Vakeita's testimony. His flesh and blood were the key witnesses.

Zeek Bey drank two cups of water out of the sink. "MO, I don't see how you drank that nasty water. I can't drink it. It hurts my stomach."

"After a few burps and passing gas a couple of times and you'll be alright. The body has more water in it than anything. All I drink is water. I don't drink sodas, Kool-aid or juices like you. I'm a water man," Zeek Bey said. He downed another cup of water. "Bad, but good. Do you know anything about fasting?"

"Naw, tell me."

"Fasting is about getting inside the inner self. Knowing, mastering, and controlling the inner self. It cleans us from all that negative. That is why we don't eat, drink, and try not to entertain negative thoughts during the time when the sun is out. When you can't spot the sun anymore, that's when we start filling the body back up. Most of us misunderstand what we just went through and believe that now is the time to fill the body back up with a lot of polluted toxicants and foolish thoughts."

Chapter 12

Chase waited beside the door, waiting on the SHU officer to return in five minutes like he had promised. Chase read over the old lockdown sheet.

NOTICE

TO: USP PETTY ROCK INMATE POPULATION
SUBJECT: LOCKDOWN OF INSTITUTION

Due to the recent incident, the USP will remain locked down and all privileges suspended until further notice.

SUSPENDED PRIVILEGES include, but are not limited to:

TV   TELEPHONES   COMMISSARY
ICE   HOTWATER VISITATION

The following WILL OCCUR daily:
  * Sick call and medication distribution in the unit
  * Mail picked up and delivered.
  * Bag lunches in cell.

SHOWERS & LAUNDRY EXCHANGE will be considered at a later time, depending on the lockdown and in accordance with BOP policy.

The other half of the page repeated the message in Spanish for the inmates who had not completed their mandatory English as a Second Language studies.

The SHU inmates had an advantage over the general population during lockdowns. They had a shower in their cells and could take showers at their own convenience and as often as they liked.

Chase looked out the cell window again, futilely hoping to see the officer. The steel box on the cell door directly across from him attracted his attention. There were fifty cells on his range, twenty-five cells on each side. Ten of the cell doors had the metal box attached.

These boxes had never held any importance to Chase, and he really had not even wondered about them until today. "Celly, why people got them boxes? They sit on some penitentiary spenders. Ya heard me?"

"Guys always taking their food slots. Every time the COs feed them, somebody going to try to stick their arm out there and hold the slot hostage. They do it because they be wantin' some hot water, clean laundry or probably because they need to see somebody like a lieutenant or counselor. Some do it just for an extra tray, while others just do it for attention. Round, them folks built those boxes especially for a dude named Quick. Young boy was always wildin' out.

There also was a hillbilly back here with long hair and a wild-ass beard. That fake-ass gangsta refused to step foot on the compound. Round, if one of 'em wasn't raisin' hell, the other one was."

"What's up with the dude across from us?"

"That's Pussy Peter. He raises hell too. He can't stand to be in the cell alone. He'll kick on the door and hold the slot until they give him a celly. The young sissy say his baby momma daddy turn him out. He ran up in pop's daughter, and pop ran up in him for running up in his daughter. Peter look like ET's twin brother."

Chase looked at his celly. His celly's feet were propped up on the fold-up green mattress, and he was still holding his pen. "Celly, how many books you done wrote?"

"I'm on my seventh one. I have three more to write."

"You got a baby library, ya heard me?"

"I just have a passion for writing. I started off writing music. I wrote four albums, and then I started writing novels offa my albums. This bid will make the way for my future."

Peter put his whole face in the cell window, giving Chase a clear view of his ET features. He nodded at Chase, and Chase nodded back. "What up playa? My name PP," Peter said, trying to introduce himself.

"I see Pussy Peter tryin' to holla at'cha," Chase's celly said, laughing.

"Say, cousin, I ain't try'na play the dirty dozen, ya heard me?" Chase shouted over to Peter.

"Nigga, meet me on the rec yard," Peter replied.

"Woady, meet me on the compound and we can get it crackin', ya heard me?"

Peter tried to raise hell from behind the steel door, but Chase didn't entertain the thought because he wasn't a behind-the-door gangsta. Chase's celly assured him that once Peter's celly run up in him a couple more times, he'd be back to his friendly-ass normal self.

The CO finally made it back around to get Chase, ten minutes before the shift change. Chase snapped on him, "Man, you had me to rush and pack my shit at lunch time. You said after you picked up all the trays on our range you'd be back to get me."

"Man, I came back and got your ass, didn't I?" replied the CO.

"Man, that ain't worth a damn. Five minutes is five minutes," Chase snorted, as he was being rushed down the range. His escort put him in one of the six green dress-out cages that were used for inmates changing clothes.

"I'll be back in five," the CO said with a wicked smile.

The CO entered their house stations, which was their place of gathering where they could all eat lunch and freely leave their personal belongings laying around. He threw his backpack across his shoulder. "Number One, I need you to dress one out for me. He's already in the cage."

Ms. Coon sat behind the ten small TV cameras. The cameras revealed every part and section of the SHU. Holding the number one position, she had authority over her shift staff. Every SHU officer had a title, numbering from one to four. The number two officer was second in command and was over number three and number four.

"Oh, Number Two, you trying to hurry up and get back home to that woman," Ms. Coon joked.

"I stayed an extra hour last week for you, when you went home early to that man," Number Two joked back.

Ms. Coon had left early last week because of a dental appointment. Her wisdom teeth had been giving her problems and the store-bought medication wasn't doing a good job of killing the pain any more.

"Oh, okay, now I see what's happening. You trying to bring last week's score to today's game. Number Two, when you do favors for people, you can't throw it up in their faces later."

"Do unto others, like you would like done to you. Treat others like you would like to be treated."

"You prayin' out the Qur'aan on me?"

"No, Ms. Coon... from the Bible."

"In that case, then preach on out the door, Rev."

"Thank you, Number One, I owe you one."

"Consider us even, Champ," Ms. Coon said in good faith. She buzzed Number Two out both of the steel doors.

"Now let me get up offa my tail and dress this inmate out so I can kick him out too." Ms. Coon sprang up out of her chair and rubbed lightly across her butt, like she was trying to brush off a piece of lint. She had a habit of feeling on herself.

Chase stood in the green cage just as the number two officer in charge had left him, in nothing but his size IX boxers, 3X Kool-aid dyed shirt, and dingy-looking socks.

"Justin Chase, you supposed to been long gone," Ms. Coon informed him as soon as she arrived in front of the cage.

"Hey, Ms. Coon. What's poppin', ya heard me?"

"Go on and get undress now so I can get you out of here."

Chase followed suit like a servant eager to please. He dropped his boxers to the floor. Chase kicked them away from around his feet as he pulled the shirt over his head. At this moment, Chase represented the characteristics of two consecutive groups, as he put on display his six-pack and his manhood. Some guys always walked around with their shirts off showing off their six-packs to female officers, and then there was another group of individuals who were dedicated to the indecent-exposure game.

"Okay now, Justin Chase. You can put your little wee-wee back up now that you done showed me already."

"Ms. Coon, you better sweat the technique now. It ain't like every day you get to see a body like mines, ya heard me?"

"Boy, come on here and put ya clothes on so you can get back to the compound," Ms. Coon said.

Chase was stalling and taking his sweet time. He saved his boxers for last.

"Hurry up, my lil-bust-it-baby. Justin Chase, I'm gonna call you my lil-bust-it-baby."

"Oh, yeah," Chase said smiling from ear to ear. "And I'm going nickname you Wet-wet."

Ms. Coon had given Chase the private name of the Ne-Yo and Plies song, Bust-it-Baby, and Chase had given Ms. Coon the private name that Plies said he named his boo.

Ms. Coon let Chase out of the segregation by pushing the button with her left hand while she used her right hand to brush against her butt. When Chase stepped back onto the compound, everything was back to the normal routine. The jungle was full-fledged back into the swing of things.

The gorillas, snakes, pigs, and baby orangutans were doing what they do and the compound mascots were back to their routine, which was being straight up and down donkeys.

Chapter 13

Romeo walked on A-Yard normally. That's where he would see Shakur playing chess. Shakur would be on A-Yard all day because he didn't play on the other yards. On C-Yard, Shakur could not concentrate on his chess game with someone constantly shouting, Head's up because softballs stayed flying. If a softball game wasn't going on, one of the teams would be out there practicing, or the guys would create a batting competition. Those white balls always promised to interfere with everyone's task and break their tranquility.

On B-Yard, the handballs would constantly be making their way over by his table from the handball court. The handball players would holler for the guys at the tables to throw their balls back to them, and Shakur, not being the rude type, would usually break his concentration to assist them.

"I'm on the block, gentlemen's. Get'em while they hot," Cox shouted as he coasted up the sidewalk with fifty burritos in a clear plastic trash bag. "Beef burritos and fish burritos."

"Johnny get money," Romeo shouted.

"Come on and support my hustle and get you a couple of burritos?" Cox asked.

Cox's name wasn't Johnny, but that's what Romeo always called him. It was short for Johnny Cochran, since Cox claimed he was like that with the law work.

"Say, Cox. I need you to file for me on that crack law. When you think can help me?"

"Come see me in about two days. Right now you need to get a couple of these burritos."

"Johnny get money," Romeo chanted. "Cox, man, you seen your Muslim brother, Shakur? I know he don't go nowhere but on A-Yard."

"Him and the guy in the wheel chair on B-Yard sittin' at the table playing chess. Now come on and get you a burrito or two?"

"Johnny get money," Romeo hollered, walking away.

Cox knew Romeo was not going to buy any burritos. All Romeo was going to do was holla his famous saying, Johnny get money. Cox taught Romeo how to make burritos when he had first arrived. Cox was the king of burritos.

He had taught several more of his Muslim brothers the game. They all had short terms in the burritos field, but Cox was the #1 chef and the people said his Muslim brother Ali was not too far from taking the #1 spot away from him. As soon as Ali would think Cox would lighten up, Cox would tighten up.

Romeo walked through the gate to B-yard; two handballs were laying by Shakur and Sten's table. As

Romeo drew closer to the table, he saw another blue handball by Sten's wheelchair.

"Hey, homie, throw them balls. All of 'em mines," said DC Mike.

Romeo slipped two flyers on the table--one beside Shakur and another one beside Sten. "Brother, you're in the nation, ain't you?" Romeo addressed Sten as he retrieved the handball by his wheelchair.

"Yes, I'm with the Nation community," Sten answered.

"Good lookin', homie," DC Mike shouted as Romeo was throwing all three balls towards him. "Romeo, what is this?" Shakur asked, slightly glancing at the paper as he was moving a pawn. "That's a paper telling you that you and your Muslim brother can come speak at the chapel on October 16th. Shakur, you always around here talking to the young guys, now here's you chance. Don't get scared now."

"Romeo, remember I fear nothing but Allah," Shakur replied.

When Sten and Shakur sat down to play chess they put their religious differences to the side. They dealt with each other as respectful individuals. They stopped playing chess to read the flyer. The thought of what Mr. Pete said one day during a chess session slipped through Sten's lips, "I think we can make a difference here and now by coming together to let the people see the things that been holding us back."

"What is that--that been holding us back?" Shakur asked, laying the flyer on the table.

"A misunderstanding of unification," Sten noted looking into Shakur's eyes.

"So what is it that we going to do about bringing the universal understanding together?"

"You just said it. We will come together universally by bringing our different religious organizations together to speak on this Day of Atonement," Sten explained.

"That sounds like a good idea. We need to reach out to the other religious groups and have them to join us to speak out on this day. I been thinking. I know the force is moving me in this direction, I just do not fully understand it right now. I will just have to ask Allah to continue to guide me down this path," Shakur said.

Organized religions through a vision will become a thing of the past as it stays in this day and time. Organized religion is the # 1 thing of separation. Each organization, each organized group teaches superiority and inferiority. I'm better than you. You're not going to make it into the Kingdom of God or the hereafter because you don't do things this way or that way. In other words, people believe that they know how to pray but in reality, they don't. They believe that if you don't perform in this way or that way you will not be heard. Most people do not know that they just going through the motions and worship or some just following rituals in the things that they do.

If we believe in the one God, then we must truly understand the one God and walk in that path. Anyone can walk in that path regardless of the title that they claim that they are under. We must do away with titles and positions and come together as one... and follow and believe in one God in that straight path.

When one takes on a belief, in time you'll see the reflection of that belief in their characteristics or at the least through their ritual. These rituals can be many different things. For example, where they wear a part in their hair, if it's just hiking up their pants to a certain length, the growth of their beard, or other rituals they might take on depending on their new-found belief.

Shakur and Sten set out to find Zeek Bey. They found him on   A-yard exercising with his Moor brothers. Zeek Bey wore gray sweatpants, a white wife-beater, a white headband and his white Nikes. His bald head was damp with sweat. Their exercise was super-sets of burpies with the kick-outs.

Shakur and Sten stood their distance until they saw Zeek Bey's crew decide to take a break. They called Zeek Bey to the side. They both greeted Zeek Bey with "Peace, Mo." Zeek Bey fired back with Islam.

"Did you receive one of these flyers yet?" Shakur asked, holding the paper in plain view.

"No, what is it?" Zeek Bey asked.

"It's the beginning of our beginning," Sten revealed.

"Beginning of what?" Zeek Bey asked.

"A unification of all people," Shakur suggested.

"How can we unify the people?" Zeek Bey asked.

"By doing something that never has been done with religion and with the races of the people," stated Sten. "We are going to unify with the different races and with the different religion of the people on Atonement Day."

"What is the Atonement Day stuff all about?" Zeek Bey asked.

"That is the day that we are going to make history and change history with the races of people and the religious misunderstanding of the people," stated Sten.

"What is it you want me to do?" Zeek Bey asked.

"By unifying with us on this mission," Shakur instructed. "By bringing the people together on the Atonement Day."

They came up with the idea to set the plan in motion the week before Atonement Day. Zeek Bey, Shakur and Sten took it upon themselves to finance a gathering to feed the entire prison yard, regardless of race, religious beliefs, or gangs. They told everyone to just come out to have a unity day, where they would eat the food that was provided by the three of them. The prison yard could not wait to get a free meal. Anytime something is given out free there would be no ending to the lines. The prison tower guard could not believe what he witnessed, and he jumped on his radio to tell some of the guards to see what the gathering was all about.

Chapter 14

Zeek Bey, Corroll Bey and Gather Bey ran five miles. One thing about the Moors, you were going to see a couple of them exercise daily. If not in a group, then as a couple. They were going to sweat that poison out of their systems. They took turns leading their formation. Every Moor got his day to play drill sergeant. He would lead his brothers in the exercise that was the easiest for him but the hardest for the others. Everyone had their own favorite exercise; some kind of callisthenic which they mastered in.

Zeek Bey was a beast in squats, he could not be matched. He could do fifteen hundred straight. Corroll Bey was the fastest runner on the compound. He would give the person he was racing several car lengths lead, then run them down, waving to them as he passed. Gather Bey was a burpees man. He could and would do a thousand burpees straight and still go run ten miles. Some people don't understand that the body is a machine.

As Zeek Bey was making his way back to the unit, he saw Mr. Johnson feeding the birds. Mr. Johnson fed the birds three daily meals, just like the institution gave him three daily meals. In the morning, Mr. Johnson would feed them his biscuits, for lunch he would feed them his light bread and for the last meal, Mr. Johnson would give the birds his cornbread. He took it as his responsibility because he felt as though he needed to feed the creatures that crept and crawled on the Earth, as well as the birds that flew above the heavens. It gave him a sense of importance by doing the work of his God by providing and lending a helping hand to those who were in need.

When Zeek Bey walked into his cell, his celly was slumped down in a chair, looking like he had lost his best friend. Once his celly got to worrying, stressing or thinking too hard, he would eat as if he could eat away the problem. Four soda cans sat on the table alone with empty bags of chips and candy bar wrappings.

"Brother, you suppose to eat to live, not live to eat!"

"Mo, I'm going through it with my baby momma. She says I call my own child too much. She said the psychiatrist said I need to stop talking to my son so much."

Zeek Bey felt every bit of his celly's pains. He could relate to the issue because he had experienced similar problems.

"Once something comes into your life she will always be in your life as a part of you, even if you cut her off. It's nothing personal between you and her and as for your seed coming to or growing up, you must not stop the growth due to your separation. You have to maintain a connection because it's an issue of your seed maturing to its full potential. You don't want him to be mentally messed up in the head due to your selfish reasons. It's a cycle that must be broken. You must get her to understand it's not about you and her, it's deeper than that due to the fact that generations have been set in place and there is an aim and purpose for that. When a child is born that's native, that's a gift from Allah." Zeek paused and sat on the toilet. "Celly, my son's mother told me I can't be a father from jail! Did you just hear what I just said, brother?"

"Yes!"

"Our women used to depend on us. They took her and made her dependent, and she became independent of us, because she had her own. When we were in this servitude condition, they took the woman's independence from us when they gave her the little house on the plantation, fed and sheltered her, and made her depend on them. She became independent from us and now depends on them. That is still what is happening today. The woman is still making more money than the average Blackman. This is why women have lost respect for the Blackman. Only a few were actually there for the woman. Most of the time, in the average work of the Blackman, he had to be away so that he could clothe and feed her. You didn't see his work, and did not see that he was the provider. You only see her, and thought that she was independent, but she was really dependent. This tired the next generation. We didn't understand the work of the father. We thought we could just make a baby and move on. We thought Poppa was a rollin' stone, as we seen it. We misunderstood the guides of the father, and had no real understanding of the father figure. You see, your son's mother may still see you as that person you were when you came in. She has not looked at you in the light that you are shining in now. In other words, she does not look at you as the man you have grown into. The mirror image that she is reflecting on is a hindrance in y'all's relationship. She will not get or let that old mirror image die away. She has to look at you in this day and time as the man you have grown into. Once she recognizes and sees you for who you are today, your relationship will improve down a positive road. Now, celly cell, kick rocks so I can get ready for a shower," said Zeek Bey.

Twelve guys sat in the lobby waiting on their individual turn to be reviewed by team. There were a total of twenty-seven inmates on the list. The other guys would be paged or hunted down by the unit officer.

You were required to see team every six months. However, if you were within six months of your release date, you would see team every ninety days. During team, you would be seated with your counselor, case manager and unit manager. Sometimes it would be only the two of them who happened to be available.

"Say, Slim, some people say Petty Rock is fucked up, but I like it because this shit is gonna rock. Niggas get their man around here, Joe," said DC.

The counselor stuck his head out of the office door. "We're ready. Let me have the first man."

The first and second person were not going to tongue wrestle about their place in line, but from the third man on down, they had to be on the lookout for someone trying to cut the line, because everyone wanted to run in and out of team and get it over with. Some inmates would try to waive their team. Why show up and get their time wasted? They knew there was nothing that the team could say or do to help them. One of the female case managers had stated loud and clear that if they had a life sentence or over twenty-five years, there wasn't anything she could do for them.

The first guy watched the case manager look through his jacket, otherwise known as his inmate file. She frowned as she wiped a lace of stringy hair out of her face.

"Here, sign these," Counselor Sed demanded as he pushed a couple sheets of paper in front of the inmate.

"What you want me to sign it with, my hand?" the guy asked as he spread both of his empty palms.

"Oh, that's my bad, I thought one of your fingers was full of ink," Counselor Sed joked as he passed the guy his personal pen.

"Wotson, you need to get in a GED class," recommended the case manager. "Do you know how many days you're losing without going to school?"

"How many?" Wotson asked with an attitude.

"Wotson, they give out fifty-four days a year in good time, but you get only forty-eight because you don't have a GED."

"I'm losing six days, huh?"

"If you enroll in a GED class, you'll get fifty-two days a year." "Four mo days, huh? Yeah, fuckin' right."

"Why don't you just get your GED and you'll get the whole fifty-four days?"

"Yeah, you'd like that, wouldn't you? After I graduate they'll pay me that lil twenty-five dollars. Damn that GED, I ain't doing shit for the system!"

"Do it for yourself," the case manager encouraged, brushing the hair out of her face once again.

"I'll do this shit like Mandela. All y'all gotta do is leave me the fuck alone!"

"Unbelievable. Where do all you people come from?" the case manager said out of frustration.

"Son, you need to take some type of program so you can better yourself for society," advised Counselor Sed.

"Man, do you know when my gotdamn out date is, man?" Wotson huffed in a negative voice. "My out date is 2088. I'm twenty years old. How the fuck you think I'm gonna live eighty more years in prison? What's the average age a person lives to? Seventy, eighty? Man, y'all folks done bumped your fuckin' heads around here. I got a ton of decades to do and y'all talking about a fuckin' GED."

"Calm down, son, calm down," counseled Counselor Sed. "Why so much profanity?"

"Hey man, don't call me your son, cause I'm not your fuckin' son! Alright? Do I make myself clear? Man, didn't you say you was a preacher?" Wotson addressed Counselor Sed as he stared him down with an angry look.

"Yes, I'm a preacher. Yes, I'm a man of God."

"Well then, do your damn job and go out there and tell the young people about a fucked up nigga like me! That's y'all real job, the Lord's word. Go counsel and preach to the people." Wotson stood up and started walking towards the door.

"You have two more pages to sign," informed the case manager. "Fuck'em. I ain't signing shit. Be grateful I signed the shit I did."

As Wotson rushed out of the room, a guy jumped out of his seat and started racing towards the door. His intentions were to go in and pick up where Wotson had left off. "Say, Woady, I'm next. I was second in line, ya heard me?" said Chase. The line-jumper returned to his seat and Chase knocked on the door.

"Come in," Counselor Sed invited. "Didn't we just have his team about a month or so ago?" he asked after seeing Chase.

"Yes. He's under thirty days of his release date," updated the unit manager.

"Have a seat, Justin Chase. If anybody should be standing up in here, it gotta be me," wolved Counselor Sed.

"I don't understand why all y'all short, fat, bald-headed guys always try to play tough, ya heard me? Try that tough man shit on somebody who got a lots of time and see what will happen to ya. I know what I gotta do wit'cha, I just gotta catch ya by ya self," Chase remarked, getting him and his counselor some one-on-one time.

"What you gonna do when you catch me by myself, Mr. Justin Chase?"

"It ain't about what I'm gonna do, it's about what you gonna do."

"Justin Chase, what you want me to do?"

"Nothin' but what you always do when we by ourselves."

"And what is that?"

"You smell like fear and I always see the fear in your eyes." "Justin Chase, what you trying to say, I'm trying to show out?" "Shit, you ain't trying to. That's exactly what you're doing."

"You just messed up then. Now I'm going to add you to my Cage of Rage class. You can look forward to being on my roster."

"And I second the recommendation that you take the counselor's class," said the case manager.

"You people can recommend all you want, but just because you recommend I eat a bowl of shit doesn't mean I'm gonna eat it. Didn't y'all two just sit there and hear the boss man when he said I was under thirty days to my release date?" Chase looked at the unit manager. "Boss man, tell ya people one mo' time how long it will be before I'm free as a bird."

"Justin Chase, just because you under thirty days doesn't guarantee that you'll walk out that door. You're a knucklehead and with that attitude you're liable to run that little bit of time up any day now if you're not careful," Counselor Sed told him.

"You're a lying ass," Chase replied. "You can stop holding your nuts on me."

"I'm not saying that it would happen, all I'm saying is you need to act like you are trying to go home and start thinking like you are trying to go home. I saw the last softball game you had. I was standing right there," Counselor Sed said. As he pointed to the small window, Chase saw that it was directly in front of the softball field.

"Man, I don't wanna talk about that shit. Let's talk about my halfway house papers."

The case manager licked her right thumb. She shifted through a couple of papers in Chase's file. "You'll get twenty-three days halfway house."

"Michael Jordan?" Chase cheered.

"What Michael Jordan have to do with anything?" asked the case manager. During her sixteen years of working in the system, she still hadn't gotten accustomed to all the slang language.

"That's the number on Jordan's jersey," the counselor explained. "Now-a-days, instead of saying twenty-three, these youngsters will say Michael Jordan instead."

"Man, keep that halfway house. I'm gonna do all mines right here. I'm bring it to the door like Mandela."

The case manager looked at the counselor. Now he could translate Mandela. She had heard that term a lot but didn't know what it meant either.

"The extraordinary African leader's name brings them strength and hope. They feel like Mandela did all his time so now they can stand strong and do their time," the counselor filled her in.

Counselor Sed sniffed Chase over. "Justin Chase, what kind of cologne you have on? That's a different kind, ain't it?"

"Man, why you always worryin' about what kind of earl I have on?"

"Because I know you can't say oil," counselor Sed started laughing.

"Man, I'm from the home of broken English, but if you keep on bullshitting up in here, I'm gonna make you hit the deuces, ya heard me?"

Chapter 15

Zeek Bey sat at one of the four library tables, reading through law books searching for a case that could help relieve some of his prison sentence. He scanned through the Shepardize. The Shepardize book would provide cases in each circuit throughout the country.

Big G from Florida assisted Zeek Bey. Big G followed the Hebrew Israelite lifestyle and wore long dreadlocks. Even his beard was one long dread. He was tatted with the Father, the Son, and the Holy Spirit tattoos. Big G was the firstborn to this generation of King David, lion of the tribe of Judah.

"Mo, I'm going to help you give back some of this time. We going to find the loophole. The courts are good about making mistakes. We will find a case pertaining to yours," said Big G, as he laid an armful of books on the table. "I need your case number, the date you got sentenced, and the address to the courts. I'm going to type up a letter asking the courts for sort of an extension on your appeal because we are a little late."

"That lockdown delayed me."

"You should've sent it out handwritten."

"Twin had my papers. I didn't even have it myself."

"Then he should've handwritten it, that's what I would've done."

The two guys at the table started making more noise as they played cards. "The people in UNICOR got tired of lookin' at you sittin' around there lookin' stupid, so now they got you over here sitting up in the schoolhouse looking stupid. You got a stupid Casino game," Mike said, being sarcastic, and Slick laughed along with him. It was okay for Mike to call him stupid, because he had given Mike the name Stupid Mike.

Mike had more sense than he put to use. Mike put that show on just to get his way. He would make you underestimate him, and once he had you laughing, he had you. That was Mike Summer's ace in the game.

A dark-skinned bald-headed guy walked over to the table. "Peace, brothers," he greeted Big G and Zeek Bey. "Say, Mo, you heard from my homie Bush yet?"

"Your name's New Kirk, right?" Zeek Bey asked. He then remembered that the Brother hadn't introduced himself by his alias, so he corrected, "Brother Terrence X, right?"

"Yes sir," Terrence X replied.

"Brother T, where you from again?"

"Norfolk, Virginia."

"Oh, okay. Naw, homie, Bush never holla back yet," Zeek Bey said.

"Bush told anotha one of my homies he was going to send him some flicks and a few dollars," Terrence X unfolded.

When a guy leaves prison, it is like when a person visited the graveyard. When they leave the graveyard, they don't send pictures, money orders or anything else of value back. People in the graveyards will not be needing those things. Unfortunately, it's the same way for some of the people who are left behind the penitentiary walls. They are not physically dead, but the memory of them is dead.

Shakur, Zeek Bey, and Sten sat on a bench by the soccer field. They stayed completely out of the soccer players' way. They weren't watching the soccer game, but were enjoying one another's company as they built each other's universe.

Shakur was always one hundred percent focused into their conversation, but his eyes were always roaming the rec yard. He watched what person ran with what person, and always observed all the grouped-up gang members, so he would be aware of everyone's affiliations. Shakur noticed Mississippi continuously looking off in their direction. He locked eyes with the guy twice. Shakur didn't know Mississippi personally and they had never said one word to one another, but they were familiar with one another's stats. Mississippi knew Shakur was a Muslim that was 100% on his Deen, and Shakur knew that Mississippi was a hustler and was living off the land.

Shakur's eyes did not miss out on Mississippi's steps as he made his way around the track.

"Do one of y'all know this brother walking up on us?" Zeek Bey asked Sten and Shakur. He was really directing the question at Shakur since Shakur had been at the institution for four years and played out on the yard a lot.

"Naw, I don't know him, Mo," Sten replied.

Shakur didn't respond. He just continued rubbing and combing his beard with his fingers.

"Excuse me, good brothers. Muslim brother Shakur, could I borrow a few minutes of your time? I was told you might be able to assist me concerning this matter," Mississippi said, with both palms parallel to his shoulders.

Shakur excused himself from Zeek Bey and Sten, took eleven steps over and asked, "What is it you think that I could assist you in, my brother?"

"One of your homies borrowed thirty books of my money. I came to you trying to resolve this matter in a peaceful way, knowing this thing could get ugly for that kind of money."

"Hold on, little brother... who are you talking about?"

"Your homie Cole... I see you kickin' it with him from time to time."

Shakur exhaled, "I normally don't get into this kind of nonsense, but this is a small matter and consider that debt paid. I'll have one of the other brothers to give you that before the day is out. Peace, brother." Shakur walked back over to Zeek Bey and Sten.

This was a small matter to Shakur. Mississippi was getting bent out of shape about something that was small and petty. It was a breakdown of how prison could reduce you. Prison can break people physically, mentally, emotionally, spiritually, financially and otherwise, the financial value system would break down from people getting hundreds of thousands of dollars to thousands turned into stamps. The breakdown process would begin when people got caught up in this world of the penitentiary. They often would not have the value or the morals and principles that they once had in the outside world. In this inside world, a few stamps could add up to a lot of value. Those stamps might add up to $5 or $125, but either way an amount that could get a knife put in you or a lock upside your head.

If you defaulted on a bill on anything over $125, it was pretty much an automatic death attempt. That is what prison will do to your value system; break you down to the lowest common denominator.

All seven chairs at the poker table were filled, and Cole occupied one of the chairs. He stared across the table as Slab raised the pot five more dollars. Cole's eyes trailed on down the line as the guys around the table began to call by throwing a book of stamps into the pile.

Damn, if all them callin' then I can't win, Cole thought as he threw in fifteen stamps as well. "I call, lay down and let me see what you got!"

Slab looked at the houseman to make sure that it was okay with him, and the houseman nodded. Slab laid down two deuces to match the other pair of deuces on the board. Four of a kind was the best hand. "O.G., cut it and push it," Slab said, laughing.

"Yeah, you needed them four deuces to beat me," Chuck admitted, spreading out all five card and displaying three aces and a pair of threes, which was second best.

"Damn, man, you had a beautiful boat... I see now why you called," John said, displaying his five cards, all clubs.

"Man, I knew you had them damn ducks. I don't know why in the fuck I call for," growled Cole. "But, hell, I just had to pay to see it."

"What you had, goofball?" Chuck asked Cole.

Cole laid his five cards face down, but Bo-low turned over his hand. Cole had a pair of fours and a pair of fives. "Shit, Cole, you don't have a damn thing. You sittin' here givin' away free money. You the goose that laid the golden egg."

"Man, I'm so far in the hole, shit, now I got to call everything and play every hand," justified Cole, speaking the God-given truth.

"Cole, man, you chasin' Jason," Twin joked.

"Cole, you ain't got the second best hand. You have the worst hand at the table," Uncle Ben said.

"I just had to pay to see it," exhaled Cole.

"You could've saved that money and seen it for free," replied Pone. Everyone already knew that thinking was not one of Cole's best qualities.

Cole felt a hand connect with his right shoulder, and he looked around to see Shakur standing behind him. "C, miss a hand. I need to speak with you for a minute."

"Shit," Cole gritted under his breath. "Deal around me for one hand, but whoever dealing next deal me in. Chino, make sure I'm in the next hand, alright?"

O.G. nodded. He needed Cole to get lucky and win some of his money back. Cole was down $75, which amounted to about fifteen books of stamps. One good pot, he could break even and possibly win a few dollars.

"Brother Shakur, this can't wait until yard recall? You see I'm doing my thug thizzer," Cole teased with a smile.

"Say, Cole, dude pulled up on me, saying you owe him a piece of change."

"Man, these niggas kill me. They wanna be tough loan dons, wanna be big ballers and shot callers, and they cry about these few coins. "

"But bro, that's the man's property. You can't get mad with him for asking about his. You know as well as I know that debt isn't nothing heavy, but you know this is not the world that we came from. This is anotha world behind this wall, and so when you deal with people behind this wall you have to keep in mind that most of 'em never had two of anything, much less two hundred dollars. Are you ready to get a life sentence for two hundred dollars? Think about this with intelligence when you dealing with the value system. For that couple dollars, if you don't have it on time, you may get killed or have to kill one of these fools about nothing, because that's what it all adds up to. I'm going to leave it like that and let you think about it." Shakur walked away leaving Cole looking stupid. He did not want to continue back and forth with Cole about nonsense.

As soon as Cole had left the poker table, three officers and four Rec officers raided the poker table and confiscated all the poker chips. The staff members lined everyone up against the wall, giving them a thorough pat-down search.

John Doe had nothing to do with the card game, he just happened to be in the wrong place at the wrong time as one of the officers gave him a direct order to empty his pockets. Fu Man Chew carried on like he had made a hell of a bust when he confiscated John Doe's candy.

"Give me your ID and come see me at the Lieutenant's office on the next move," he ordered John Doe.

When the move was announced, John Doe walked over to the Lieutenant's office. Fu Man Chew invited him into his office and closed the door. "You want your candy back?" he asked John Doe. "I'll give it back if you tell me something. Tell me what's going on out on the compound. Who's got the dope? Who's got the knives?"

"Man, I'm no fucking snitch," John Doe snapped, feeling disrespected. "I didn't tell in my case, so what the fuck I look like tellin' you something to get a half bag of creamer and four funky-ass juices back for? Man, you have a fucking million snitches on this fucked-up compound. Ain't that enough?"

"I'm try'na get a million and one," Fu Man Chew replied truthfully.

"There's one outta every hundred that get away, and I'm that fucking one," John Doe barked and stormed out of the office.

Fu Man Chew thought about what another guy told him when he was asked for information. Switch to Geico, it'll save you money. He couldn't care less about the inmate's rights. Let him tell it, the prisoner didn't have any fucking rights, and they were all here to be in his service as his pet pigs, bitches, snitches and do boys. Putting a prisoner's life in danger was his second nature, and he wasn't going to lose one bit of sleep over it.

Seven hours later, John Doe's partner got busted for a cell phone and word got out that John Doe had been over to the Lieutenant's office earlier, so the shot caller took the inmate.com and ran with it.

Once they located John Doe, four soldiers begin to put in their work, stabbing John Doe in nothing but his face, chest and neck. Two staff members rushed over to try to end the attack but found out they were not untouchable. They died in the line of duty, along with John Doe.

If Fu Man Chew would have invested a couple of minutes to read over John Doe's file, he would have learned that John Doe had been incarcerated for twenty-five years straight and had stayed at war with the staff, throwing body waste on them or spitting in their faces. John had no respect whatsoever for their law. They had punished John Doe in every form possible.

John Doe never paid any attention to the authorities. He would tell them to fuck themselves and their pussy-ass threats would go in one ear and out the other. They always threatened to lock him up. It never failed John Doe would always scream, The hole ain't nothing but a different part of the jail. I'm already locked down. Fuck you and fuck the hole!

What Fu Man Chew failed to realize if he would not have abused his authority, everyone would still be alive and breathing. One small petty-ass situation turned into a bloodbath and a nightmare. Staff that work in the prisons have the prison's life and future in the palms of their hands, and if they aren't careful, they can also put their co-workers into a deadly situation as well.

Chapter 16

Mr. Ben saw the new arrivals coming into the dorm and he set out his barber kit. Mr. Ben always cut the new arrival's hair for free. He didn't want them walking around looking like cavemen. He wanted them to look like the human beings that they were. Mr. Ben was the best in the unit with the scissors haircuts. Mr. Ben was from Harlem. He had been down for many years, and he felt the guys in the unit were his family. When they would first come in he would cut their hair, drop jewels, and give them a care package which consisted of several food and hygiene items. Mr. Ben felt as though one hand washed the other, and both hands washed the face.

"Hey, all y'all come over here," Mr. Ben called out to the four new guys. When they reached Mr. Ben, he began to speak. "They call me Mr. Ben, and I'm going to cut y'alls hair for free. Who wants to go first?"

"I'll go, sir," said one of the guys who really needed a cut and a shave.

Mr. Ben swung the green cape around the young man's neck. "Young brother, if you ain't been to hell, you're here now. Your destiny and your faith are in your hands! You can make this time work for you or against you. If you know better then you'll do better. Now, young man, it's like they say... if you want to hide anything from a Blackman, put it in a book. Just like now, they have programs here but the youngsters don't want to program. Son, get all the free education and programming that these people are throwing at you left and right. Utilize your time wisely and take advantage of all this free education. You can come in here and make something out of yourself or you can bullshit around and go back out there the same. You have a second chance I don't. I have an elbow and some change."

Blind man #1 started choking when he heard Mr. Ben's sentence. "How much time you got, son?"

"Forty-eight months."

"Then you have a little over forty-eight hours to get yourself together," Mr. Ben said. "When I came into the system, they were giving out numbers I never heard of. They were trying to lose people behind these walls. You lucky they didn't bury you alive."

As Shakur walked into the unit, he noticed the guy in Mr. Ben's chair. The orange and white transport shoes told him everything he needed to know. A bus had come in and Mr. Ben was doing what he did to every new guy. He would speak to them in a father's language, and everything he said would be positive and about bettering themselves. Mr. Ben wouldn't give propaganda conversation the time of day. You would never get anything negative out of him. He would always find something positive out of a tragedy or a bad experience. In his book, he believed that everything in life happened for a reason, no matter how bad the situation might be.

One day a server put the smallest piece of fried chicken on Mr. Ben's tray as a joke. He knew Mr. Been loved some fried chicken because he would always ask for the biggest piece on the pan. Mr. Ben thanked the guy for the small piece and thanked him once again for looking out for his best interests. Mr. Ben said he didn't need to be eating all that fried and greasy food. Another incident occurred where a youngster stole $40 worth of Mr. Ben's commissary. Mr. Ben said the youngster must have needed the groceries since he took it. The whole unit was upset about the youngster's lack of loyalty. They beat him almost to death and returned every piece of Mr. Ben's property. Mr. Ben then gave the items back to the youngster and asked him if that little bit of commissary was worth having the locks and socks slammed across his head. After that, the youngster made sure that Mr. Ben kept extra issues of fried foods. Mr. Ben made sure the youngster ate off his $40 a month allowance of commissary.

"Mr. Ben, I see they done snuck the crowd through the tunnel."

"Shakur, you know how them people do it from time to time. They make the crowd avoid the crowd. They in control. They allow the wars to break out when they want to. I guess they didn't feel like watching the show today. They feed the wolves to the wolves, the lions to the lions, and the gators to the gators. They know they could feed the lambs, ducks, and their snitches off all season round."

"Mr. Ben, I'm next, right?"

"Brother Shakur, how could you not be? We lock in our meals."

Shakur's penitentiary money was considered counterfeit to Mr. Ben. He would not accept any store items or stamps from Shakur. Shakur could get haircuts, shaves, and all the razor linings he wanted from Mr. Ben for free. Mr. Ben's stamps and food items were no good to Shakur as well. They were both penitentiary rich.

Shakur would return the favors by sharing meals with Mr. Ben. Shakur would chef up a couple of meals at least three times a week, sometimes more when they served pork. On pork days, Mr. Ben looked forward to Shakur's microwave dishes. The fried rice, nachos, burritos, fried mackerel patties or dirty rice. Shakur could also make a good banana pudding from scratch.

"Oh, man, I hope them deuces don't go off, because then that tower holla Todos al piso, it will be another day I can't get another dollar," Popper Charlie said upon seeing the guys with the bus shoes. The shoes always made a person stand out like a sore thumb. If a bus came in and you didn't see all the new guys, all you had to do was post up at the chow hall, and you couldn't miss a one of them.

"Mr. B, I like how you look out for all the new guys."

"Brother Shakur, I'm only doing Allah's work. Allah deserves all the credit, not me. Now days if it ain't right, then it ain't me. Back in the day, if it wasn't rough, it wasn't me."

"Well, Mr. B, in that case you stay you, and don't let anyone bring the beast or the devil side back out of you."

"Brother Shakur, I was the devil himself. These young brothers are out there faking it and just meddling in the game. They didn't want to see me or cross my path. Brother Shakur, it's like that movie, Get Rich or Die Tryin '. Fifty should have made that movie based on my life. In the streets of New York, I thought every grain and piece of gravel was my property. I actually thought the whole city belonged to me. Yeah, brother, I was young and dumb too once upon a time. I once was blind but now I can see and I truly thank Allah for protecting me! Brother, the old people always would say God takes care of the babies and them damn fools. Would you believe that, Brother Shakur?"

"Why would I have any other reason to believe anything different?" Shakur answered the question with a question. Shakur heard the story from many different guys from New York City about how Mr. Ben used to terrorize their city. At his highest level, he thought he was untouchable. Mr. Been had seen death. He looked at death and had no fear of death. He thought he could take on the biggest and baddest of them all. Ignorance is totally blind.

Mr. Ben stuck drug dealers up that you didn't rob because of their reputation. He didn't see any of that. All he saw was his .38 or his double-barreled shotgun in your face, breaking you down--breaking you of all of your worldly possessions that you had on you.

He would go through a whole crew of people by himself and tell them they had to pay street taxes to him. One of those days, he lined them all up: the number writers, the dope dealers, the store owners and the regular street hustlers and told them all that their street taxes were due. They all agreed to pay Mr. Ben the taxes but little did Mr. Ben know that he would not be collecting a dime. They told him to meet them on the avenue at 1:30 a.m. Mr. Ben walked right into their trap. When he arrived, they started raining gunshots in his direction. He hit the ground and pulled out his raggedy little .32 caliber pistol. Car windshields and the bark on the trees was being shattered from their .44 Magnums that were coming his way. In his desperate attempts to make it out of the situation alive, Mr. Ben cut loose with his .32, getting off enough shots to allow him to crawl away on his hands and knees. This only frustrated him that much more. He told himself that if he made it out this deal alive, he would be back.

Mr. Ben did make it out, and reviewed the mistakes that he had made. He knew he had to come up with a team of madmen like himself. Three days later, Mr. Ben recruited five people that he felt would be able to help him out on this mission. First they would pull off a robbery that would give them the cash to supply themselves with the things they would need. The gas station robbery ended up giving Mr. Ben a five-year prison term. The end result was that his team went down and so did Mr. Ben. However, during his five years, Mr. Ben had grown and had a whole new vision--still violent—to return and take the streets over.

On Mr. Ben's first day of release, he walked into one of the number writer's stores and told them they had to pay their street taxes. The owner of the store was behind the counter when he walked in, but had his head down getting something for a customer. When the owner looked up and saw who was in the store, he said, Aww, shit, you back here with that dumb shit.

Naw, I'm just coming by to let you know that I just got out today, Mr. Ben told him.

The owner of the store, being an old head from the neighborhood and seeing Mr. Ben grow up, felt kindness for Mr. Ben. When he realized that he was no longer in danger he came around from behind the counter and embraced Mr. Ben and told him, I'm not doing as good as I used to, but come on in the back with me. I have something you may be able to use. He gave Mr. Ben some shoes, shirts and pants. All the items were brand new and came from people who had gone out and boosted from name-brand clothing stores.

To go along with that the old-timer went into his pocket and gave Mr. Ben $500 and told him to come back tomorrow and he'd have some more for him then. That day Mr. Ben continued on his mission. He went and got with his old gang members and called a meeting together in the old club house. About fifty gang members showed up, and Mr. Ben began telling them his old plan of having the street people paying their street taxes. Once again he told the dope dealers, number writers, store owners and street hustlers that it was time they had to pay. He told them that most of the money would be going back into the community. They were going to buy trash cans, clean the blocks up, paint the front sidewalks and make the area a better place to live.

Mr. Ben told the people the consequences and the penalties that would go along with execution of these plans. He said if someone went to jail, they would help out with lawyer's fees and money for commissary, and their families would be taken care of as well. He explained that some might even die in completing this mission.

The audience responded by saying that it sounded good, but they needed him to kick it off and get it started. He told them he couldn't start it without them. That was the mistake he had made the first time, and he had gone to prison trying to do it by himself. However, they still thought that Mr. Ben needed to try to do it alone.

He called the meeting to a close and put the next step of his plan into motion. He went to the northside and bought a .32 pistol and then headed over to the southside and met with some other people. They told him they would give him a shotgun the next day. That night he called his childhood sweetheart. She told him she had to go to work in the morning, but they would get together tomorrow.

His next call was to his main man. His main man picked up the phone and asked how he was on the phone without calling collect. Mr. Ben told him he was no longer in the penitentiary.

Where you at then?

Mr. Ben took the phone from his ear, Listen. Mr. Ben let him hear the noisy crowd behind him. You hear that noise?

Yeah!

Then you know I'm in the saloon.

Which bar?

Mr. Ben gave him the location to the bar. A half hour later his main man walked into the bar. They went through the manly embrace, handshake and talked about the future. After a few hours they left and their crime spree began.

The next day, Mr. Ben picked up the shotgun and went back to the number writer's store and picked up $300. Then he went and got with his childhood sweetheart and stayed with her for the night.

The second day, Mr. Ben went to a neighborhood clothes store and told the man that he thought was the man that he only had a couple of hundred dollars and he needed to get clothes for the next few days.

I don't have a problem with that, the storeowner assured him. You will get your money's worth. Little did the salesman know that Mr. Ben was talking about getting much more than the couple hundred dollars he was going to spend. The salesman began gathering shoes, underwear, undershirts, dress shirts and a cashmere topcoat. When it was all said and done the sale bill was a thousand and some odd dollars. Mr. Ben pulled out the $500 and his prison ID card.

The salesman looked at the identification card, What can I do with this?

The identification card was just to let the salesman know that he would be back to spend some more money with them or he would be back in the penitentiary. When he told the salesman this, the salesman replied by saying, I have to ask the old man if I can do this.

Mr. Ben looked over at the old man, who had heard everything that was being said to the salesman. When the salesman said that he would need to talk to the old man, the old man had never taken his eyes off of Mr. Ben, and just nodded to the salesman to let him know it was okay to make the deal. In that deal was an agreement that the store would never become victim of a stick-up. From that day, Mr. Ben and the old man became friends.

After he purchased the clothes, Mr. Ben went home and took a bath, and then began his mission. He got the shotgun and pistol and went over to the southside to his partner's house. Mr. Ben then left his house and went to the grocery store a couple blocks away. When he entered, there were only three other people in the store.

Mr. Ben made a purchase at the cash register, and as the sales clerk rung up the total bill, Mr. Ben pulled out the shotgun and the pistol. Put everything in the bag, he told the clerk.

The clerk obeyed the order and put the money in the bag. Mr. Ben took the money and buzzed out of the store. He ran down the street into the alley leading to another alley, and then through the back door of his apartment building. He went into the bathroom and put the pistol and shotgun, along with the money, in the dirty clothes hamper. Mr. Ben called his partner into the bathroom.

What the hell you call me in here for? What the hell you sittin' on the floor for? his partner asked.

Just come in and look in the hamper?

Horse looked in the hamper and saw the weapons and the money. What you done?

You know what I had to do.

Then why you didn't come here and let me know?

We talked about this shit for years, ain't no need for us to keep on talking about it. Let's just put it into action.

Horse dumped out the money. It totaled $1,500 so after they split it up they walked away with $750 each. And that's how the new robbery team was formed and started.

From that day, they set off a string of robberies, kidnapping, mayhem and murders. Mr. Ben and Horse went out to rob drug dealers. They would put them in the trunk of their car, kidnap them, and take everything they had. They would send them back to their stash houses and make the drug dealers bring back whatever was in there, which led to many shootouts. The robbery team then began snatching legitimate people who were bank employees and check cashing agency owners.

They just could not stop. But it all came to an end after they had to put two armored truck guards to sleep one day during a robbery. Finally their criminal careers unraveled on the hard streets of Harlem.

Mr. Ben managed to get himself put back into the servitude condition with a life sentence plus 35 years.

Chapter 17

Playa changed the mop head. He wanted to re-mop the R&D floor once more with a cleaner mop before he buffed the floor. Playa would always leave the floors looking glossy and wet. He would mop the floor with ice water before quitting time. Every morning, when the staff walked into the building, the floors would welcome them into their work area with a smile.

Playa shoved three scoops of ice into the fresh mop bucket of cold water. He put the bucket against the wall out of the staffs way.

"Excuse me, Playa, for tracking up your floor," said one of the female staff as she cautiously walked over the wet floor.

"It ain't nothing but a floor," Playa responded as he took a break to watch the female until her bottom jiggled clean out of his sight.

Playa mopped half the floor before he stopped to admire his work. The floor looked like it was freshly waxed. "Naw, I ain't gotta buff this baby today. This ice water is doing the magic trick. Ice, ice, baby. Ice all up in the jailhouse taking care of that hard nard. I re-rock the floor," Playa mumbled.

A bus had arrived, so Playa planned on skinning that entire side, with the intention of buffing it first thing in the morning. That would give him something to do.

Thirty-nine people were on that bus. They got lucky and arrived at 9:30 a.m. They all received hot meals and not the old stanky bag lunches. They still had to wash their food down with the Kool-aid packs. Their meal was chili over rice, the second version of shit-on-the-shank as the convicts called it. The first version of shit-on-the-shank was gravy with small chunks of beef poured over grits.

The guys swallowed their meals. They were hungry and knew they would not get anything else to eat until the chow hall fed again after the 4:30p.m. count. So they gassed up their stomachs with that diesel fuel, chili mac. Shit on the shank beat nothing at all, any day. Any food was better than no food, the guys thought as some of them soaked up the loose chili juice with the remainder of their two slices of white bread. The food service staff sent extra food trays because all the leftovers were going into the trash. But let a bus arrive on fish, chicken or hamburger day, and they would not be offered an extra tray. The kitchen staff would lock all the leftover meats in the freezer. The kitchen workers would have the opportunity to earn the fish on fish day, to earn chicken on chicken day, and hamburger on hamburger day, according to who worked the hardest and did the most snitching.

The new arrivals watched Playa sling the mop across the floor a few times. They knew that Playa had a good job. He was his own boss and Playa was getting a Unicor grade-one pay. As long as Playa kept the floor shined and the trash cans dumped, he could sit back in the air conditioning and wait on his $108 per month institution pay check for doing the small bit of work.

Playa's job wasn't like the regular institution jobs. He had to maintain a certain standard. He had regulations and rules he had to meet. It was in his verbal contract upon getting hired.

Playa's khaki outfit had to be ironed. His shirt had to be tucked into his pants at all times. It was mandatory that he wore a belt, no sagging allowed. He could not come to work looking like a bum or show up late. If he broke a rule twice, he would be fired. Playa was pushing a mop bucket to the mop closet when Tray L rushed up to the holding tank door. "Say, woady, they got people up here from the N.O.?"

Playa paused as he gave Tray L his full attention. "It don't work like that, my man. It's a car thing."

"What do you mean by a car thing?" Tray L asked, because this was all new to him, it being his first time in the Feds.

"It's like this: every state got its own car. For example, I'm from Texas. Houston, Dallas, San Antonio, and all the surrounding cities in Texas... we all as one."

"So what you trying to say, round? Louisiana all as one?"

"Basically, yeah. Who all around your city is your car, I can't name' em for you, playa, cuz I don't know your state."

Un-fucking-believable, how can we be in the same car? Family with the enemy! When niggas from Baton Rouge, Kenner and Hammond hate on a nigga swagger from N.O. because us niggas some true gangsta,. Tray L thought. He mean-mugged Playa. "Man, is there anybody here from CP3 that you know of?"

The rest of the bus inmates did not ask any questions. They were just sitting there afraid and let Tray L do all the talking. Playa had to ask him this question, "Say, Woady, what's your name?"

"I'm gangsta Tray L from CP3. Any nigga from the N.O. know about me. Man, just ask any nigga out there do they know Tray L."

"I got'cha. I'll see you when you hit the compound," Playa said.

Chase sat in the room smoking a blunt and drinking a quart of white lightning as Killer danced and sang around in the cell.

"Shoulder, chest, pants and shoes. Wipe me down, cause I'm on, I'm on," Killer sang Lil Boosy, Webbie and Foxy music.

There was a blanket in the window to prevent the compound COs from looking into their window while making rounds. The front cell door window was also covered with a black cloth. Chase had built a box to hold eight speakers. His room sounded like a house speaker. When the guards did their body counts, they would always give Chase a direct order to turn down his music. They just did not want it done during their counting session because sometimes the music interfered with their counting, causing them to have to recount.

Before the song came on, Chase and Killer were talking about how the Feds system put their feet down on a Blackman's neck. They just wanted him to stay down and out. They were reminiscing and tripping on how much time they had gotten!

Killer was light-skinned with a good grade of hair. He was a one hundred percent brother, with both parents being black. His first case, he received probation for the dope. His second case, Killer got sixty months for a gun. This time Killer got caught with three K's and four and a half ounces of heroin. Killer's cases ran wild. He was sentenced to forty-five years for the drugs, and twenty-five consecutive more years for each weapon. Killer spent his days like Chase, getting drunk and high. They would go to bed high and wake up getting high. They didn't reach for a morning breakfast or a cup of coffee before they reached for a bottle of liquor or a blunt.

Killer picked up a bottle of lightning and took four big gulps. "Damn, round. Dude didn't give us the first pull." Killer shook the bottle up and watched the liquor bubble up. "This shit isn't grade A. The nigga gave us the last pull.

This is some grade C shit! Ya heard me? Man, I oughta go stab that bitch in his fuckin' neck!"

"Killer, its some good shit. Your system is just used to it already. Round, you're a fuckin' alcoholic, you been drinkin' lightning for twelve days straight. Now your system needs something stronger." Chase took a swallow and frowned up. "Man, that's some grade A shit, ya heard me, round? Dude wouldn't try me with that sucka shit. He wouldn't play with his life and health like that with a nigga like me."

"Damn, JC, you about to go into the world?"

"Don't worry, round, you know I'm gonna look out for you. Round, I'm not going to get out that door and forget about 'cha."

Killer nodded, "Fo sho, fo sho."

Four knocks came on the door with a pause, followed by two more knocks. Chase smiled because he knew who the knocks belonged to. There was only one guy on the compound who would carry out such a unique knock.

"Enter," said Chase.

Playa walked into the room. "I'm just in time, if I would've waited until Friday to stop by I probably would have missed out."

"Naw, woady, this shit 24/7 everyday of the week. This food and medication so a real nigga like me can function! Ya heard me?" barked Killer. "Say, round, you did say you was from Texas, right?"

"Yeah, I'm from Texas."

"Big Texas, taste this lightning and tell me is that shit watered down or what?"

Playa looked at the bottle of lightning and it looked very, very tasty. He could feel it now burning as it slid down his throat, leaving a trail of fire until it hit his belly. "Killer, I don't drank until the weekend. Through the week, I gotta stay focused. I got a sweet job that I can't afford to lose."

"Say, Playa, what brings you over to our neck of the woods? Round, by me seeing you made me think the day was Friday," blurted Chase, after taking another pull of the jailhouse liquor.

"I stopped by because a bus came in today," Playa stated.

Killer slumped down in his chair. "How many people?"

"Bout twenty-five to thirty, I really didn't try to count 'em, but one dude keep talking to me. He said his name Tri Pell, Tire L, something like that."

"Where he from?" Killer asked, sitting straight up in the chair and sitting the bottle of liquor between his legs.

"He said he from the same place y'all from."

"From the Third Ward?" asked Killer.

"Yeah," Playa nodded and confirmed. "He said everybody from Calliope Projects would know who he is."

"From my projects and the nigga name Tire L or Tri Pell," Killer mumbled and let his intoxicated mind rumble.

"Round, you tryin' to say Tray L?" Chase asked. All the alcohol in his body vanished because it was suffocated by anger.

"Yeah, that's him. He's about in his mid-thirties. I'd say he's about thirty-six maybe thirty-five," Playa mused, trying to put Tray L in connection with Chase and Killer as much as possible.

"Yeah, I know him. He's from our hood. Good lookin', woady. I gotta hook my rounds up a care package," said Chase.

Now Killer's intoxicated mind knew who Tray L was. Tray L was the person who had murdered Chase's big brother. Gangsta B and Tray L were around the same age. Tray L had killed Gangsta B because he had taken his girlfriend. Tray L's girl left him to be with Gangsta B because she dug his style. Gangsta B was hard on a guy, but sweet on a female; however, if a female ever got out of line, he'd handle her no different than he would a hard-leg.

Playa excused himself and left Chase and Killer alone to continue their party. He knew if he stayed any longer that it would be a war trying to escape the temptation. He would have a bottle up to his mouth in no time and a blunt digging from the corner of his mouth.

"Yeah, we got that bitch now," said Killer.

"Now Killer, I'm going to personally lay the nigga the fuck down."

"Round, let me do it for you; I have a fresh hundred and twenty years."

"Naw, he killed my brother. I wouldn't feel right. This something I gotta do by myself."

Killer stared at Chase as the sweat crawled down his face. He could smell the alcohol coming out of his pores. Killer smelled like he had used a whole bottle of rubbing alcohol as cologne. His whole body felt as if it was actually breathing. Killer palmed the twelve inch murder weapon on his side through his shirt. Killer's face carried the image of an angry bull. He could smell blood and see death. Killer could see himself throwing a powerful jab into Tray L's body, penetrating the knife deeply and twisting it. Killer looked at his tightly close fist. He slowly reopened it, hoping to see a palm full of Tray L's blood.

"Yo, Chase. You jumped out of the car and ran with my pistol. You see, I couldn't rest until I came to prison. Now I'll take this bitch-ass nigga out for you."

Chase turned up his bottle of liquor and Killer did the same. It was as if they were in a race trying to beat one another to the finish line, and Tray L would be the winner's prize.

Sten sat in his room thinking about some of the things the most Honorable Elijah Muhammad had said on the Pale Horse tape. The messenger couldn't have said it any better. Our people are truly riding the Pale Horse to destruction.

There was a knock on Sten's door. "Come in," he hollered.

"Brother Sten, come outta that room. We ain't in Marion on a 23-hour lockdown anymore," Lil Red joked with Sten.

"I'm just sitting in the room meditating and thinking about what the messenger said on the Pale Horse tape. Why don't you come out and watch part two with us Friday, Blackman? You see, it really ain't nothing to do around here anyway but watch videos and soap operas. Yes, sir, Blackman, come on out and get you a good hour of teaching so you can learn about that Pale Horse what most of us still following behind. Yes sir, Blackman. Can I look forward to seeing you this Friday?"

"Brother Sten, I don't want to make you no promise because our word is all we got, but I'll try to make it. I stopped by to see did you want to play a game or two of chess but I'll catch ya a little later."

"Hold up, hold up now, Blackman. Let me enlighten you a little bit about the Pale Horse before you walk away. Listen, the Pale Horse led us down the wrong path. Now the reason why I use the word us is because I once was into the things the Pale Horse brings about. The smoking, getting high, gambling, drinking and trying to murder off our own people. Yes, sir, Blackman, it's time for knowledge, wisdom and understanding of the Pale Horse. Yes, sir, Blackman ..."

Lil Red cut in on Sten, "Brother, I'm not as knowledgeable as you. I don't know nothing about this Pale Horse thing."

Sten gave Lil Red one of the messenger's smiles. "But, Blackman, you can become knowledgeable. All you have to do is put forth an effort. It's easy, just come out and watch the tape with us Friday. You'll see."

"I'll see you Friday, Brother Sten," Lil Red said, leaving Sten to finish getting into his tranquility.

Cal couldn't wait until the brother left Sten's room. He walked over and knocked twice. "Peace, brother Sten," Cal greeted, walking into Sten's room and seating himself, not even waiting for Sten to invite him to a seat. Cal looked up to Sten as an advisor. He always asked Sten for his opinions. Sten smiled because he knew that Cal wanted to talk about some kind of bad situation he'd done landed himself in, as always.

"What can I do for you today, Blackman?"

"Brother Sten, this guy who always owes me money, he always drag me when he owe me, but now I owe him a few dollars. I have it, but I want to drag him like he always dragging me."

Sten nodded, "Blackman, see you could never treat him fair because the more fair you treat him, the more unfair he'll feel. But when you deal with people, you'll see the value in them because everything will reveal itself in time. Blackman, don't let his characteristics rub off on you and you play out and live his characteristics. If you do then you'll become him and lose your identity of who you are. You feel me?"

"Yes sir, brother Sten, yes sir."

"Blackman, you know tomorrow is the Day of Atonement. You come out to the chapel? There are going to be several good speakers there, as well as myself."

"Yeah, Brother Sten. I'll be out there so I can steal some knowledge."

Sten smiled again because Brother Cal always had a way of putting things. "Listen here, Blackman. You don't have to steal the knowledge because the knowledge can't do us no good in the graveyard now can it?"

When Sten stated the most Honorable Elijah Muhammad, Cal sat up straight. He braced himself for the long, long ride that Sten was about to take him on.

The telephone rang. Annie sat at her desk studying the Qur'aan. She would read a section daily so by the end of the year she would have digested the whole Qur'aan.

Annie lived Sunnah and she gave it her best effort to be a walking Qur'aan. She dealt with her sons by the Qur'aanic way and not by her own ways. Annie was a single parent. When her son's father walked out on her, she did not look for another male to be their father or role model. She returned back to her deen. Annie depended on Allah to guide, teach and protect her sons.

Even though when her husband had walked out of her life it had broken her heart, it had been for the best. He was leading Annie off the righteous path and down the path of destruction. Annie cried for uncountable days and nights and asked Allah day in and day out what her and her two kids were going to do.

She had counted on their father to provide and to protect them. However, Allah blessed her with the best job that she could ever had prayed for. Now teaching at a Muslim school, Annie taught the fourth graders and also taught a Salat class. Annie let her students know that they have to always be in the remembrance of Allah and that Allah was the best of planner. She loved teaching and her students took pride that Allah had blessed them with a strong, knowledgeable and God-fearing person such as Sister Annie.

"Mom, don't worry about the phone, I got it," ShaBazz shouted from the kitchen. He was thinking about the girl who he had finally given their phone number to.

Annie had no intentions of answering the phone anyway. She was going to let the answering machine demonstrate what it was made for. If the phone call was important, the caller would call back. Once Annie picked up the Qur'aan, nothing or no one was going to take her away from the Qur'aan.

"Hello," ShaBazz answered.

"This is a pre-paid call from a federal correctional institution. The caller's name is Shakur. If you wish to accept this call, press 5 now. If you wish to block future calls from this caller, press 7 now," said the automated phone message.

ShaBazz held his breath as he pressed the number 5.

"As-Salaamu 'Alaikum," Shakur greeted.

"Wa 'Alaikumus-Salaam Wa Rahmaa Tullaahi Wa Barakatuh," ShaBazz returned, giving his brother a higher greeting.

"Where's Mom?"

"She reading the Qur'aan."

"You still reading yours every day too, right?"

"Yes."

"So, ShaBazz, what this I hear about you trying to carry out one of my summers?" Shakur asked.

He gave his little brother time to answer, but ShaBazz was at a loss for words. He didn't know how to answer the question. He was also afraid and hurt that his big brother was not there with him.

"I don't know what got into me that day. Satan the devil whispered in my ear, and I let him trick me. I don't know what else to say, Shakur."

"At least you know the truth. Now with that truth that you know, little brother, you have to act on the truth knowing that Allah is the only true reality when them discombobulated thoughts come into your head by the whispering of Satan. You have to look at reality and know that the devil is only trying to mislead you. What are you looking for?"

"I'm looking for my big brother."

"You know where I am at. Are you trying to end up in hell like me?"

"Not really, just trying to be near you."

"Little brother, this is no place that you want to be near! It would hurt me to my heart to ever know that you ended up in hell like me. I want you to be bigger and better. I want you to be able to take my misfortune and use it in a positive way. Let no one or nothing guide you but Allah. Take my advice and use it where it would benefit you. Don't try to walk in the path of the dungeon, you understand, little brother?"

"Yeah, I understand, but it's hard out here without our father and without you, big brother."

"Don't ever feel as though I'm not there. I'm always there. Not in physical form, but spiritually and mentally. All you have to do is think of me and I know that you will get a positive thought about whatever the situation may be. I know this, little brother, because I live my life here in a positive manner. I didn't want wrong to come to me so this is why I'm always trying to feed you something on a positive line. I know that I would have to do more to nurture you in a better direction. So from here on out, little brother, listen to me and take heed to the things I will be telling you very carefully because one false slip up and your life could be over. All I am asking is that you listen to me and allow Allah to guide you down the straight path."

"What's it like in prison?"

"It's hell. Don't take hell to be as something spooky and that's up underneath the ground. That would be giving you a misconception of what hell really is. Hell can be a state of condition, a state of being. You could be in the worst condition of your life and you could be in hell right here on Earth. Did that answer your question?"

"Not really. You see, me and my friend want to know how the prison life really goes."

"I just explained to you that it's a state of being in hell. Now you want to know the silly nonsense that goes on and takes place in this place? Is that what you are asking?"

"Yes."

"Well, first you have to deal with your mental state of mind, state of being.

If you are looking for prison life to be a vacation, then you are dealing yourself a delusion. Prison can be used in many different ways. You can use it to better your condition mentally or you can allow it to break you down physically, as well as mentally. It can be used to further your education, and it also can be used to further the career you have chosen. It can be used in one of the most beautiful ways of all and that is to give you time to get to know yourself. It is all about what you are looking for and what is on your mind. If you are looking for the negative, you will surely find it! If you are looking for the wisdom, the knowledge and the understanding, then you will have to seek it. There's not a whole lot of that sitting out in the open, you'll have to search for the positive. The negative will not be hard to find, it would be sitting there waiting on and for you if that's what you are seeking. In other words, prison can be what you make it to be for you."

"One of my friends said that them polices in there be trying to be all ya mommas and daddies?"

"It all depends on how you carry yourself. You can act like a sucka and they'll handle you like a sucka. They will test you to see if you are really what you say or carry yourself to be. If you fail the test, they will make life a living hell for you. But if you pass, they will stay out of your way and respect you."

Chapter 18

It was the Day of Atonement. People rushed into the chapel, like it was a government building passing out food stamps and government cheese. A line trailed out the door with a mixture of different races.

Sten, Shakur, and Zeek Bey stood in the back. They didn't need to grab a seat, because they had a special seating reserved for them. The chapel was packed and seats had to be borrowed from the other rooms. Some guys tried to shake Sten, Shakur, and Zeek Bey's hands with their old code, but they kept the handshake simple, with a firm shake.

The host walked behind the pulpit and raised both palms in the air. The crowd quieted down, "As-Salaamu 'Alaikum," he greeted. Some of the crowd greeted back with, "Wa 'Alaikum-As-Salaam." He greeted again, "Islam," and some of the crowd greeted back, "Islam."

"I greet you all in the name of peace. Many people are not aware that, when brothers greet you with As-Salaamu 'Alaikum, or with Islam, they are simply greeting you with a form of peace. My people, please look beside you and around you. I know you all have heard this phrase before, but it's a true fact, because we is all we got. When you need a few stamps or need to borrow a few soups or mackerels, I know that you're going to borrow it from someone in this very room. I'll run to one of you in a heartbeat, brother, to loan me two books of stamps, until my oldest brother catch up with me." The crowd laughed at the true statement.

Allah can and will help us overcome any and every challenge that the world can produce, but we gotta have the faith, as well as keep the faith. President Obama said change will not come, if we wait on someone else or on some other time. Harold Melvin and the Blue Notes say: The world can't change, if we just let it be, but we can begin to change the world, starting with you and me. And we definitely going to need some help. Dr. Martin Luther King said he had a dream, there will come a time when we, as the color people, will not be judged from the color of our skin, but from our character. Ms. Whitney Houston said she believes the children are the future. Teach them well, and let them lead the way.

"Now we have some beautiful spirited brothers here to lend us their voice. My good brothers, I'm not going to delay you any further from this good knowledge, wisdom, and understanding that these brothers can share with you, because all I can share with you is my problems. Problems after problems. If it's the Lord's will, these brothers can give me and you some information that could and would put us back in good grace with our Creator. I been trying to please my homies and the young ladies for too long. Now, it's time for me to try to please Allah. Without any further delay, I welcome you Brother Shakur, Brother Sten X, and Brother Zeek Bey. Will you all please give the good brothers a big round of applause," the host said, as he clapped repeatedly.

The crowd gave Shakur, Sten, and Zeek Bey a standing ovation. Shakur led the way and everyone shook a few more hands, before they could reach the stage. The host shook each of their hands and advised them to share Allah, the Almighty God's words.

"Zeek Bey, you go first, and I'll go last," said Shakur.

Sten smiled, as he had no problems with going in the second spot.

"I greet you brothers with the greetings of peace," said Zeek Bey, as he looked around the small crowded room.

"The majority of my brothers have unintentionally invested more

of their time to incarceration, than they have lived as free men. My point is when one claims to know better, then one is supposed to do better. I know from experience that common sense is not always so common."

"Tell 'em, Mo." Pleasant-E whispered.

Zeek Bey's Moor brother, Antwon, stood up and yelled, "Listen!"

Zeek Bey wiped the sweat off his stone face. "I can't use the term that it disturbs me sometimes, because I wouldn't be saying the sentence accurately or speaking my true heart. It touches me deeply and frequently, when I look around at my young brothers, who are my children's ages. The sad part is that within these bloody walls is a lot of extraordinary talents going to waste."

"My young people, we were not born as savages. We shouldn't want to grow into that animal. You young guys are the future. Adding your name to the game is truly a waste of energy. Life is beautiful, only if you give it a chance. Yeah, you only live once, so make the best of it, if not for you, then for your mother or for your kids. I'm not content with my environment, that's why I speak out. I've allowed the system to suck all the youth out of me, and so did my father. The majority of us have that, I don't give a crap attitude, from growing up without both parents, but please don't cheat yourself out of life, because you truly deserve better, and I only want better for my people. Let's destroy that cycle that runs in our family occupation. As OG Bobby Johnson's baby mother said to him in the movie, South Central, You been to jail, your daddy been in jail and now your son going to jail. People, research your true history. Find out who's the real kings and queens, the real chosen people."

"Identity comes not from what rolls off the tongue, but from how one performs. Life is one giant stage. Never ever forget, it's not how one begins the race, but how one finishes it."

"In the Holy Koran of the Moorish Science Temple of America, there is a chapter titled: Misery. Chapter 44, page 55, verse 20 says: Man forseeth the evil that is to come; he remembereth it, when it is past; he considereth not that the thoughts of affliction woundeth deeper than the affliction itself. Think not of why pain, but when it is upon thee, and thou shalt avoid what most hurt thee."

"There is nothing that man cannot avoid. This Chapter tells us so. We know when we're headed down the wrong path. We should be able to steer ourselves back in the direction of righteousness, when we put our minds to it. It is the patterns of our thoughts that bring us out of righteous mindful ways. If I too do harm to someone, to afflict pain upon him or her, I have already afflicted pain more times upon myself. When in the presence of evil, when it has caused pain upon someone, do you think that it will not cause pain upon you, because you keep it good company? Remember the saying, Misery loves company? And when you know that you've put yourself in a situation that you'll be stuck in for a while, like prison, you become miserable, because you don't know how to get past it. Find the affliction in your life, and heal it with Allah's grace. Be always prepared to give an account of thine actions, and the best death is that which is least premeditated. My people, please bear with me. There are so many issues that desperately need to be touched on more so now then ever, I'm going to swerve in and out, because I only got ten more minutes of fame."

"It's time for us to be universal builders. Society places man on a beast level, when in actuality he is much higher than a beast, and now he's beginning to excuse himself. People place value on material things. Materialism becomes their god."

"The people also say we use only 10% of our brain and the other 90% is not being used. Let's prove them wrong and let's awaken our household and especially our community, because our young generation needs us." Zeek Bey paused, as he pointed to a couple of individuals. "And it can start with you, you, and me, we can better our society. Some of us were straight savages, straight beasts, but Allah has cleaned our souls. Allah loves people who repent."

"Some people profess to have the truth and knowledge of the truth and ain't doing anything with it. In the quest for knowledge, many people choose many different ways to attain the truth, which is power, which is also the light that turns on our consciousness. There are many ways that one goes about his search to attain ultimate truth. You have also had people that state their path is the right direction. To that jewel, we call enlightenment, but what one fails to understand is that there are many paths that will take you to the destination, just as a highway has many exits and turn sections. It applies to our growth and development, meaning one shouldn't limit themselves to a particular understanding, without traveling down the many paths. Meaning, if you're on a quest to becoming a universal builder, you will have to study all things in life regardless to whom or what.

You'll have to look, learn, listen, and respect one's ways of life."

"Now listen to this, history repeats itself, because we don't review the past. Some of us were savages. We pursue happiness in the wrong way. We had the characteristics of a savage. A savage is one who has lost all knowledge of self and is living a beast life. He or she does things on instinct. They don't think. Some of us tried to live that lifestyle of the rich and famous off the backs of our poor and ignorant people. Our little twist was only ghetto fabulous. Our egos push God out. That's when we act other than ourselves and pick up the character of a savage. It's not our nature to be un-Islamic, you pray to God, God doesn't condone evil. We cause ourselves, our family and loved ones heartaches, pain, and so much suffering."

"Know thyself, know thine enemy. We need that guidance. Without guidance, it's like our people are on the Titanic, and they will crash into the iceberg. When crack came to town, lots of people's morals and principles went out the window. It was about the mighty dollar and getting high. Crime rate went to its highest peak. Robberies, homicides, prostitution and all kinds of other things. The youth no longer respect themselves, let alone the elders. They turned away from their parent's guidance. Now, the younger generation seeks to obtain their respect from the streets. All they respect is two to the dome, and riding on chrome. Our young people need to be prostrating, repenting, and be bathed in Holy water. We come up from hell, we didn't fall from Heaven. I used to be scared of religion. My mother used to drag me to church, and she used to leave me. I would give her a head start, then I would ease right back out the door behind her. Allah sees all things. Allah sees in the past. Allah sees in the future. If you don't join the Nation of Islam, then join the Moorish Science Temple, or the Sunni community. Get under some kind of religious umbrella and prove to the people, we are not a menace to society."

"Now, this is the last thought that I want to leave you with. Guys, any male can be a daddy, but not just any male can be a father. See, now a father is different from a daddy. A father is going to be there for the child. If he's not physically able to be there, he is going to walk him or her through their development and growth in life. The father is going to school and will guide the child throughout their life. He's going to walk them in the right direction. He's going to give them better choices to choose from than he had. He's going to assure their comfort as well as their protection. A father's whole thing is to protect and properly guide them through their development and growth in life."

"It's just no one thing that defines the father's obligations and responsibilities--the father knows his job and carries it out to the best of his ability. He might not be in a position to help financially, but he's going to do the best that he can under the circumstances, that he presently may be in. The father's whole job is to do what he can do.

Sometime, we want the father to be there physically, but unfortunate circumstances may not permit him to be. That doesn't mean that the father is not a father. You have to look at the father's work and what he's able to do. When you see that work, you will know and recognize it as the work of a father."

"Our kid's future can't be the path that we walked. We have to guide them to a brighter and better future. Our path of destruction will not be the choices that we will leave for them to follow. We will make better decisions to guide them, so that their choices will be better than ours."

"Providing that some of us were able to walk in a bright future, then we will guide our children to walk in that path that we have walked. I'm not trying to fly George Bush's flag; I'm not trying to toot George Bush's horn, but George Bush, Jr. is a prime example of having one of your children walk in your path for the next generation."

"Only Allah knows how many of us have other brothers to raise our seeds or seed. May Allah enlighten and continue blessing all the single mothers."

"Now, as I finally close, do you remember the song called Self Destruction? We all know that America has a serious problem. Now our race has a serial self destruction. Brothers, wake up. If the East Coast know that they have a serious problem, then I know the South should be aware as well, and we don't need a scientist to tell us this black-on-black crime gotta decrease, do we? I leave you like I greet you."

Zeek Bey pounded on his chest twice with a closed fist, then threw a peace sign in the air, "Peace."

The host stood up and shook Zeek Bey's hands again and congratulated him on his beautiful speech. He walked over to the pulpit. "Will you please give that brother another round of applause? Now peoples, y'all leave me no choice, but to re-ask the same question that brother Zeek Bey asked. Do we have any scientists in the house? Do we need to have a scientist in the house? Now y'all give another round of applause to our next guest, our next speaker." The host clapped, as Sten made his way to the pulpit.

"I greet you all in the name of peace."

"Peace," echoed through the building from the audience.

"I'm a little under the weather today, so gentlemen, I won't hold you all too long, but I will try to give you something sweet and short, that you can digest. I don't know what I'm going to say, but I do know, that I have to say something. I asked Allah to speak through me to you. There's so much needed to be said, but I have very little time. The Chaplain, he ain't never seen so many brothers in here before at one time. I heard him tell another brother to take his hat off in the house of God. I also heard him tell another brother to not be cursing in the building of God. My people, do you really, really know the house of God? Do you really, really know the building of God?"

"This is the house of God, this is the building of the Creator, and this is the temple of Allah," Sten stated, as he tapped himself on the chest. "We have to start taking better care of our body. Some of us use to take care of our car better than we took care of ourselves. We spend lots of money on the outside of our bodies to look good, but we get filth and pollute up the inside with all kinds of garbage and trash. You know the Most Honorable Elijah Muhammad started out teaching the people how to eat to live, but the Europeans are trying to act like it was all their idea. They are trying to steal and take all the credit. They get their benefits. They are always going to get caught with their hands in a Blackman's cookie jar, but guess what, people. They don't get the credit, because all the credit goes and belongs to Allah, to God alone."

"The people said we are sub-human, three-fifths of a human. Dr. Martin Luther King marched for civil rights. Elijah Muhammad advised him that we needed to be marching for our human rights. Although, Elijah Muhammad respected Dr. King and likewise, Dr. King respected Elijah Muhammad a great deal."

"A brother spoke to me once and said, Morning, good brother. I replied to him, Ain't nothing good, but God. I'm only a servant and the good things I do or say only come from the Creator Allah. Allah has cleaned all our hearts. We are not enemies anymore. It's time for us to grab a firm hold to the rope of Allah. Al-hamdu lillaah, Allaahu-akbar. 24/7 I try to stay in the remembrance of Allah. It was Inshaa Allaah that I made it this far. I'll stay in Allah's car."

Sten looked around and saw there was mostly young guys in their late teens and early twenties. If they are not carefully and properly guided, their future will become some of the hardcore criminal past, Sten thought. "My young people, if y'all don't stand for something, you will fall for anything. If there's a way, then there's a will. The old folks said, before I reached the age of 15, 16, or 17, I'd be in this place or have gotten killed."

"Chasing that dirty, dirty American dollar set trends for other suicides to follow, but, brothers, please don't follow my path. There are so many positive things that this life has to offer."

"In the street I made a name, but I caused my mother, grandmother, and auntie so much pain. They attach trouble to my name. The new me is about uplifting, instead of disrespecting and trying to destroy our culture."

"Our crime rate has to stop. Our high incarceration numbers have got to stop. In the graveyard, it's time to set the alarm clock. Living fast and dying young ... my people, this has got to stop. Allah spared me, so now awakening the people is my occupation. Yes, it's my job. Let's join hands to decrease the youth incarceration. Let's become brothers from different mothers, for the cause of saving our future generations. Let's stop being the one to cause trouble, and become a part of the solution to the struggle."

"Now it's time for men to stand up and be men. Let's get in Allah's car. Nobody's gonna love y'all and protect you like Allah. I'm God's son, you're God's son. We are all God's sons. We all can be like a walking Qur'aan. I leave you brothers with As-Salaamu 'Alaikum," Sten shouted, putting his hands up to his ears.

"Wa 'Alaikum-As-Salaam," the audience shouted, returning the greetings.

The host walked over to the pulpit, clapping. "Now my dear brothers, here's the last speaker. Please, put your hands together for our brother, Shakur."

The crowd rose to their feet, giving Shakur a warm welcome. The Chaplain and the Tower Three CO walked into the room. The tower guard had traded places with another one of his co-workers, so he could be present on this day to hear brother Shakur speak. He had heard bits and pieces of brother Shakur's counseling several times from the tower. It was not the same as being only a few feet away.

Shakur stood over the pulpit, searching the crowd for familiar faces, to see who was looking and searching for knowledge. His eyes landed on the Chaplain.

"Chaplain, you ready to take your Shahadah today? We would love to have you as our Muslim brother."

"Thanks, but no thanks," the Chaplain produced a fake smile. "I get my knowledge from the Bible and my blessing comes from Jesus."

"I greet you brothers with a word of peace. I'd like to thank Allah for allowing us to come together on this beautiful day. Allah has a plan for each one of us. Yesterday is history, tomorrow's a mystery, but today is the present, so let's unwrap our gift. My dear brothers, it's sad to say but there's a must that I put it out into the open. Everyone today has failed our youth. Christianity, Judaism, Islam, Jehovah's Witness street organizations. Our youth today killing one another is at an all-time high. There's not a time in history that we have been killing one another like the rate of killing today. The rate of killing is higher than at any other time. If you don't believe it, check the rate of black-on-black crime. We are in this condition for the very reason we must re-educate and reguide our youth back into the community. To be community people, we have to teach them all over. We have to teach them that with unity they will be able to overcome any differences or obstacles that may try to stay in their way. They must re-unite and stand for one another to overcome. I tilt my hat to America. Even though it's a young country, it don't give a damn about your nationality. Whether you're Chinese, Japanese, or from the Philippines, etc. America's not concerned about your culture or your religious beliefs, rather, America's concern is about improving the condition of your people. Don't get me wrong, I'm not trying to fly the flag for 'em. The eagle of the flag represents that this country rises and flies high in the sky like an eagle. The other countries are undeveloped, because other countries stay within their country."

"They try to use their own kind, their own people. They make the mistake of placing themselves within perimeters. Once you draw a circle around yourself and don't step outside that circle, you hinder yourself from your full development. You overlook knowledge. No other wisdom, knowledge, or understanding is accepted from any other, but from your higher rank Superior. We must not be infant-minded. Allah wants a man to travel the earth, and while traveling the land, a wise person will universally build. Knowledge is supposed to be sought from the womb to the tomb, from the cradle to the grave. Some people are living in darkness and have no sense of direction. My dear brothers, the people's minds, ears, hearts, and eyes need to be reopened.

They need to come out of their la-la land and come face-to-face with reality. I'm not going to blame everything on the white man," Shakur said with a smile. "But when they conspired to bring drugs into our communities, they consciously made our people become assassins against our own race." Shakur paused, and smiled once again. "Since 2-Pac and I share the same name, Shakur, that is, I feel the need to say his words verbatim. I come to bring the pain, hardcore to the brain, I'm going to overlook the fact when he said why keep explaining the game, when the people aren't listening and stuck in position. Please know this, when the people supplied our hood with weapons, we became assassins of one another. We fall victim to one another, doing the job for them. We're doing the dirty work. Yeah, we're putting work in for the enemy. We're killing two birds with one stone. One of you is going to hell," Shakur said, while nodding with a mean-mug on his face.

"The other one will be confined to a 6-by-6 cell. You think you're winning, but you're not. You are losing all the way around the board. You'll probably have the guy's son more than likely grow up with a bitter and negative outlook on life. Soon as the opportunity presents itself, they're ready to unleash the violence, ready to assault someone and have no problem with carrying out a murder. They overlook their future. They don't present their freedom long enough. They don't live life long enough to utilize it, or to see their God-given talents."

"When the conditions get rough, it changes the mentality of the people. They gotta eat. They start taking desperate measures. Day by day, their ungodly ways will not go unnoted, but first, before one can begin to find self and to gain knowledge, one must attain knowledge of self and have to know thyself. In order for one to know thyself, they have to know who they came from, who they are, and where they came from. We as a people from North America have lost the truth. Knowledge of self, and where we came from. Some people will say we were taught to act the way we do toward one another. I would differ that, because I know once you are taught something, you will come into the knowledge of that, and you will know that you know. I know that we were conditioned to think and act in the foolish ways that we do. Once we go back and find out who we really are, we will no longer act the foolishness towards one another. We only do these negative things towards one another, because we've been hit in the head and thoroughly robbed of the knowledge of ourselves. We are here today to get back on the right track, and that is by gaining the knowledge of who we are, and where we came from. We will do away with the negative image that we were told about ourselves. We will research the truth and find out that we came from great people, who were living in a great condition. Christopher Columbus tricked some of our people to go back with him. He took them to his Queen, and when he got there with our people, he said, these are the most civilized people I have even seen, and like I promised you, I have brought back gifts, and I give these people to you as gifts, so that they can be your servants."

"The Queen said to Christopher Columbus, I can't take these people as a gift and use them as servants, because you told me that they are the most civilized people that you have ever seen. You must return these people. I can't use them as servants."

"Christopher Columbus begged her to take the people as a gift, but the Queen refused and had him return the people to their rightful land. Columbus came up with the idea of bringing some more of our people back with him, and this time he stripped them of their clothes, jewelry, and pride."

"He told the Queen, These people have no God, and they are the most uncivilized people I've ever seen."

"The Queen said, I can take these people and give them our God, our language, and our way of life."

"That's when we were tricked into slavery. Now, people, listen, and listen good, because my time is up. I want to leave you all with this."

"God and Satan the Devil were talking, and Satan asked God to extend his time. God asked Satan why he should do such a thing. Satan told God that if he would just grant him a little more time, he'd have everyone deviating from God's path. God then told Satan, You can have them all, but my chosen ones."

"Now we look at the condition the world is in today, and the lives that people are living. We can truly say that Satan has led us all astray, but now there are a chosen few that are striving to get back on the right path of the almighty God. Sometimes, people follow their beliefs with blinders on and it leads them down a narrow tunnel. They see things only one way. With their beliefs and understandings, they can do things and have no remorse, no sympathy and no regrets. All the wrong we do comes from Satan, the devil, and all the good things we do comes from Allah alone. Allah tells us in the Qur'an, I have created you different hues and colours, so that ye may get to know one another, so that ye may be brethren. Guys, now it's time for each and every one of you to join our brethernly hood. The extraordinary Africa Leader Mr. Mandela said, if you want peace, then you have to work with the enemy. May Allah be pleased with him and continue to strengthen as well as bless his family. Most of all, if it's the will of Allah, the forth coming young generation will be strengthened from his wisdom and name." Shakur shouted "Harr," which is the Africa word that brings forth strength. "Now my people, I leave you with the same greeting, I greeted you with... Peace."

The Chaplain saw Shakur heading for the exit door, and he walked over beside Shakur and whispered, "Brother Shakur, I like the outburst you made about me. Anytime you feel the need to talk to me, you know where my office is."

"Chaplain, I don't do house calls," Shakur replied, while continuing to make tracks towards the exit doors. He could feel the Chaplain's eyes on him, so Shakur looked back with a smile and threw the Chaplain a peace sign.

The youngster who had written on one of the fliers, "There oughta be a program in the Chapel called, Increase the Killing and support the Violence," shook Shakur's hand and said, "Brother, sometimes a person can say the right word at the right time." With that, he walked away with his head down.

"Lil Brother, that was Allah's doing, not mine. The Creator worked through my sinful body to get to you. Little brother, you'll be alright, 'cause I know Allah is definitely not finished working with you youngsters, yet."

Chapter 19

Twenty-one hours after the Atonement, Counselor Sed exited through the double doors. He trailed the sidewalk towards his unit. The compound was covered with people.

All six towers immediately zeroed in on the crowd, thinking tension was in the air. However, there wasn't; everything was copasetic. All cars were having a meeting with their people. They were making it known that all the unnecessary petty propaganda would no longer be tolerated. Borrowing money with no intentions of paying it back, breaking into lockers, stealing people's radios, when they left them in their chairs, stealing people's sweat suits out of the laundry bags, stealing tennis shoes, or just stealing in general would not be tolerated. Guys were tired of going to war over thefts or homies, who smoked the weed and cigarettes and didn't want to pay. There was too much good and innocent blood being shed and wasted. Guys who didn't cause the trouble would have to go to war, because of his homie's ignorance. Too many people were catching longer sentences and longer out dates, getting set back on their parole dates, or getting injured, going to kill or be killed over some unnecessary foolishness. Now, the individual who broke the rules or committed an unlawful act would have to cut the field--go shake on the double doors. He would have to tell the law he needed to lay down, meaning go to the SHU, where he would remain, until he transferred to another institution. If he came back out, he'd get those locks on a belt slam dunked across his head or get stabbed up. Maybe even murdered, if he couldn't run fast enough, or the hospital didn't get him patched back up in time.

The individual who always caused these problems would often be in the hole saying his car was scared to go to war, so they checked him in, but if he would look at the situation from a different angle, he would see that his homies sent him up top for his own protection. They were saving a mother's son. They were giving him the opportunity to make it back to society in one piece. The individual would still blame his homies for being weak. Sometimes, a person's own car would beat their people to death with locks, until the law enforcers arrived. They would punish him for putting them in that life-threatening situation.

Wotson broke away from his homies, as Counselor Sed rounded the corner by the exit double doors, by the chow hall. The counselor's black shades, bald head, and shoes were all shining.

"Yo, Counselor, hold up, and let me get a couple seconds of your time."

Counselor Sed looked up and saw Wotson, "You better catch up."

Wotson jogged a few steps and before long, they were side by side. Counselor Sed shortened his stride giving Wotson the opportunity to catch up.

"Say, Counselor... man, about the other day at team, man, I was having a bad day. Man, sometimes this time gets to me."

"Wotson, you have to learn how to do the time and not allow the time do you."

"It's easier said than done. Counselor, man, you just doing your eight hours and hit the gate."

"Wotson, you don't have to apologize to me. There was no offense taken. I do take it into consideration that sometimes one of y'all will wake up on the wrong side of the bed. Wotson, I got eighteen years under my belt. All I need is two more years, and I can retire."

"Two mo years, and then you be outta prison, huh?"

Counselor Sed stopped walking and threw his tote bag further up on his shoulder to a more comfortable position. "Wotson, let me tell you something, son. These people gave you this time! This is man-made law. God has control of the future. They say one thing, but God may turn around and do another thing. The courthouse can get wiped out by a tornado. Lots of cases get overturned. They coming out with new laws daily. Who knows, parole will probably come back into effect in a year or two. Wotson, do you believe in God?"

"Yes!"

"Do you believe God gave up his only Begotten Son, for you and me?"

"Man, we God's sons," Wotson said, looking serious.

"We, meaning you and me!" Counselor Sed asked, as he pointed to Wotson first and then back to himself.

"Ain't no question."

"Then son, you need to start acting like you're God's son, instead of running around here carrying on, like you try'na do the work of the devil. Look at'cha. You sagging, so you think God would want his son to run around here with his tail all out?" Counselor Sed saw the crazy look in Wotson's eyes. "You can't get mad, because you set yourself up for that one."

"Well, Counselor, you better ease on down the road, before you set yourself up for a right hook, and I'll knock all that gray offa ya glass chin."

"My short hook mo powerful," Counselor Sed said, while closing in on their distance. As he walked even closer to Wotson, punching him was the last thing that would happen. He leaned in close, getting in Wotson's right ear, "Son, you know you have an Angel on both shoulders, right? The Angel on your right shoulder records all your good deeds, and the Angel on your left shoulder records all your bad deeds."

"Man, how you know that?"

"Umm huh, Wotson, you didn't think I know that, did you?" Counselor Sed continued, as he made his way towards the unit.

"Say, Counselor Sed, how you know that?"

"Umm huh, umm huh," Counselor Sed mumbled, as he tried to walk in a cooler tough-man way. "It's a Muslim thing," he yelled over his shoulder.

"Man, you're a Christian. You ain't no Muslim. You just been studying up on my religion."

"Didn't you say outta your mouth that we both are God's children?"

"Counselor, man, kick rocks. Press the gas on down the street."

"As-Salaamu 'Alaikum, my brother."

"Wa 'Alaikum-As-Salaam to you, Counselor Sed."

Sten sat on the sideline keeping score, as Shakur and Zeek Bey took on Abdul Jalil and Saeed Hamza in basketball. Shakur went up for a jumper, but Hamza stripped the ball from his hands and then tried to shoot a jumper himself. Shakur blocked the ball and got it back. This time Shakur took Hamza to the hoop, making an easy lay-up.

"The score is now tied up, gentlemen, 15 to 15. Whoever makes the next basket will win the game," announced Sten.

"Akh, let me stick Shakur. I'm tired of sitting back watching the brother use you. Let me get him some." Abdul Jalil said.

"It's the game point now. You shoulda said that in the beginning of the game," Hamza responded. "But watch this, I got him."

"Both of y'all can stick him, you see what I'm doing. All I do is check out the ball and stand back out of the way and let my man do his thing," Zeek Bey said. As he stood at the top of the key, dribbling the ball between his legs and around his back.

"Mo, this last bucket on you, can you handle it?"

"Naw, Shakur, I'll let you do it."

"Brother Sten, can you make the last bucket for us from over there?" Shakur asked, joking.

"I don't know, but I'll try it," Sten answered, as he acted like he was getting ready to shoot the invisible ball.

Zeek Bey bounded the ball, throwing Shakur a bounce pass. Shakur rested the ball on his hip, as brother Hamza reached at the ball a few times. Shakur's ball-handling experience refused to let the ball be stripped away. Zeek Bey ran over giving Shakur a pick. Shakur faked like he was going to use the pick, but he didn't and that move brought about a head-on collision with the two teammates. Hamza and Jalil bumped heads, as Shakur raced to the goal, making another easy layup.

"We the best, my triad brothers," hollered Sten, as he wheeled himself towards the goal. Shakur passed him the ball, but Sten missed the shot. Zeek Bey threw the ball back to him, and Sten missed that shot too. This time, Zeek Bey put the ball in the hoop.

"We made it that time, Brother," said Zeek Bey.

"That's right, Mo," breathed Sten.

"Yo brother Shakur, I see you still got it. I ain't gonna try to take nothing away from your game, Akh," stated Saeed Hamza.

"Brother Shakur is the truth," Abdul Jalil said, in Saeed Hamza's face.

"My good brothers, that's why I won, because I had you both on my team," Shakur joked.

"Naw, we would've won, if Abdul Jalil would've made the lay-up. That man was under the goal by himself, and he still could not make the lay-up," said Hamza.

Abdul Jalil shook his head, "So now you are going blame everything on me, huh? What about you missing that lay-up before that, trying to show off by trying to make a fancy lay. It did not have to be fancy. We just needed a simple lay-up, just one basket."

The Georgia crew played on the other end. IBN, Bar None, Sally, and Pop took on Reco, Nard, Orlando, and Dope Boy. Lucky had next down. Jesse stood on the sideline drinking coffee. Jesse swore up and down that he was a pimp, and that a pimp didn't play basketball, but every time Jesse would see this certain Caucasian female, he would say, Bitch, where my money? People liked to do their time off Jesse, since that day he jumped clean off the top tier balcony, hollering about he could fly. Jesse broke both ankles, both legs, and both feet.

"Homie, where ya ho at?" Pop asked Jesse. He just wanted to get Jesse crunk up, because he knew Jesse had a story and conversation for everything.

Jesse rubbed over his black shiny, wavy hair. "Homie, I don't know where my hooker at, but she better have daddy's money, when she do show up." Talking about the devil, the devil showed up. The female was prancing down the sidewalk with her big-faced sunglasses on, her high heels knocking on the pavement, as she strolled in their direction.

"There she go, Jesse. Get her," Baby ATL cheered him on.

Jesse strolled over to the fence. He always carried his coffee cup around with him, like it was his pimp cup. "Ho, you been out screwing all night. Where's my money?"

"Yes, daddy. Ya ho been out hookin' all night long, but I don't have any money!" she joked back with Jesse.

The whole court rang out with laughter. They stopped playing ball to listen to the famous Jesse. Shakur smiled, as he saw IBN walking towards him.

"Wha's up, Big IBN?"

"Just tryin' to get some rec, bro."

"So how did that lil demonstration play out?"

"Shakur, since they knew I was like Johnny Get Money,   Ra-sheen tried to handle me, as if me and Johnny Get Money were cut from the same cloth. The imam told me to go around to all the people the brother owed, and tell them I was going to pay the bill and give him ninety books. I buck the hock, I don't break bread."

"Sheed was good for always calling a brother a jacked-up joker, or always hollering about Allah done exposed somebody. Now they would see that he was truly the jacked up joker, and Allah done exposed him. Sheed told a brother he needed stop writing that urban novel foolishness, Sheed was on his second urban novel. The crumb-snatcher was thirsty. As long as the brothers fed his palm, he was cool, but I'mma make D'ua for him."

Shakur threw his right hand on IBN's shoulder. "Brother, some people become victims to their own greed. Lots of times, they'll say they are waiting on the hereafter and that they fear Allah, but their actions will reveal them. I'll speak with the imam, so he can revisit that sanction, because he can't put you in a hardship. Plus, that money supposed to go into the baitul-Maal."

"Did I hear y'all say something about ninety books?" asked Zeek Bey.

"Mo, that's a story within a story," IBN responded.

"I ain't come to prison to be nobody's follower. Fonky, I'm not cut from that cloth to be nobody's donkey. I'mma old dawg. You can't teach new tricks, so you can miss me with all of that gang-fested bullshit. Until I die,

I'mma chase that bread and walk with the same breath. Wish I could drill a hole and pour knowledge in the young generation's head. You can't do much without the education, don't allow being the bad guy to become your occupation. Live fast and die young. That's only a cute saying, not the future for no one's son," Pop rapped off looking into his homie IBN's eyes. Then he asked IBN to ask his Muslim brothers, if they wanted to run full court.

"Shakur, you heard the man, wha's up?" asked IBN.

"It doesn't matter to me," Shakur replied.

"Say, Bar None, who you playing with? Your Muslim brothers or the homies?"

"It don't matter to me, I'm just trying to get some rec," Bar None replied, as he started rolling up his pants legs and putting on his wristband and headband.

"Bar None, is you ready?" asked IBN.

"How you know?" Bar None answered, the question with a question and using his favorite words. You could ask him a question that required an answer, but he still would fire back with a, How you know?

Soon as Shakur inbounded the ball, the deuces went off and the tower intercom rang out. Everybody get on the ground, in English and Todos al piso, in Spanish. Staff and COs raced from all directions to one of the units. They came from rec, the education department, other units, Unicor, laundry, the business office, and the mail room. Facilities officers, Unicor officers, SHU officers, the warden, assistant warden, captain, lieutenant all came running along with three COs with machine guns that carried hundred-round clips.

As the shakedown crew was in motion, they all were taking turns shouting, Get down on the ground. Some staff wanted to boast around their authority more than others. They stopped running and walked up to a couple people and individually demanded that they get on the ground. A minority obeyed, but the majority refused to sit or to kneel on the ground. An education teacher stopped running, because he was out of shape and could not run the full distance. He took his frustration out on the guy leaning on the fence.

"Didn't you hear the orders to get on the ground, inmate?"

"Man, I'm not getting' on no ground," snapped Duck. "What you think, you got a bunch of chillins around here? Man, you better look around you. You in the penitentiary. This ain't no boy's club."

The education teacher held out his right hand wiggling his fingers, "Let me have your ID!"

"I don't have one, they already done took it."

"Took it for what?"

"Cause I keep walkin' across the grass."

"You stay right here, until I come back," the education teacher said. As he raced off to the crime scene.

He had just used Duck as an excuse to build his wind back up.

"Man, didn't I just tell you, that you ain't got no damn chillins around here," Duck scolded.

Everybody stood around wanting to see what had happened in the unit. They knew a serious war had gone on, because if it wasn't, there wouldn't have been reason for the three gunmen. Guys started forming around windows at that unit and pretty soon, someone from some car was going to get the news.

"Yard recall! Everyone report back to your assigned yard! To your assigned unit! Now!" the officer in the main tower shouted, over the loudspeaker.

The inmates next to the windows did not move a muscle. They thought the tower officer was retarded and just wasting his breath. Other staff ordered the groups to get away from around the windows repeatedly. The crowd needed info and without it, they were going to stay huddled up.

Assassyn walked by a window, and someone started banging on the glass. Assassyn banged back, "Say, New Orleans."

"Yeah, wha's up, woady. Who's that?"

"Say, homie, I'm from RO City."

"Say, round, wha's going on in there? Ya heard me?"

"Man, you Tree's celly, ain't it?"

"Yeah, I'm Tree's celly. My name Assassyn. What's going down in y'all unit?" Assassyn asked, as he stood as close to the window as possible. The guys from Louisiana were considered their homies, because they all sat together.

"Say, Assassyn, y'all homie, Chase, stabbed up anotha one y'all homeboys. Chase stabbed him in the neck and the police say dude is dead. The dude he stabbed was a new dude. He ain't been here all that long."

"A new dude, huh?"

"Yeah, he just got here on that last bus," RO City reported. He was doing his best to make Assassyn know Chase's victim.

"Yeah, I appreciate the info. Good lookin', round. I gotta get on back to the unit, 'cause you know how these white folks be trippin'," said Assassyn.

He saw the ten officers, as they spread throughout the yard. They were running guys away from the windows. The officers were hoping to detain the crowd, before a crazy war broke out, because they had not discovered that Tray L and Chase were homies and in the same car. The staff did not know this murder was planned and there would be no retaliation. Everybody from New Orleans had known Chase was going to murder Tray L.

"Say, Tree, the homie, Chase, took Tray L's ass out. I told you that lil one was bout it, bout it. Chase earned them stars. I ain't put shit on his chest. Ya heard me?"

"Yeah, but Chase still should've let Killa done it for him," Tree replied, picking at his medium-sized afro. "Woady rode like a true soulja for his brother Gangsta B," Tree added, slipping on his red and white bandanna.

Ty positioned the 8-ball and leaned on the pool table. Ty and Cole used the 8-ball, as most players would use the cue ball. He made a good break on the very first try. Ty knocked in four balls--two high balls, one low ball, and the cue ball. Ty confiscated the cue ball, which he and Cole considered the eight ball, out of the side pocket and put it back into the huddle. Cole did not see this, because he was too busy watching Mississippi. Even if he would have seen Ty, Cole would not have protested, because if he had knocked the cue ball into the pocket on accident, he would have put it back onto the table as well. Cole and Ty made up their pool rules, as they went along. When someone tried to correct one of them concerning a pool rule, Ty would say, Slim, find you some business. Don't worry about what the hell going on over here on our table. We don't follow rules; we break rules.

The rec room had a music room, a hobby craft shop, and an exercise room, but nothing interested Cole, but the TVs. Cole was a sports maniac. He loved sports so much, that's almost all he watched. Nothing else mattered to him. Cole wasn't really interested in this pool game, but he and

Ty had to do something, until the next ten-minute move came.

A ten-minute move meant you had exactly ten minutes to get to anywhere on the compound. After ten minutes, you would be locked into whatever location you where for the next hour. On a move, people would always be rushing somewhere like rec, pill line, other units, their housing unit, laundry, or commissary.

"Yo, Ty. Check out ole boy," Cole said, with a head nod.

Cole brushed Ty up on Mississippi telling Shakur about his debt of thirty books of stamps. Mississippi tried to explain to Cole, that if he would have handled his business by paying him his money back on time, then he wouldn't have had to put Shakur in their business. Mississippi advised Cole that there were no hard feelings or love lost between them. Mississippi was just tired of the song and dance that Cole constantly put on him. Mississippi knew this was the only way that he could get his money. Mississippi made it known that they were still cool, but business was business. Everyone knew Cole would pay like a cow shit in the road. He would piece-pay you. He paid his poker bills, as if it was a layaway.

Ty looked in Mississippi's direction, "Ha, ha, ha, naw, naw. I'm laughin' at you suckas like ha, ha, ha. Naw, naw, naw."

Ty and Cole would always do this, when they saw a guy trying to be too much, or when they saw a guy trying to play like he was a big boss.

"Say, Ty Tilzo, these niggas start getting a few stamps, so people will like 'em and love 'em. These niggas around here chasing statue liberties, when they ought to be trying to tear the library door down."

Mississippi walked over to their table. "Big Cole, wha's up, money?"

Cole started doing the Shawty Lo dance and sang the hook. Mississippi found it amusing. He didn't have a clue that Cole was belittling him. Young Ty Tilzo had a field day laughing. So happened, the remix video came on, and Ty put the volume on sky-high and started singing the hook once again.

"Young Ty Tilzo Bilzo. When the artist first hit the stage, they say I'd like to thank the fans for supporting me. These niggas around here act like I need 'em. Shit, I'm make 'em rich. I'm gonna cut back on my vices."

"Cole, you got too many vices," Mississippi lectured. "You ballin' out of control. Baby boy, ballin' get ballers outta control."

"When I hit the streets, look me up on poor man dot com," Cole snorted.

"Playboy, I'll spend three dollars wit'cha," Mississippi said, being sarcastic.

"Yeah, and when I get rich, you won't find me on poor man dot com no mo. I'm gonna step my game up. You'll have to log on to my line, www rich man dot com."

"It don't matter, cause right now, I got a stamp tree," Mississippi fired back.

Cole and Mississippi verbally assaulted one another for the next eight minutes. Cole ended the conversation with "Mississippi, you should be about two stamps away from being a stampanaire."

Chapter 20

The blazing angry sun hung high in the clear blue sky. The temperature was every bit of a hundred and ten degrees. On sweltering days like this, the prison officials hung a black flag from the center tower, indicating no physical activity was to take place on the yard. The flag fought with the breeze that did nothing to cool anyone from the summer heat.

The prisoners on the yard did the same thing they did when the black flag was not hanging from the tower. They totally disregarded the flag. To them the sun was energy. They weren't concerned with heat strokes. The Mexicans, blacks and Native-Americans did not fear skin cancer; they were people of the sun. They were raised up bathing in its red glaze. The guys played handball and basketball without a care in the world. The only thing that was on their minds was defeating their opponents.

The inmates assigned to keep the water kegs filled on the three compound's sections stayed busy refilling the cambro kegs every hour when the ten-minute moves were called because everyone was devouring the water by filling personal coolers, drinking from coolers and using water from the kegs to wet and cool themselves. This was done by the guys playing basketball, handball, and working out.

The guys at the yard tables who were gambling--playing poker--kept their focus and concentration on the fifty-two cards, upping the ante on bets and getting paid. The heat was nothing to them. They hoped it distracted their opponents majority of the poker players wore wet towels on their heads to deflect the heat.

Lorenzo and Ky were getting their run on around the USP's compound. They ran the outer perimeter of the whole compound because the track was too short to give them the speed and distance they needed to get a good workout. The track was for little dudes in the running game. Zo and Ky were running on what was considered the big boy circuit in the joint. Zo pushed Ky to run faster and further every time they ran. They didn't jog, they ran. Lorenzo would tell Ky that if they pushed themselves at running it would be easier for them to push themselves in their educational and occupational pursuits.

"I'm finna go back to them streets, get me in one of them colleges, and get a good job and take care of my daughter," Ky fired back without breaking stride in their frenetic pace.

"Wise man, that sound like a plan. You can bullshit me, but in the long run, just don't make as ass outta yourself," Zo breathed, stretching the distance between him and Ky.

Lorenzo would turn his Walkman up on full blast because the music motivated him. The music made Zo bust them laps quicker, in addition to Lorenzo getting a kick out of convicts on the yard stopping what they were doing to see how long the yard running would last.

Lorenzo tied his T-shirt around his head to hold his broken headphones in place, and it resembled a turban. The fellow convicts played on that with their taunts, jokes and jibes. Ky had fifteen days left of his incarceration and these last days had him worried. The twelve years he'd done was the easy part. Ky did not know how he was going to cope with society. Despite Ky's frustration during the run, he took it in stride and used it to go hard. He really liked and admired Lorenzo like a brother.

Lorenzo was a thinker. He knew how to stay out of trouble and moved forward on progress and his release date in this prison volatile and often violent environment. Zo was passing this necessary ability on to Ky.

Lorenzo and Ky sprinted past Shakur as he stretched. Shakur looked at Zo for the second time. He remembered Zo from somewhere. USP Florence, USP Beaumont, USP Pollock, or USP Atwater, Shakur thought. Yeah, at USP Atwater. Shakur stood up straight and started jogging in place. He was waiting on Zo and Ky to come back around so he could join their two-man train.

A guy dressed in gold nylon shorts, shirtless, and wearing a white headband sprinted down the football field. Shakur got a better look at him as he was walking back up the field. Shakur jogged over to the sprinter, "Say, brother, don't I know you?"

"Brother Shakur, cut it out."

"Nate, I thought that was you. How long you been here?"

"Bout a month."

"I haven't seen you because that's about how long they had us staying on our own yard," Shakur said, shaking Nate's hand.

"Where you coming from, Nate?"

"From Atlanta," Nate answered as he wiped sweat off his face. Nate looked like he was in his mid-20s. He and his son looked like brothers. When people saw him and his teenaged daughter together, they would be surprised to learn that Nate was her father. Nate looked like he was too young to be a father to teenagers.

"Nate, how was it back in your days when you grew up in Alabama? Was it hard for a brother?"

"Not really. No harder than it is for a Blackman anywhere else. Shakur, it wasn't all that crazy like people claim it was in Montgomery. You know my homie Wendall in Atlanta. Brother since they turned it into an FCI they shipped all the USP guys out."

"Jefferson, he's a real good brother. He has a knowledgeable head on his shoulders. And Buck is pretty good with that law work. He's the second brilliant guy to come outta Alabama besides Lionel Richie," Shakur stated. "Brother Nate, go ahead and finish getting your sprints on. I'm going to run about twenty laps around the big track. Come out after the last meal so we can chop it up."

"Alright," Nate said, giving Shakur some dap for the second time. Shakur watched as Nate shot down the field. Nate used to run during his high school years. He raced in the Olympics twice. The first time he came in second and the second time, Nate was the winner.

As soon as Shakur got in gear to run, Zeek Bey walked up, "Peace, Shakur."

"Peace, Mo. You wanna run a few laps with me?"

"Look at me. Look how I'm dressed. Do you really think I came to run?"

Shakur looked Zeek Bey over. Zeek Bey was dressed in his khakis outfit, which was crisp and creased up. Zeek Bey wore his tan Tim boots and he was sitting on a full tank. Zeek Bey had gotten two burritos a piece from Cox and Ali. Both brothers traveled the compound side by side. He shopped with them both because he enjoyed Cox's cooking as well as he enjoyed Ali's cooking.

"So where you heading?"

"Over there," Zeek Bey answered, pointing to the table where Mr. Pete and Sten played chess.

"I'll run tomorrow. I think I'll hang out with you guys. I might be able to get a few games under my belt," Shakur said as he followed Zeek Bey's idea.

"Sten, hold the belt. He's up how many games on you?" Bird asked.

"Two," Shine answered, holding up two fingers.

"Bird, Brother Sten lucky we don't have a peter-roll in chess cause I'll peter-roll him twice, back to back. But don't worry my dear brother, I'm going to glove him. I'm winning five games straight today. Brother Sten will be wearing a Michael Jackson glove."

"That glove can go both ways now, Shine. If Sten would've won three more games, you'd be wearing the one glove," Bird alerted.

"Thank you for reminding me. Now I'll play extra hard. I won't play around. I need them two games back and five more to go along with it," Shine replied.

"What you think brother Sten going to be doing while trying to get them seven straight?" Bird inquired.

"Some people like this game, but I love this game," Shine put out in the open. "That's what separates the good from the great."

When Shakur and Zeek Bey reached the table, they both greeted with the five-letter word, "Peace."

Mr. Pete and Sten both chanted the five-letter word back and Mr. Pete went on to tell them, "Brother Sten ain't taking any more butt whippings. Now he's giving them out."

Zeek Bey's eyes shot over to Shakur because he liked what Mr. Pete had announced.

"Which one of you good brothers wants next?" asked Shine as he propped a foot on the bench as he leaned over and moved his queen.

"Check," blurted Sten.

"Brother Shakur, Brother Zeek Bey, which one of you next in line to get into this line of fire?" asked Mr. Pete.

Sten had the pressure down on Shine, and Shine knew it wouldn't be long before the game would be over. He had only a pawn to protect his king. Sten had a bishop, two pawns, and a powerful knight that he was pushing up and down the board. Shine was hoping for a stalemate, but one wasn't in the forecast because Sten was far from making a mistake. He was determined not to allow a stalemate. Sten was too skillful to allow a stalemate to come into play.

"Check, Shine. The next move will be your last move," stated Sten with authority. He didn't have to broadcast that to Mr. Pete because Mr. Pete was the chess master. Mr. Pete saw that Shine had lost the battle and the war which was the main object for asking who had next, twice.

"Brother Sten beat me today as well. He got his thinking cap on," Mr. Pete enlightened. "Brother Sten beat me three games today. His game has improved well."

"What? Sten beat the chess master?" Zeek Bey blurted.

"Yeah, Mo. Brother Sten got me today. You can't expect to beat a man down every day. Today Brother Sten came out fighting," Mr. Pete said proudly.

"Mr. Pete, I won only a couple games, but you're still up two point two million games on me," Sten taunted as he started doing the loser's job of setting the chessboard back up. He was so accustomed to setting it up, he did it even when he won. Some old habits were definitely hard to break.

"Shakur, you want some of this trouble?" asked Sten.

"You might can beat Sten today," Zeek Bey encouraged Shakur.

"Mo, is you trying to get me to put my head in the lion's mouth?" Shakur joked as he made his way around the table over to Mr. Pete's seating area.

Sten tried to get the game in motion by moving his horse. Shakur was in the process of imitating Sten's move when Cole intervened. "Shakur, I got something I wanna show you," Cole said as he stood on the other side of the gate with a vanilla envelope in his hand.

Shakur exhaled.

"Go ahead, Brother Shakur, and take your time. I wanna rematch Brother Sten anyway, since he seems like he's ready today," offered Mr. Pete.

"I stay ready to keep from having to get ready," Sten replied. "Mr. Pete, you done let Sten get his voice back," Big Pat joked.

Shakur walked over to the gate. Cole held the envelope open so Shakur could look in. There were two pretty knives sitting side by side looking like two Siamese twins. The steel knives were so sharp they could cut through steel.

"I'm on the block, gentlemen. Get'em while their hot. These burritos fresh out the grease," baldheaded Halim yelled. Halim had a total of thirty-seven burritos in a nylon gray gym bag. He'd had forty until he ate three before even making the first sale.

"Brother Shakur, come on over and get you and Cole a burrito. Ali made these, homie," said Halim.

"I thought you were slanging for Cox?" Shakur asked.

"Yeah, I was yesterday, but from this day on I'm helping Ali out," Halim answered.

"So now you don't wanna work for Cox, huh?" Cole asked, addressing Halim by this government name.

"Homie buy you and Shakur a burrito?" Halim asked.

"Buy a burrito with what?" Cole asked, hunching up his shoulders. "Homie, I'm so broke that I can't pay attention. Homie, let me get a couple of them? I got'cha on the rebound."

"Cole, you and I both know you don't like to pay," Halim said, walking off.

"Kick rocks then," scolded Cole.

"I got fresh burritos, gentlemen. They been cooked in fresh grease and not in old grease. This is Ali's work. The burritos are extra cheesy and not greasy," Halim shouted. Before Halim got off the yard, he was stuffing his mouth with another burrito.

Cole turned his attention back to Shakur. "Why don't you carry a knife?" he queried.

Shakur took his eyes off the chess game and looked at Cole. "If I carry a knife, I'll be carrying a life sentence. Why would I do that? Wouldn't you think that would be doing this time backwards? Surely if I carry a knife, my intentions would be to remove someone from this planet. Brother, that is not my intention. I would leave that in the hands of Allah to find another fool to use as that example. You see, my mission is to awake the people and not to send them into eternal sleep. Those are the reasons why I don't carry foolish tools as you call a knife."

"Everybody got one, what you gonna do if you have a fight with somebody that have a knife?"

"If that ever occur, he better know what to do with it, then, instead of just having it."

"Shakur, I remember one time a dude was talking crazy to you. Why didn't you get mad?"

"Because to get mad, you would be doing just what your question is."

"What you mean by that?" Cole asked, looking puzzled. He was used to Shakur not coming clean and giving him a straight-out answer.

"To get mad is to lose all ability to deal with reason and logic. You would lose control over yourself and your ability."

"Shakur, but that's not answering my question!" Cole exclaimed grabbing ahold of the fence, now wishing that he had walked around to Shakur's side of the yard.

"I'm answering you but you just cannot see what I am saying to you."

"What is it that you're saying to me?"

"I'm saying to get mad and act out madness would make you become a mad man. Brother, you must think at all times and deal with each situation as it is. When that fool was talking, I knew that he was a fool and just talking.

279

If I was dealing with someone else other than a fool and he would have said those things and meant them, I would have handled that then and there. To react to any and every little thing would make you become a madman. Do you see, little brother?"

"I don't see nothing. I don't bar nothing," Cole replied, shaking his head.

"Well, all I can say right now is that in time if Allah blesses you, you will live to see things in a different light."

"Alright then, God body, I'll see you later on," Cole said as he followed Halim's footsteps up the sidewalk.

"Inshaa-Allaah, Cole. Inshaa-Allaah," Shakur acknowledged as he allowed his eyes to travel behind Cole. Shakur saw his homies group up on C-yard and the scene did not look right to him. The Westside paired off and so was the Southside. Shakur watched them from a distance. Those brothers were up to something that Allah would most definitely not be pleased with.

While Chris was getting screamed at, not once did he take his eyes off Cole once he saw him talking to Shakur. He was hoping and wishing that Shakur would come through the gate with Cole.

"Nigga, you make all that damn iron around here and you're scared to push? Cole running around here doing all this bullshit with people and playing games with the homies' money. He think a nigga won't blast his bitch ass. Homie or no homie, the nigga gotta be dealt with," advised Q.

Chris wanted to let the situation blow over because he didn't want to hurt Cole. Cole was his homie and everyone knew Cole's ways. If you loaned him anything, then it was like you were giving it to him.

"Big Homie, he don't owe me nothing but a book of stamps. He can have that. I'll charge it to the game."

"Naw, naw. Cole thinks this shit is a game. Now it's about the principle. We gonna teach his ass about telling lies and playing with other people's money. When he come over here, I want you to stab that nigga's ass up until your arms get tired and if any other homies get in it, I'm gonna take' em out, cause I got all day."

All day is a term of saying that he had a life sentence. Normally, lots of stabbings, murders and assaults came from people borrowing cookies, candy, stamps, and other commissary items. The borrower would claim he was going to pay it back on his store day, but when their day arrived, they'd come with some excuse and lies, claiming they were looking for something but their mother, father, brother, sister, or grandmother did not send the money order off yet. Also, this is how homosexual activity came into play, because some guys would prefer oral favors or some booty as payment. Some guys would create sad stories and tragedies about their family members. The same old stories: my son got hit by a car, my grandmother had a heart attack, or my father went to jail. People weren't concerned with sympathy; all they wanted was their m-o-n-e-y. Sometimes when you asked the person for your petta-sweat-ta they would beat you to getting mad, like you did something wrong for asking for your money.

Cole walked into Q, Chris, and Stunter's huddle. "Man, what's going on? Why y'all bunched up?"

Q whispered into Chris's ear, "Nigga, if you don't stab that nigga up, then I'm going to stab your soft ass, and nigga, you'll be in the hole for the rest of your bid. Now stab that nigga's ass up until my arms get tired." With that, Q gave Chris a push in the back.

Chris rushed forward like a madman with only one thing in mind. I can butcher Cole or I can get butchered. I'd rather it be his ass than mines. The first blow Chris threw landed on Cole's shoulder causing blood to skeet in his nappy hair and on his thick eyeglass lens. Chris rode Cole all the way down to the ground. He stabbed Cole again in the chest and again in the side. Chris stared into Cole's eyes with each puncture. He felt sorry for Cole. Chris was doing this by force and not by choice. It had to be done.

Cole's eyes started sinking back into his head. Chris's heart was beating like he owned an athlete's heart and he didn't have an athlete's bone in his body.

Tower Two dropped the bomb and yelled authoritatively through the intercom, "Put down your weapon now! Get away from the victim now!"

Chris did not know what to do. He was waiting to hear his order come from Q. Q had not told him to put down the knife or to get up off Cole. Chris pulled the blade out of Cole's side and was getting ready to drive it deep into Cole's chest when he felt Tower One's bullet rip through his back and exit out of his chest, missing his heart by a millimeter. Tower Three's bullet hit Chris in the knife hand, knocking the weapon completely from his grip. He collapsed on top of Cole. They both were in total shock and critical condition.

Straight commanded his homies to hold their knives; they were going to keister them. The staff rushed the rec yard like they were troops getting ready to fight in Desert Storm.

"Shit, back to the drawing board. We gonna go back on lockdown again," a bystander cried out.

Fat Corey, Ginmeni, Face, and his big brother Cadillac were standing over by the outside bathroom on the yard. They were too far away to see what all the commotion was about but each of them silently said, I hope it ain't one of the homies over there going to war.

Coolie strolled over. "Coolie, what happened over there?" asked Fat Corey.

"Now, Big Corey, how would I know when I'm over here with you?" Coolie replied.

"Man, that was my two homies, Cole and Chris," a guy from the Midwest spoke up sadly.

Fat Corey waited until the guy walked off and then said, "Man, Cole done got himself fucked up. Coolie, you know Cole wasn't no thinker anyway. Cole was a crash dummy."

"Gentlemen, we're officially going back on lockdown so get your burritos now. There ain't no tellin' when you're getting another hot meal. I got..." Halim paused. "I got eight left. Now don't everybody rush me at once." Halim had sixteen but his intentions were to hold the other eight for him and his celly Qawi so they could have four burritos a piece.

Chapter 21

Everybody from the shakedown crew had a job to do. A female officer dropped green duffle bags in front of the doors, while other female officers taped inspection sheets on each door. This was the time you'd see female staff officers that you had never seen before.

The guys on the shakedown crew would strip-search the prisoners one by one. They had another crew that would escort inmates to a room they designated where they would remain until the shakedown crew finished shaking down their cells.

"I need for you guys to put all your personal property into the green bags. Put all of your institutional clothing into the plastic bag, and don't leave anything in your cell. If you do, it will be thrown away," advised one of the females.

Hafidh rushed to the door. He wanted to get a better look at the woman. He'd been there for two years and this was a female he had never seen before. "Shakur, there's all kinds of broads out there I never seen before. Now I can choose me another new girlfriend."

Twenty minutes later, four male staff knocked on Shakur and Hafidh's cell door. "Come out in nothing but your boxers, t-shirts and shower shoes. Also y'all will have to remove your headgear."

Hafidh's fragile ego kicked in as he was making his way towards the door. He gave the staff a glare, "Man is you crazy? I ain't taking off my kufi and you better not touch it. Man, you work here and still don't know the BOP policies?"

The unit officer advised his co-worker that all a Muslim had to do is take their kufis off showing they weren't hiding anything . They were allowed to wear their religious headgear. The shakedown crew had a misconception since a couple doors down they had told the guys they could not wear their do-rags and black pull-over caps out of the cell.

"Y'all throw your mattresses and pillows over the rail and put all y'all's personal property in the cart down stairs. You'll get your mattresses and pillows back after the other crew finishes X-raying them," stated another unit counselor.

Shakur threw his mattress over the rail. Hafidh's passed Shakur his mattress since Shakur was the biggest and strongest. Shakur stood outside the door and let Hafidh get strip-searched first.

"Shakur, get dressed. The captain wants to see you," commanded the unit officer.

"I'm not going up there without my witness," Shakur stated while overlooking the unit.

The shakedown crew was working hard, not lollygagging. They were trying to finish this unit and move on to the next. Every staff was working and they had a system going. They were working the inmates back and forth from room to room.

"Take your celly," the unit officer suggested. "All you want is a witness anyway, right?"

"Naw, man. I'm not taking my celly. I'm taking my brother Sten and my other brother Zeek Bey."

"Brother Shakur, you're talking about the two guys who spoke with you in the chapel? I see y'all together all the time on the yard," the unit officer replied. He knew them by face and by name.

"CO, tell the captain I'm not coming without them."

"The captain said that you were going to say that. Look out the window. You talking about them two guys under the shed?"

Sten stood behind his wheelchair, pushing it back and forth, stretching his legs. That was what he called his exercise. The doctors claimed that Sten would never walk again, but Sten's baby-steps had improved. His body did not ache as bad anymore as he would travel the short distance. Sten stayed signed up for yoga classes. He was a regular. The classes had taught Sten that there was an exercise to strengthen every part of his body and to build up the body without becoming medication-dependent. Sten got an hour if not two hours of exercise every day. He would keep track of his activity on his wall calendar as his strength and ability increased. He had gotten addicted to winning back his health.

Zeek Bey stood in the center of the shed, ready to assist Sten if assistance was needed. The female guard sat on a table as she and Zeek Bey made small talk. The female guard looked presentable and wore a smile. Her voice made her sound like she was sweet as pie.

A couple of years back, Zeek Bey had caught strong feelings for a woman. This woman was beautiful, sexy, intelligent and extremely feminine, but her outside appearance did not entrap Zeek Bey... it was her heart. No matter how negative, crazy or disrespectful Zeek Bey would lash out at the female guard, she would still speak positively and conduct herself professionally.

She carried no harsh feelings towards Zeek Bey and gave him the utmost respect and the best advice that she could possibly give. The sister must have not had a taste of the ghetto lifestyle because she showed no ghetto characteristics at all.

The female guard's strong, positive attitude calmed Zeek Bey down and that was the day he started respecting female guards that deserved respect. Working in the prison system was a means for some women to escape the ghetto and also a way for them to build up self-esteem. It would make some of them think they were classified on the scale with Beyonce when it came down to getting a guy's attention.

As Zeek Bey and Sten sat underneath the shed, Zeek started thinking about how the woman was used in so many ways. He contemplated about the woman guard and his lust for the woman kicked in. He reflected about spending some time with her in an intimate way. One of the many things that triggered his lustful speculation was because of the little attention that she had showed him. She had just simply spoken with Zeek Bey and he had taken that and created all of this in his mind of how and what he would do with her and to her. This was just one of the powers that females had over a man.

The head administrator knew the effects that female officers had over the prisoners. There were times when it was needed for the female officers to use their feminism to bring the institution back to order. Looking at history, you would find that the female was always used to gain control and power of the throne. In those days, she would be the most powerful person in the land, and everyone that had a daughter was trying to get their daughter impregnated with the king's son. If that happened, that particular family would gain control over the throne, allowing them to lead over that land.

The female had always been used in different feminine ways at different times. You just had to look at how she had been used in your time to gain control.

After wars had broken out and the institutions had been on lockdown for a period of time, the head administrators would use their number one control mechanism by placing female guards and staff members in position so that all the warriors and would-be warriors could see them.

This was used to distract them. The prisoners would half-way be looking to war, but the other half of them would be looking through the eyes of lust. The guys could not fully concentrate on war when the female guards were there and were looking their best. The female guards had on their tight uniforms. Normally, it would be one button open, at the top of her blouse but now it would be two. If she spoke to an individual, he would become her number one protector because he had just fallen in love and believed that the female belonged to him. The slightest conversation from one female to a prisoner could lead to irrational thinking.

It was a known fact that it was that easy for prisoners to be lead astray through a conversation with a female guard or female staff member. She was the number one control method that was used after any major crisis. A female staff could take a prisoner and make him like putty in her hands.

Since the institution was on lockdown, all the assistant warden did was use his office for a miniature golf course and think about his 19-year-old mistress.

Candy rejuvenated his spirit. The more gifts he showered Candy with the more good things she said to him. The assistant warden loved the way Candy stroked his ego. She didn't complain about his wig piece and his habit of knuckle cracking like his wife. Candy allowed him to be the big baller and shot caller.

The assistant warden drew back to hit the ball, but the ringing of his desk phone caused him to miss the hole. "Jesus, that would have been an easy hole in one," he cried out as he walked over to spin the plastic shaped hole around towards the angle of his next shot. The desk phone continued to ring. "Go away, can't you see a guy trying to enjoy himself a beautiful game of golf?" the assistant warden waved the phone off.

For the last couple of days that the institution had been on lockdown, the assistant warden had been communicating with the staff by phone or by walkie-talkie. He always enjoyed the peaceful days of lockdown. He slipped a small picture of Candy out of his wallet. "Darling, do you think I am the best golfer in the whole world?" He chuckled and continued with the self-praises, "Don't you have faith in me? Don't you think I'm the world's greatest?" He kissed Candy's paper lips and looked at her picture one more time before he pocketed it and continued with his game of golf. He made the hole this time. "Candy, did you see that magnificent shot? This week I'm going to go out and buy you a brand spanking new BMW, one of the latest models."

"Can I get one too?" the lieutenant asked with a chuckle. He had heard every word that the assistant warden had said, but he would not manifest it because the assistant warden's love life did not interest him.

"Lieutenant, why are you here in my office? Don't you have a job to do? Now if you can't find yourself something to do then I'll have no problem with finding something else for you," the assistant warden promised. As he continued on with his golf game, he instructed the lieutenant to make rounds to every unit and talk to the guys on lockdown to see if he could obtain some information that could stop the violent season. The assistant warden had the lieutenant doing his job and making rounds for him. The lieutenant did everything but the assistant warden's paperwork.

"You told me to drop in if I had any suggestions, right or wrong?" the lieutenant asked, spreading his palms out. The lieutenant did not like this ass-kissing job, but it paid the bills and his family had to eat.

"What you got? Let's hear it."

"The very next time an inmate gets injured or so much as a scratch, we'll lock the place down and we'll do it every time," the lieutenant exhaled and immediately held his breath.

The assistant warden putted the ball eight feet closer to the hole. He wanted to make an impression on the lieutenant that he was a skillful and professional golfer, but the lieutenant knew better because he had seen him cheat several times and would congratulate him on the shot, then afterwards the assistant warden would carry on like he was a great golfer.

"I like that idea. In fact, I love it. That would mean more golf days for me," the assistant warden walked over and shook the lieutenant's hand. "LT, did you ever watch that TV show that used to come on in the early '70s called Get Smart?"

"I'm afraid that I can't say that I have, sir."

"Well, LT, ain't nothing terribly wrong with that but what I was going to do is give you the guy's name. Now your name will be Get Smart," the assistant warden complimented while smiling as he patted the lieutenant on the shoulder.

"Thank you, sir. I like that."

"Lieutenant, do you play golf?"

"I've played a little bit in my time."

"In that case, join me for a game or two. I'll spot you and take it easy on you poor guy," the assistant warden said while handing the lieutenant his golf club. He pulled another one out of his golf bag.

When the lieutenant worked late nights, he would sneak into the assistant warden's office and borrow his golf kit. Sometimes the lieutenant would lose track of time and would golf until his 4 a.m. alarm went off. The lieutenant had spent his childhood on the best of golf courses. He had been a caddy and had taken golf lessons from the best of golfers. They had also introduced him to cigars. The lieutenant was a non-smoker but he did enjoy the strong cigar smoke. He thought the thick white smoke represented power. The assistant warden just knew he was going to run circles around the lieutenant, but he had another thought coming. The lieutenant was going to beat him and teach him a few lessons from his own game.

"Sir, do you mind if I fire up a cigar?" the lieutenant asked, pulling his shirt out of his pants.

The assistant warden gave the lieutenant's question a wave. "Go ahead. I understand about you being a little nervous. If I was having to play against me, I'd be nervous too."

The lieutenant puffed on his cigar a couple of times. He looked at the assistant warden, smiling. You think the joke's on me but this time the joke's on you, he thought.

"Since I'm the veteran, you can go first," the assistant warden invited. He saw the smile on the lieutenant's face. "Say, lieutenant, if you like we could play for a small wager. A hundred dollars per game, perhaps, if that's not too much?"

The lieutenant bit down on his hundred and seventy-five dollar cigar, "That would be like takin' candy from a baby," he mumbled.

"Excuse me?"

"Sir, all I said was the hundred dollars would be just fine, sir, just fine," the lieutenant said, knocking the ball a foot away from the hole on his first try.

"Lieutenant, are you sure you haven't played this game before? God, if I didn't know any better I'd think I may have had a brain fart!"

"Sir, haven't you ever heard of beginner's luck?" the lieutenant asked while making the hole.

"You're a lying ass. That's not luck, that was all skill. Lieutenant, are you trying to hustle me? I know a hustler when I see one."

"Sir, have you heard the saying that says if it walks like a duck and quacks like a duck then it must be..." the lieutenant cut off his sentence to release a mouthful of smoke.

"Lieutenant, you've been around the prisoners too long. You're beginning to sound like them with all this duck method."

The assistant warden closed his eyes. He did not want to witness the next hole in one that the lieutenant was in the process of making. Now he wished he would have followed his first idea and called Candy so they could entertain one another with their dirty little conversations.

"Sir, did I ever mention about winning a trophy about your size in a golf tournament?" the lieutenant asked. He was talking trash now, trying to belittle the assistant warden as much as possible.

"LT, I don't care to hear all that garbage talk you pick up from the inmates. We're here to play golf, so let's play it!"

Captain D looked out the hallway window while smoking a cigarette as he watched the three figures cross the grass. Captain D's eyes landed upon the guy that he knew to be Shakur. Shakur was 6'2" 180 pounds and his body carried only 9% body fat. His top lip and head were both shaved completely bald and his thick black beard always remained groomed. Shakur would never be found in public without his black kufi. Shakur had a unique walk that could not be imitated and his stride could be easily picked out among the sixteen hundred inmates of the compound's population.

The captain returned back to his office. He wanted to put on a fresh pot of coffee in case Shakur, Zeek Bey, or Sten accepted his hospitality. Captain D glanced through the assistant warden's office.

They looked like they were on the lake fishing instead of playing golf. The assistant warden was shirtless, shoeless and sockless, and had his pant legs rolled up to his calves. The lieutenant sat back in a chair with his legs crossed, treating himself to a glass of vodka and club soda. Every once in a while the lieutenant would blow out rings of smoke.

Captain D scanned the computer. He wanted to get freshly updated, and get familiarized with the guys before they came into his presence. He sped-read over the classified files concerning where they were from, their religious beliefs and their ages.

The female escort guard lightly tapped on the door. Captain D signaled for her to come in without looking away from the computer screen. "I have them here," she confirmed.

"Please send them in," Captain D replied as he switched off his computer. Captain D had digested enough information to be able to state a few facts, instead of assuming. Now when Captain D mentioned something in particular, the guys would know that Captain D was speaking from the record and whether the allegations were true or false... that it was logged in the book.

Shakur entered the office first, Sten entered second with Zeek Bey pushing him. "Y'all gentlemen have a seat," Captain D offered.

Zeek Bey took the comfortable plush seat on the left, next to Sten's wheelchair. He left the exact same chair located to the right for Shakur, but Shakur declined and remained standing. Shakur stated that he had been laying and sitting down too long already. The captain offered them coffee but they all declined.

"So, Captain, why did you send for me?" Shakur asked, not delaying the question that had danced on his tongue as they had traveled to Captain D's office.

"I sent for you, Douglas, because the two guys are your homies and I would like to know what all this is about," Captain D responded, addressing Shakur by his first name.

Staff members would always address the inmates by their last names until they got to know them. Once they felt like they knew you or had gotten better acquainted with you to where they felt comfortable with you, they would start calling you by your first name or even by your nickname.

"What's the static on my homies? How they doing?"

"Cole got stabbed up pretty bad, but he'll make it. Chris, after he recuperates, will be sent to ADX and he will be prosecuted for attempted murder and not manslaughter. He is facing no less than a life sentence."

ADX was a prison where inmates stay locked in their cells for 23 hours a day. They got one hour of rec in a dog cage. They celled alone, had rec alone, ate alone, and had no contact visits. Their visits were conducted through a bulletproof glass, and they read all their mail from a screen.

"Douglas, I'm trying to make my prison a safe population. If we come off lockdown today, can you guarantee me that your homies would not go to war with one another again?" Captain D asked as he tapped his pen on the desktop.

"Now how would I know that? Only Allah knows what's best."

"Douglas, your homies would listen to you. I have seen how you, Sten Peabody, and Zeek Wilson speak to the people. Douglas, you once sat in this office talking on the phone to one of your people in USP Playa Palace and you convinced them to stop warring with one another. Now you're trying to tell me that you can't bring this little mediocre war to an end that is already in the palms of your hands?" Captain D asked as he walked away from behind his desk. "Would you even give it a try for me?"

"Captain, I would try to reason with the people. I will try to get my homies to do away with this unnecessary bloodshed, but I would do it only for their benefit and on their behalf. Nothing lays before my hands. Pull them out and I'll talk to them. I'll leave the situation in Allah's hands. Now you have a good day, Captain," Shakur signed. He wheeled Sten out of the office, leaving a trail for Zeek Bey.

"Thank you, Douglas, for coming," Captain D thanked him with a wave .

He called each living quarter that needed to be notified for them to release Shakur's homies from the units so they could attend the meeting that was about to take place on the yard. The sooner Shakur could reason with them, the sooner they could come off lockdown.

Shakur looked over his homies' faces. "What's this I hear about homies going to war over a book of stamps?"

"It wasn't about the money. It was about the principles," JJ spoke up.

"Do you know what principle is?" Shakur asked.

"Niggas need to stop playing games with people's money and shit wouldn't happen to 'em. One get outta pocket, he get dealt with," Rock stated.

Shakur rubbed his face. He couldn't believe what he had just heard . "Is that what you build your principles on? How would you explain it to your son or your daughter that you are never coming home because someone violated your principles about five dollars worth of old stamps? Do you think your children will look at that as being principle? Or will they look at it as you being a damn fool? You weigh it up and do the math on it and tell me what it adds up to."

JJ bit down on his bottom lip, "Man!"

Shakur cut in on JJ, "Naw, I want you to sit back and think about it."

Mel, Rabbit, Tim, Bird and Boleg, did not try to speak because they all knew that Shakur was speaking the truth. Mel shook his head, he didn't really have anything to say. He knew that Cole was totally wrong about how he was always taking the homies and other people for granted, but still, Cole did not deserve to be butchered.

"Look at this and weigh this up and understand that you got two good men that just got hit up about some ugly used up government stamps that didn't add up to ten dollars. You got rats that put people in prison and told on their grandmothers, but nobody is making a move on them low down and dirty, no-good peoples. You have to think about it before you make a move on a good man. What makes a man good is when he stands up and takes his own medicine. He don't tell on any and everybody just to get back out there and be no good to the other people that's out there . You see those two good men stood up and held their own. The petty crimes according to the jailhouse rules did not add up to the punishment. You have to think twice before you punish an innocent man. I'm not saying that they were wrong for the petty little crimes that they committed according to the penitentiary rules and codes. I'm just saying that they are two good men and that kind of punishment should not and cannot be given out to good men. We have too much dislike for one another, and use every little opportunity to show that dislike. We take the smallest thing and use it to hurt or destroy one another. We have to build a unity unlike anything ever was built so that we'll know our dislikes for one another and do nothing that will warrant unjustified action. We have to keep the street beefs in the streets. We don't have to love and bow down to one another but we do have to lend a helping hand when it is needed to one another. We are not in the state. Here in the Feds we have to become a family. We have to stand on that and live it. We have to start coming out and functioning together, playing basketball, playing handball, exercising, etc. etc. We have to put meals together and eat together. Not in the chow hall, I'm talking about putting a meal together on the yard so everyone can see the unity that we are showing and then maybe we ourselves will see the unity. Until we take a step to come together, we will not be together. If we don't come together here and now, then I don't see it happening in the near future. Before anyone can build an alliance together, they will have to come together, socialize with one another to make that happen. Divided, we become individuals. Unified, we become strong as one."

Officer Waylo stood forty feet from Shakur and his homies, giving them their privacy. The stocky officer was known to tackle the attacker within a heartbeat, and wouldn't call it quits until he wrestled the weapon away. The brave-heart Caucasian guy showed no fear and that was how the dangerous prisoners had learned to respect him. He earned every bit of that respect. Waylo never feared for his life during his twenty something years of being an officer, until a car surrounded one of their homies and decided he had to go up top. They planned to carry him to the lieutenant's office until Waylo stepped into their path asking what was the problem.

This bitch gotta go, demanded one of the mob.

Okay, put him down and I'll take care of it from here, Waylo said.

Once they slammed their homeboy on the ground, he sprang to his feet. Waylo grabbed him by the arm. Let's go, you know the process. Your car doesn't want you on the yard.

Fuck them bitches. Fuck them pussy-ass niggas, they don't run shit, the guy spit and was willing to fight to stay on the miserable compound. He wasn't in his right frame of mind, because there wasn't anything worth fighting for. He should have been glad to get away from all them broke, miserable, and gossiping-ass guys. They did more gossiping than women. The majority of them were nobodies on the street and now that they had come to jail wanted to be somebody important. They loved all that unnecessary political bullshit. Their lockers were empty, account on zero, and they should have been coming up with a plan to make some money instead of being stuck on bull shit.

Once their homie tried to snatch away from Waylo's grip, again the car closed in. If Waylo hadn't had his black shades on, they would have seen the fear in his eyes. This was the first time Waylo's five senses had encountered fear, but little did he know that the car was there for his protection. They protected him from their other homies.

"Everything good?" Waylo addressed Shakur since he and his homies had started shaking hands and doing the brotherly hugs.

"Only Allah can answer that question."

Waylo and the other five lieutenants were accustomed to Shakur giving his Creator all the credit, so in their mind, everything was well.

"Waylo, you told the people about the shot calling days, did you?" one of the lieutenants said, smiling.

"I can," Waylo replied, smiling back.

Once he discovered Shakur and his homies were waiting, Waylo rapped off, "On Mondays, it's the Indian's day to call the shots, Tuesday is the white man's day, Wednesday is the women's day which is why you never see us on those days because most of us take the day off and call in sick. Thursday is the undercover he/she day. Friday, that's the Blackman day to call the shots. Saturday, that's a free day, anybody can call the shots and Sunday is the Hispanic day to make the decisions."

Shakur and his group shared a laugh with the lieutenants, but deep in Shakur's heart, he was a firm believer that Allah called the shots seven days a week, and his five salats, seven days a week kept him in remembrance of Allah. He didn't have time to entertain foolishness, let alone give it the time of day.

Up and Downs
I've been put down, pulled down,
Let down, and sat down,
Talked down, brought down,
Hauled down, and shackled down.
I've even been beat down, knee down,
Chased down, and maced down,
Knocked down, locked down
Chained down, and plain down.
I still get stared down, sneered down
Tied down, and tired down,
Worn down, torn down,

Took down, and shook down.
I've sometimes held my head down, said down,
Laid down, but never stayed down.
I've always jumped up, stump up,
Got up and plot up,
Keep up, reach up,
Stood up, and held my hood up.
I still flame up, aim up,
Bang up, like I came up,
Hang up, range up,
Crook up, and keep' em shook up.
I kick my feet up,
I speak up, and heat the tree up,
Stepped up, crept up,
Fed up, gotta keep my head up.
Stash up, cash up,
Get my bread up, just in case I mess up,
I know the hate's up, face up,
I pray up, and hope God open the gates up.
-by M. Cannon

Chapter 22

The prison library was divided into two smaller rooms. In one side were the tables, books and typewriters. There were also four TVs with built-in DVD players that sat on desk-like booths. The library carried a variety of historical, religious and animal DVDs.

The prisoners had to provide their own headphones. The headphones were mandatory requirements to keep the TVs from distracting others. The other side contained computers and typewriters. The library staff made room for the computers which gave the prisoners more access to cases and information concerning their particular offenses.

The computers were not like computers in society. These did not do tricks. These computers were in prison as well. They had a word processor on them so you could type letters and do legal work, but to print you had to send the document over to a printer in the CO's office, so they could see exactly what you had done.

The resources were limited. There were bars on the library windows. When prisoners looked at the bars on the windows, it should have made them want to fight the government harder and work even more frequently on their cases. They had been captured and held hostage against their will and forced back into slavery. However, some people just laid down and did not fight. They were content with their long sentences and didn't have a fight muscle in their body. They were just too lazy to learn, study, and research their case. They would constantly make excuses that they were ignorant of the law, and instead would escape reality by playing card games, dice, or sports. They did not realize the majority of everyone had errors in their cases, which they could use to give back some of their time. The resentencing would give them a lesser sentence.

Most inmates did not act like a cat or a dog backed into a corner. Some people were chasing any and everything that could help them escape reality. One brother actually turned down parole. After being incarcerated for twenty-three years, he was afraid he could not cope with society. He stated he would rather die in the penitentiary.

Zeek Bey did exactly like Jesse advised him to do, read up on his case and other cases like it. Jesse was from Texas and was a knowledgeable Mexican guy who was willing to give assistance and advice to the people who were trying to give back their time. Jesse believed in fighting until there was not a breath left in his body. He spent all his time in the library. Jesse worked in the library and refused to work any place else. The only slave Jesse was going to be was a slave to his case and his efforts to win back his freedom.

Zeek Bey walked over to Jesse's desk. Jesse was typing away and looked up briefly. "What's up, Wilson?" Jesse greeted Zeek while continuing typing. Jesse and Zeek Bey always addressed one another on a last name basis.

"Ramirez, I hate to bother you but is it cool for me to ask you a couple of questions while you are typing?"

"Sure, I can type and talk, too."

"Say bro, is anyone using this chair?" Zeek Bey asked the brother who sat at the table. Zeek Bey could have just collected the chair, but he wanted to ask the brother out of respect. The guy glanced up from his newspaper. He wanted to keep the chair beside him just in case one of his homies came into the library but went ahead and let Zeek Bey have the chair. His homie could get another chair with ease from a different table, the same way Zeek Bey had gotten that chair.

Zeek Bey sat down beside Jesse's desk with an open law book. He was careful not to lose the page. "Ramirez, I read this case similar to mine and the guy got away with a lesser sentence than me. I don't understand how that could have happened. I read three other cases and didn't any of them receive time like I did," Zeek Bey said. He had markers on all four case pages so he could show Jesse and let Jesse read each case for himself.

"Now, Brother Wilson, you know I don't have time to read over those cases but what you need to do is check on the guys' criminal histories. See how they were enhanced. You have to look at everything that happened in the cases. See what they all did different, Brother Wilson, and that could be your way out. Study all those cases you're talking about. Make copies of them all and I'll look over them for you one day this week. You have a copy card?"

"Naw, but I can get a couple of them from my brother Shakur, he keep 'em."

Jesse stopped typing and went into his wallet, collecting two copy cards. "Here, bro, try to have my copy card back by store day."

"I'll bring them back to you tonight," Zeek Bey promised.

Zeek Bey put the chair back where he had gotten it from and raced to the copy machine. Today was his lucky day-there was not a long line. There were only two people ahead of him. Zeek Bey could make all the copies and make the next ten-minute move so he could find Shakur and replace Jesse's two copy cards.

Sten laid on the weight bench. He was on his sixth set. Sten could bench press 325 pounds, but usually worked out with 225 pounds. The two wagon wheels became lighter and lighter to Sten as the weeks went by. But on the days that he was sore, the two wheels were no feathers to him. Benching was the favorite part of the exercise to Sten.

Zayd had him exercise a different part of his body five days a week. Zayd was his personal trainer. Sten allowed Zayd to be the drill sergeant, since Zayd had been in the army.

"Brother Sten, you're doing real good. You're pushing double your weight," Zayd said as he took off his glasses to wipe his face and beard free of sweat.

"Yeah, I got like that because of all those pushups you had me doing."

The doctors did not expect Sten to ever walk again, but he could stand and take baby steps by the grace of God.

Zayd started off by taking Sten into the physical fitness room. They would lie on blue mattresses and run through a deck of playing cards. They would add up three cards after Zayd had peeled them off the deck, and that was how many pushups they would both do. As the pushups became easier for Sten, Zayd began picking up Sten's legs, making the pushups become uncomfortable for Sten, but helping his back, arms and chest to attain mass and a firmer definition.

Ten wide, ten medium and ten diamond shapes, Zayd would command. Sten fought his arm and leg pains to fulfill Zayd's authoritative commands.

Zayd joked as he helped Sten back into his wheelchair. Sten puffed out his chest and displayed his biceps. "Zayd, that ain't no cornbread, light bread and water. I'm getting' money."

Zayd laughed, "Okay, then. Bag up some, so I can get some money too."

While Zayd was getting his set in, Sten let his eyes roam around the weight pile. Three TVs were mounted on poles. One stayed on BET, another one stayed on news and the other one could be changed at request. A group of brothers had a super large dice game jumping off in the corner. Put together, they had more stamps than a post office. The stampanaires were palming big bags of stamps like they were palming big faces... a couple of hundred dollars worth of stamps in their hands. You couldn't tell that they weren't still the man.

The guys who tried to bet loose stamps were called crabs because they only had small money, usually one book of stamps. They were trying to turn crumbs into bricks or maybe win a few extra stamps so they could buy a cigarette, a bottle of wine or fill their stomachs up with Ali's or Cox's burritos.

The hustling game didn't stop, because a hustler got caught. The penitentiary hustlers were like the hustlers on the streets. They still got to eat and wear the expensive gear and have the finest of everything. The motto was to make a dollar a day by any means necessary.

Spider used a portion of the weight pile as his tattoo shop. He was the best tattoo artist at USP Petty Rock. The Mexican did all his tattoos without a pattern. People would just tell him what they wanted. Spider had people lined up trying to pay him in advance as if they were trying to line up for the dining hall to get that T-bone steak the institution fed every New Years Day.

A mosquito the size of a fingernail flew by Zayd's head, and Zayd tried to slap the mosquito. Sten informed Zayd that he didn't need to kill it. Zayd hit Sten with the reality that nasty mosquitoes are baby vampires. They were bloodsuckers. When the mosquito bites, they leave teeth prints that carry and spread germs.

"We got a good hour workout in today, Brother Sten," Zayd confirmed, putting on his long-sleeve shirt.

"What we back on tomorrow?" Sten asked, hoping it wouldn't be something that would leave him sore.

"Tomorrow is super-sets, back and shoulders," Zayd said, knowing Sten did not like doing ten super-sets. "That's when you sho-nuff gonna get good money."

Sten exhaled to keep from complaining. "Back and shoulders it is, Blackman."

Zayd went into his water cooler, pulling out two ice-cold apples. He passed one to Sten. "If you don't eat the whole apple then you ain't an apple eater."

"That's what I'm talking about. Brother Zayd, you stay looking out for a brother's health. Good and cold is this baby. I'm going to eat the stem and all," Sten replied before biting into the apple. Zayd always gave Sten a fresh well-iced apple after their workout if he had managed to smuggle a few out of the chow hall.

"You want me to push you back to your block?"

"Naw, I'm going to the court to watch Shakur play ball."

"Then I'll push you to the basketball court," Zayd insisted. He pushed Sten to the gym's front door so they could beat the crowd to the metal detector.

Shakur spent $100 on a pair of Timberland boots. He played basketball in them day-one after buying them from commissary. He'd been playing ball in them every day since. Shakur and his free rec mob won five games straight, and now that it was a ten-minute move, Hamza wanted to go in.

"Akh, that TV can wait," stated Shakur. "They'll show that same movie three days straight."

"I know, but, Shakur, I told you before I started playing I was leaving at 2:30. I gotta go watch the institutional movie."

"You ain't gotta go in, you wanna go in," Shakur corrected.

"Brother, you know I'm a TV fanatic. Where you found me at?" "In front of that TV."

"Alright then," Hamza huffed giving Shakur some clap. "There come y'all another playa. There come ya Mo partner," Hamza reported, pointing at Zeek Bey as he was heading in their direction.

Zeek Bey was dressed in sweats but he had no intention of playing any type of sports. Zeek Bey wanted to talk about them four cases he had copied. He had been talking to another guy in the library about those four cases earlier, and the guy hadn't been able to help him other than tell Zeek Bey that he hoped that Zeek gave some of his time back.

"Man, shit. He can't play ball. I played with that brother. He made us lose the game," one of Shakur's teammates recounted as Zeek Bey reached the court. Zeek Bey heard the comment. He laughed, and greeted Shakur.

"Peace, Akh."

"Peace, Mo, come on run a game with us. We need a man."

One of the opponents looked at Zeek Bey. "Man, that dude is a hacker-master. Leave him on the sideline."

Now Shakur was wishing he would have just run around the field. He could have gotten a good sweat on by himself. Guys on the court were always crying and complaining about something. If it wasn't one thing then it was another. Zeek Bey laid his law work by the pole. He put on the headband that he kept in his pocket as Sten wheeled up.

"Blackman, I found a couple of cases might help a brother out," Zeek Bey said, ready to share the news that had gotten his hopes up high.

"Tell me about it after you dunk a couple balls," Sten taunted, laughing.

"You mean after I make a basket or two, don't you?" Zeek Bey replied. He licked his fingertips and as soon as he stepped onto the court one of his teammates passed him the ball. He shot it and it went into the hoop.

"That's one bucket," Zeek Bey said, licking his fingertips again while waiting on the ball to be passed back to him. "Hey, brother, let me get my change," he said to the brother who had received the ball.

"Oh, my bad," the guy apologized, throwing the ball back to Zeek Bey.

Zeek made another basket. "That's anotha point, Brother Sten. You keeping track, right?"

"Yes, sir, Blackman," Sten answered.

"Yeah, that shit look pretty when you by yourself. You ain't gonna make one basket during the game," one of Zeek Bey's opponents predicted.

"Let's go, brothers, ball in," Shakur announced as he smacked the ball twice as he stood out of bounds. "Do y' all need a check?"

"Naw, good brother, play ball," the guy answered who was guarding Shakur.

"Give my man the ball," the guy hollered who was guarding Zeek Bey. Shakur granted his wish. As soon as the ball touched Zeek Bey's hands, he shot the ball, missing the whole goal. Zeek Bey clapped and rushed down the court to set up a defense.

A five-foot guard brought the ball down court. "Don't bring it on my side. I'm a shot blocker. I'm gonna slap your ball over the fence," Zeek Bey threatened. The point guard redirected towards Zeek Bey, accepting the challenge. He protected his ball and called himself trying to bully his way in on Zeek Bey. Zeek Bey performed a clean block without any body contact.

"Foul!" the guard cried.

"Foul?" Zeek Bey hooted. "Bro, I didn't foul you. That was all ball."

The point guard ran up on Zeek Bey, "Nigga, you did foul me, nigga!" His teammates shook their heads. They knew Shorty was going to bring some shit to the game like he always did. Shorty wouldn't be Shorty if he didn't.

"Damn, Shorty man, we was having a good game until you came along," one of his teammates complained.

Shakur started walking towards Zeek Bey and Shorty. "Say little brother, why you calling people the N-word?"

"Shit, my nigga, you want some? You can get some too. Shit, I love fighting big niggas," Shorty screamed as he dropped the basketball, walking up on Shakur.

Shakur looked down on Shorty who was biting his bottom lip and had his small fists balled into knuckles.

People always wanted to share and spread their misery. Shakur abhorred and detested meaningless violence because he was confident in himself to the point that it made enemies. Brothers on the court knew Shakur's outlook was positive. They stood back wondering how Shakur would go about this situation, formally or casually, meaning all business or more relaxed.

Shakur looked away from Shorty as he rubbed his beard and collected his righteous thoughts. "A person should never use the   N-word. The slave masters called us the N-word to degrade us. Then when he gave the house brother a couple of field brothers, the house brother would speak to them with my nigga. He clearly used the word in the way that told them that he owned peoples. It's important that we bury the N-word because if a Caucasian calls you a N-word, you still feel the pain."

"Then what you wanna do, dog?" Shorty still challenged. Shakur and the guys knew that Shorty was not a physical match for Shakur, so Shakur spanked Shorty mentally. "If you call a man a dog, that's God spelled backwards. You saying he's a backwards person and that he's not a God-minded and God-body person? Look up the word dog in the Webster's Dictionary. It means a worthless person. So that's what you think of your friends? My dog, my boy, my N. Those are terms we need to do away with!"

Shakur paused to collect the expressions from each individual's face. He looked down at Shorty. Shorty was gone! He looked up by the gate. Shorty's feet were beatin' up the pavement while everybody was listening to Shakur. Shorty went to hang out with his crew where dog and nigga were their very first communications and socially accepted.

"What's up my niggas? What's poppin', dog?" Shorty greeted his crew.

Chapter 23

As Ms. Coon rolled the blue phone down 300 range, inmates repeatedly asked to use the phone.

"Put in your cop-out," Ms. Coon replied as she continued her journey. The SHU had a policy: Guys in the hole only get to use the phone for fifteen minutes, once a month. Phone calls could be broken down to the minimum of three five-minute calls. Your counselor, case manager, and unit manager could approve for you to make an emergency phone call. If they did not have time to let prisoners make the call in their presence the warden could also approve calls.

Ms. Coon looked in Chase's cell window. Chase was lying on his stomach writing a letter. The SHU cells were much different from the population cells. A Special Housing Unit cell had showers in the room but there were no lockers or chairs. Some rooms had immobile steel desk tables mounted to the wall and some did not. All the door's windows were protected by steel chicken wire to prevent prisoners from breaking out the glass and using it for a weapon.

Depending on the circumstances, a prisoner in the hole could be comfortable in the situation or the hole days could become a living hell. If a person was in the SHU because they had checked in or had a separatee on the yard and were awaiting transfer, they would have their property in their cell with them-radio, food items, novels, and magazines. Now if the person was in the SHU because they broke the law, then they would be castigated to the fullest. They would have no radio, no food items, no novels and certainly no magazines. They would catch pure hell. Their nights and days were longer and more miserable. They'd get through the day by exercising, day-dreaming and reminiscing on the past.

The solitary confinement could strengthen you physically and mentally, just as it could destroy you physically and mentally. All SHU inmates had to look forward to were three hot meals, one hour of recreation and mail call. After that last meal, they'd tell a few gay jokes and call it a day. The majority of them would be in bed before 9:00 p.m. The SHU inmates were going to get the proper eight hours of rest and plenty of water in their system.

"Justin, you still want the phone?"

Chase rolled over to find Ms. Coon standing by his door. Ms. Coon rocked her Shirley Temple hairstyle. She wore no makeup. Ms. Coon's face gave off a natural glow. Ms. Coon opened Chase's food slot before searching for a phone jack. Chase got out of bed and collected his towel. He sat on the toilet neatly folding his towel.

"You know you better put something over this flat," Ms. Coon warned. "You can't lay the phone receiver on the steel tray flat."

"I know, Ms. Coon. It done got me already," Chase assured her, making her aware that he already knew once the steel cord made contact with the steel flat, the phone line would disconnect every time. The people you were talking to would think you hung up in their face. Ms. Coon stood by the door waiting to see if Chase got through. She did not take Chase through the stupid routine by asking him for the area code or the phone number, nor did she ask who he was calling. All Ms. Coon's two ears wanted was to hear Chase speak through that phone so she could move on.

Ms. Coon's job was not to sit there and listen to Chase's conversation. Everywhere in the fed system, they have an assigned officer around the clock listening to and recording all the prisoners' conversations. The Feds couldn't care less what language the inmates were talking in, they could have it translated. They called the ghetto language, hood codes, and thug talk their second language. They even solved tongue language.

Chase's 16-year-old brother answered the phone. Anyone who was hustling in the streets of New Orleans in the year of 1994 who was still alive was considered to be an O.G., especially if their lives revolved around the streets. The guys who lived past the age of fourteen were also considered to be an Original Gangster.

Chase's brother pushed hard down on the number five button to accept the phone call.

"Chase, wha's poppin', woady? I bet y'all niggas livin' good in the Feds, ya heard me? I heard y'all got swimming pools, tennis courts, cash money and wearing street clothes. One of the rounds say where he at they got soda machines and ice cream machines."

Somebody had been misleading Chase's little brother. It was possible that some of the activity could carry on in camps but there would never ever be a swimming pool in a federal prison.

"Big Bro, I need me a good connection-hook me up with one of them kingpins there, ya heard me? Get me a good connect with one of them millionaires."

Chase hung up the phone. He was even more frustrated that he didn't even get a word in. Chase had called home to let his mother know he would not be coming in the next two days as planned or anytime soon.

He did not call to listen to his brother's falsehood propaganda. Ms. Coon reappeared at Chase's door. "Did you talk to the person you needed to talk to?" Ms. Coon asked as she saw the look of disappointment on Chase's face.

"Naw, I didn't get to talk to my mother. I'll just write her. It would probably be best if I wrote her anyway," Chase said as he made his way back to his bunk.

"You left your towel on the flat."

"Just throw that shit on the floor," Chase instructed as he started back to writing his letter.

Ms. Coon followed Chase's request. She locked Chase's flat back and marched back down the hall with the telephone. Guys on the range repeated their first question and Ms. Coon repeated her same answer by advising them to put in a copout requesting to use the phone. "No copout--no telephone."

"Hey, Miss Coon, you think I can use the phone tomorrow?"

Ms. Coon did not need to ask for a name because she knew everybody's voice on each range and only one person called her Miss Coon. "We'll see what tomorrow brings, Justin Chase, because tomorrow isn't promised to anybody."

"Damn, Ms. Coon, I see ya got some bullshit wit'cha. Shorty, you know a nigga try'na work that phone tomorrow too now, girl," someone shouted.

"Child, please. You need to take ya hot ass back to the compound. I'm not going to be runnin' you the phone up and down the range so you can call the DEA. Y'all need to stop snitchin'... y'all becoming the government women."

"Woman, you think you're a celebrity back here in the hole now, don't ya? Ms. Coon, your hands look rougher than mines. Lady, you look like Steve Urkel."

"Oh, I look like Steve Urkel, huh? Just remember that Steve Urkel will be feeding this range for the whole quarter. So at chow time when I get to your door, you swallow spit and continue talking all that Steve Urkel shit."

"Ms. Coon, Ms. Coon. I was just talking shit," the guy yelled and started beating and rapping on the door. "I'm not myself right now, Ms. Coon. The devil made me do it."

"And the devil told me not to feed your damn ass tomorrow," Ms. Coon replied as she continued slinging and throwing her hips from side to side on down the hall.

"Get his smart ass, Ms. Coon! Ms. Coon, that's right sweetheart, make his back pockets touch his back. Ms. Coon, what you told that hot-ass nigga to do, Ms. Coon? Swallow spit and talk shit!" someone hollered down the range trying to hype Ms. Coon up. Once someone on the range put that battery in Ms. Coon's back she'd spend the remainder of her eight-hour shift out on the range. Ms. Coon liked working in the hole and had worked in Special Housing for a year straight because SHU prisoners make her feel special.

Ms. Coon argued with guys day in and day out, but by the time of her shift change, she had forgotten about that quarrel. Ms. Coon ran the hole. The hole was her house. Ms. Coon was the judge, jury and executioner.

"Ms. Coon," the same guy called out who had stated Ms. Coon looked like Steve Urkel. This time he called out Ms. Coon's name in a friendly voice, as he looked over the menu.

"Yesss," Ms. Coon answered in a sexy voice.

"Ms. Coon, you look like the bottom of a flip-flop."

"Ya momma," Ms. Coon responded laughing.

"Ms. Coon, you look like the bottom of a monkey's ass."

"Ya momma!"

"Ms. Coon, you say something else about my momma again, tomorrow when I go to rec I'm gonna hit you in your hard-ass face!"

"Boy, please. Ain't no man ever put his dick-beaters in my face before and I can't never say what you may do, but if you do put your hands on me, I'll beat you up so bad that your momma will feel it." Ms. Coon took care of that response.

The whole range took over the conversation. They verbally assaulted the guy as well by tripelizing Ms. Coon's response. 300 Range was the segregation tier. No-one had a radio in their cell. They beat on the door all day and all night rapping and taking turns as well as singing. They entertained each other when Ms. Coon wasn't there to entertain them.

Mr. Brown had studied Shakur from a distance many times and wanted to meet the brother. He wanted to walk up to him, shake his hand, and thank him for all the time, energy, and attention he was giving the people. Now the opportunity had finally presented itself. Nothing stood between them but air and opportunity.

Mr. Brown grew up in a church, and two years after his arrest he took his Shahadah, joining the Sunni Muslim Brotherhood. After about sixteen years, he decided being a part of the community was no longer for him. Mr. Brown refused to put an invisible leash around his neck and put the handle of the leash in the hands of another prisoner and allow himself to be guided. Mr. Brown battled with his so-called prison brothers for his unlawful ways as well as for theirs, due to his history of being a street soldier. Among the group, the majority of the guys did not have a loyal bone in their body and besides, Mr. Brown had never been a part of a gang and did not come to prison to join one.

Shakur is an approachable guy, very approachable, Mr. Brown reasoned with himself. Besides, he is a child of God With that being on his side he walked over to Shakur and greeted, "As-Salaamu 'Alaikum."

"Wa 'Alaikum-As-Salaam and Barrka too," Shakur replied, giving Mr. Brown a higher greeting. Shakur knew Brown was a Muslim and respected his wished to remain circle free.

"Brother Shakur, I like how you are awakening the people. We are the chosen people and the people truly do need Allah in their life. I always advise the young bucks that Muslims pray five times a day so we can stay in the remembrance of Allah."

"Al-hamdu lillaah," Shakur said, meaning All praises be to Allah.

"Brother Shakur, blessings do come in disguise."

"Akh, I'm a living witness," Shakur said, smiling.

"You know, brother, lots of people would've looked at my thirty-year sentence as a curse but now thanks to Allah, I've accepted this bid as a blessing because that's all it truly was, Shakur. I was selling dope, tooting powder and wilding out calling myself a player, a gangsta. I was insane, off the chain. If I wouldn't have gotten busted, I probably would've put that sack in my son's hands."

"Allahu 'alim," Shakur said, meaning Only Allah knows what's best.

"Destroying their future, not giving them a chance at life." Mr. Brown's eyes grew glossy. "Brother Shakur, it pains me to elaborate on the conduct of a drug dealer and now I'm ashamed of myself for being one. DD stands for Drug Dealer, but on a more conscious level, it stands for Death Dealer. That's because no matter what, everyone who is dealing drugs is passing death to the next person, whether it's a foot soldier or a drug addict, the end results are the same. Death in some sort or fashion. I was destroying our people giving that poison to the homies, telling myself, I was helping them eat. Really, I was just taking them away from their family, leaving their babies' mommas to be fathers as well." Mr. Brown lowered his eyes to the ground. "Now I see why they label a drug dealer as a low-life and scum-bag."

"We as individuals are not bad people," Shakur began. "At the time, you did what you thought was right, did what you call eating, but now Allah has opened your eyes. When people don't know much they can't do much. That's why they say knowledge is power. Prison has opened lots of our eyes, and prison has saved lots of lives. The young brothers out there trying to kick the door down to come to jail. So did I, so did you, and look what happened. We both are in the

midst of Allah. Who knows, by the youngest trying to tear down the door, it could be a sign their trying to come and learn about Allah, learn how to worship Allah, learn how to be a better father, and a better son. They are seeking knowledge and if they continue knocking, the door will be open."

"Inshaa-Allaah," Mr. Brown said.

"Inshaa-Allaah," Shakur replied, meaning If it's the will of Allah, and added, "Allahu'alim," meaning Only Allah knows what's best. "Allah guides who he chooses and puts the ones on the straight path that he's chosen and allows who he chooses to continue traveling down the path of straying. I'm a soldier for God. It's not about hurting the people but about awakening the people. We gain blessing by assistance the people, the people of all different walks of life."

Chapter 24

After the thunder and lightning finally finished arguing and cussing, all the hell-raising, they loved it when Mother Nature shed tears, leaving their land muddy and water puddles.

The rain always brought about tragedy and caused misery to surface. The handball players couldn't play handball, basketball players couldn't play basketball, and all other outdoor activities came to a stop. These activities were needed. Without it, it left prisoners without a good way to relieve their stress, keeping them cooped up in the units against their will.

There were ninety-six prisoners to a unit. That's ninety-six chances for a war, fight, or stabbing to break out, because misery loves company. Guys always wanted to share and spread their misery, but today was a good day. Both football teams were not going to let the water puddled field stop them from winning the jailhouse Super Bowl. Each team wanted to be victorious over the other. Even the four towers looked forward to this wet event. They had unconsciously joined the prisoner's fan club. They shared the athletic enthusiasm with their co-workers, wives, friends, and other family members.

"Hut one, hut two, hut three," the quarterback announced.

He looked to his right and to his left, making sure all of his homies were focused, "Huh hut."

He received the snap and jogged back a few steps. The quarterback threw the football as if he were throwing a spear at one of his enemies. The ball landed in the center of his homie's chest. The quarterback started snapping his fingers doing the Chris Tucker dance. All he had on were his boxers and a wife-beater t-shirt. He always stripped down before every game. Prisoners and staff had grown accustomed to the quarterback's skinny frame.

"I put on for my city. I put on for my city, on-on for the city." The quarterback was singing the Young Jeezy hook as he did the cheerleader's dance. He was moving his arm along like he had pom-poms but all he was doing was snapping his fingers.

Crusher raced up behind the quarterback. He picked the guy up, dumping him head first into a semi-large water puddle. "Naw, Shawty, I put on for my city and I came all the way down here just to make this shit the Georgia Dome."

The quarterback raised his head up. He looked like a wet and muddy tadpole. "OK, mothafucka, you can bet your ass that I'm gonna get'cha back!"

On the football field, any kind of crazy contact was acceptable, especially on wet days. You were likely to see teammates throwing their other teammates in the water puddles. The guys were on that field for two reasons and two reasons only. That was to make body contact and to have fun. They wouldn't let this opportunity get by them for nothing in the world. The guys on the sideline would be craving for a piece of the action. They would be wanting to knock someone into the mud or wanting to get knocked into the mud themselves. The only thing a referee called was a touchdown, so the players knew better than to look for a call. Players on the field did not bring their knives to the game, but they brought their guerilla game. They threatened and promised to knock one another in the dirt, and actually carried out their friendly threats. They relieved peer-pressure, stress and built-up tension in this game. Each individual felt twenty pounds lighter after the game.

Staff members found wet days to be entertaining. They would go to doing the rain dance. In society, they had women wrestling in the mud, but behind the walls, they had the famous mud football. They all sat on the concrete table and watched the football game. Shakur and Zeek Bey ate the peanut butter and jelly crackers as fast as Sten could make them. Neither one of them was hungry. They were just getting addicted to Sten's new invention. The peanut butter and jelly crackers were different and the combination of salt and sugar gave them a tasty taste. Sten spread peanut butter over six saltine crackers.

"Now this time we have two a piece," he said while spreading the grape jelly.

"Naw, brother, you'll knock out three a piece. I'll make me a couple," Zeek Bey replied while picking up the crackers.

A group of gangsters passed them by. Every single one of the group was sagging. Sten shook his head in a depressing way. Shakur saw how Sten looked at the young guys but he did not know what kind of effect they could have left on Sten.

"You know them?" Shakur asked.

Sten's eyes locked on the group again. He let his eyes travel a few steps with them. "I never did tell y'all brothers about how I got confined to this wheelchair."

"Sten, yes, you did. You said you had a shootout with the police, and that's how you got paralyzed," Zeek Bey answered, loading his mouth with a cracker sandwich.

"That day I could have got away. I wouldn't even be in this chair. I was running backwards, and my pants fell down to my ankles. Blackman, that was the day sagging cost me my freedom and almost cost me my life. Brothers walk around sagging, never knowing when a war is going to break out or when they might have to run. I just hope to God that their sagging don't cost them like it cost me."

Zeek Bey stopped chewing. He felt every inch of Sten's pain. He promised himself that now he would start telling the people about that sagging. Some guys sagged shirtless. Their butt-crack would be exposed to the public view. Wasn't anything but men walking around in the penitentiary, but guys still would come out of the shower in nothing but their boxers and sag all the way to their cells. One guy would wear gym shorts and khaki pants over his boxers and still would manage to sag all three, his butt-crack still hanging all outdoors.

"Brother Sten, I just don't know when the people are going to start pulling their damn pants up. I guess it's going to take a tragedy among their circle for them to wake up. That's when they'll probably take heed. Naw, they ain't trying to hear it from an outsider. To them, we are nobodies because we don't get down like they do. I hope they wake up before a tragedy wakes them up," Shakur stated.

"Some people still believe they have to test the water," remarked Zeek Bey.

"Nope, they don't have to touch the stove to see if it's hot. You have babies and small kids that know better than that," Sten commented as he looked off for a second. "People got it twisted by the old sayin', Experience is the best teacher. I'll never forget one of the questions my Muslin brothers asked me. Now I'll ask you guys the same question." Sten drew three imaginary circles on the table. "This hole has one snake. The second hole has two snakes, and the third hole has three snakes in it. Now which hole are you going to stick your hand into?"

"Neither one of them," answered Zeek Bey.

"You have to stick your hand in one of them," Sten replied.

"You know we are going to take the hole with one snake," Shakur spoke up for him and Zeek Bey. He wanted to let Sten get his point across.

"Surely, anybody in their right frame of mind is going to take the hole with one snake, but now let's be realistic here. How many people do you see doing things with sense? How many people we see around here acting out with sense?" Sten questioned.

"Not many," Zeek Bey answered.

"Now you see my point," Sten said, reaching for a cracker. "Good point taken," Shakur added.

Mr. Pete and IBN parlayed on the wall up by commissary. Mr. Pete watched the game and IBN scanned C Rec Yard. "Mr. Pete, look over there."

Mr. Pete followed IBN's direction and smiled upon seeing Sten, Zeek Bey and Shakur as they sat at the table. "Let's go over there and see what the good brother's up to," fired off Mr. Pete.

"I see y'all having a picnic. We come over to the party," said IBN as he and Mr. Pete approached the group. IBN sat down beside Shakur.

Mr. Pete greeted the group with peace, and immediately addressed IBN's comment. "You know, brother IBN, back in my time when you heard a white person saying let's have a picnic that was their way of saying let's go hang us a colored guy," Mr. Pete updated.

"I won't be using that word no more then, Mr. Pete," IBN assured. Then he addressed the crowd with, "What's the word for today?"

"Drank plenty of water and drive real slow because you know you have to drive for these other drunk drivers," Zeek Bey spat into the air. In other words, Zeek Bey was saying to be patient and stay humble, because on the positive and righteous path you have to think for the next brother. You can't let him trick you into going back down the wrong path. Zeek Bey knew IBN's character. IBN was a good brother but he'd been living a wild life and he wasn't fully ready to give it up yet. IBN still enjoyed that dungeon lifestyle.

"So, what y'all gentlemens up to?" Sten addressed Mr. Pete and IBN.

"Brother Sten, you know me. I like the outdoors-- fresh air," Mr. Pete blurted.

"Yeah, Mr. Pete, ain't nothing like that fresh air," Shakur added.

Brother Curtis passed by and he greeted the group, going on to say, "I would hang out with y'all good brothers but I got a classroom full of good brothers waiting on me. They're depending on me to show up."

Brother Curtis gave clarification for not being able to be among their circle in the company of good men. They knew he was a computer tutor. Brother Curtis strolled on down the sidewalk with his gray gym bag thrown across his shoulder as he sipped on a cup of coffee.

Brother Omar jogged by. He promised to come back by the last hour before recall. Brother Larry stayed outside on the yard every day and all day. He was always present among the circle. You would always find these gentlemen and knowledgeable brothers grouped up on the yard. But to the prison yard, they were known as the chess crew because they played chess every day and all day when they were not exercising.

Shakur, Zeek Bey, and Sten enjoyed these brothers' company because they all would bring some type of knowledge to the table. They would discuss and debate on worldly issues, day in and day out. Each individual had their own method and could see through the murky and cloudy water. Not one single person was on a narrow path. They all carried a broad horizon of thinking.

The prison loudspeaker erupted, "Ten-minute move is open." People rushed out of the gym. The chaplain lady took her sweet time opening the Religious Services door and the education teachers patrolled the door at Education, releasing approximately fifteen people at a time. They didn't want everyone to crowd the metal detector at the same time. The metal detector distance from Education was about the length of a football field. Ms. Healthy was posted up by the metal detector. Her duty was to make sure every prisoner went through the metal detector. If Ms.

Healthy turned her head for a second, guys would try to slip past her. An older gentleman placed his gym bag of law work on the table top.

"How are you today, Mr. Raven?"

"I'm alright, Ms. Healthy. How about yourself?" Mr. Raven answered, firing back with a question of concern.

A young guy walked around the metal detector. He walked up on Ms. Healthy.

"Why you ain't asked me how I'm doing?" he addressed Ms. Healthy. She pulled her windbreaker close and gave the young guy a get-outta-my-face-boy look.

"Ms. Healthy, I been locked up fourteen years straight and I feel like I been walking through hell with gasoline drawers on the whole time!"

"Mmmmh, now go on. I'm gonna pray for ya," Ms. Healthy said, turning her attention away from the young fella. She had to go through this with him Monday through Friday at 9:00 a.m. because the guy went to school.

The young buck began impersonating Stevie Wonder while clapping and trying to sound as if he was the artist. "Make me feel like I'm in paradise. Give me what I been missing."

Ms. Healthy smacked her lips. She acted like she did not hear the young buck's question. She was fed up with hearing the young wanna-be's slick comments. When Mr. Raven exited the door, it was so hot that he saw heat waves.

"Mr. Benjamin, can I borrow your umbrella?" he joked. Mr. Raven always cried out when it was super hot.

Unique stood in the grass sparring in a circle, using his left hand. His right arm was behind his back and not once did he change pivots. Unique rotated from jab to hook, sweat and salt creeping out of his pores.

"Unique, hot as it is out here, I don't see how you can do it. You're a better man than me."

"Mr. Raven, I wouldn't feel right if I didn't do this. Mr. Raven, I see you put your gloves up for the kitchen. Now you're boxing for your freedom. I like that."

"Unique, guess what they told me?" Mr. Raven asked and then answered his own question. "They said now they can keep some bell peppers and onions."

"Hu, hu, hu, hu-hu-hu," Unique breathed as he threw the two-piece combination three times. "Mr. Raven, it ain't about who can hit the hardest, or who can throw the strongest punch. It's about who can control the space," Unique stated as he still stood boxing around in a circle, but don't get me wrong, Santa Claus. When I do hit a joker, I'm trying to punch clean through him."

Mr. Raven rubbed his gray beard. He liked to be called Santa Claus.

"Hey, Unique, where Santa Claus go?"

"Santa Claus go straight to the ghetto," Unique chanted for Mr. Raven

"God Body, you go ahead on. I'll see you a little later. Merry X-mas!"

"And Merry X-mas to you, Santa Claus."

As soon as Mr. Raven rounded the corner, Cole's cousin, Fin, walked up. "What's goin' on, Mr. Raven?"

"How's Cole doing?" Mr. Raven asked him immediately. "You know Cole was a good friend of mine. I hope he doing alright."

Mr. Raven's words fell on deaf ears. Fin stared at him, because he, himself too, did not feel sorry for anyone who was playing with other people's money.

"Man, that nigga Hoodstyle playing games with my money like this shit a game. The nigga got three books from me three weeks ago, claiming he was going to the store."

"Let some go sometime. It'll come back to you three times," Mr. Raven dropped a jewel, like always.

Fin wasn't trying to hear that. Hoodstyle was going to pay that money and Fin wasn't going to Hoodstyle's homie about the situation because Hoodstyle came and got that money, not his homie. Hoodstyle used it to his advantage. He and Fin were cool. He did not think Fin would trip on him because of their so-called friendship.

Mr. Raven put a little bit more pep in his step. He was determined to distance himself as far away from the commotion as possible.

"Say, Hoodstyle, you just gonna continue to bullshit me about my cheese?" Fin asked, with death in his eyes. "So you just gonna keep spinning me with this petty-ass shit, huh?"

"Bro, I swear on my momma, I swear on my kids. I ain't trying to take nothing from you, God as my witness."

"Petty-ass nigga, it's been three fucking weeks!" Fin spat.

Hoodstyle's eyes grew large. His homies were watching to see how he was going to handle this situation. "Oh, I'm petty, huh?"

"You got-damn right, you petty! You're a petty-ass mothafucka just like the rest of these mothafuckas," Fin replayed. Reaching into his front pocket, putting his knife rope on his wrist as he also palmed his 14-inch murder weapon.

"Nigga, you the petty mothafucka askin' a nigga about that small-ass cheese on the fucking sidewalk. Nigga, I hope you ready to use that iron, cause I got mines! Petty-ass nigga, let's rock!" Hoodstyle spat the death words as he went under his shirt pulling out an ice pick.

The knife fight began, Fin and Hoodstyle danced around like two boxers. Neither one wanted to take the first swing. Hoodstyle was scared and Fin was glad of it. They stalled for a couple of minutes and then a miracle happened: Shakur, Sten and Zeek Bey rushed over.

"Man, somebody please tell me I didn't hear this correctly. Man, y'all out here about to waste blood about some stamps? Is y'all brothers out of your minds?" Shakur asked. Looking at his homie Hoodstyle, he said, "I'll pay the three books."

"I'll pay one of them," Zeek Bey volunteered.

"I'll pay one too," Sten added.

"Big dawg in the house," someone shouted, performing his ignorant outburst several times, until his crew aided and assisted him by barking like a dawg. The guy brought his pep rally to an end with two words, "PETTY ROCK!"

As lots of us get older, we begin to convert from working for and with the devil and return back to our God-fearing ways. We learn there are no rewards in doing all the wrong things. Nothing good surfaces from the negative. Now we strive to make it to heaven. We work to get through the pearly gates and strive for paradise. We can achieve this super-large goal by assisting others. Our darkness can be the light in the youth's tunnel. Our little light can truly shine and just maybe it can help the young generation to walk through the realms of temptation and look further than that ghetto-fabulous wall they have built around themselves. Hopefully, they'll stop dealing themselves this false illusion of becoming ghetto rich.

We all need to be like no other than Jacob and wrestle with the Lord and refuse to walk away until we receive a blessing. God is a good God, a merciful God. The good part about it, we can repent sincerely as many times as needed because God knows we are not perfect people. The Lord loves it when we come and ask for forgiveness.

Now myself, I am no walking saint, nor am I able to be labeled as a mentor because sometimes I can talk that talk but can't walk that walk, but I'm 100% out for the young generation due to the fact Allah has opened my third eye. It's a Hadith that says all the good a person does goes into the bones but all the evil he does will last forever. So that explains my reason why not to play the mentor role but that doesn't stop me from testifying how the Lord has cleaned my heart. Now I am almost a complete human being. I enlighten the people of my bad decisions and poor choices. If it's the will of Allah, my trials and tribulations will and can be a wake-up call. The savage way of life shall not be the young generations' future. They can capitalize from someone's misfortune. Like the saying goes, 'you can learn lots from a dummy.'

I sincerely apologize to everyone who I have intentionally or unintentionally made a part of my struggle. People often try to judge, but only God can judge. God knows everyone's heart, so all we need to do is continue making our good outweigh our bad, as well as continue trying to do the Lord's will by doing good deeds which I call making a down payment on heaven. It is hard to please people, and even harder to please the Lord. I am no saint or angel, but I thank the Lord that I'm not the person I used to be. Now I know everything in store for me comes from the Lord because nothing in life happens unless it was the will of Allah. God allows us to experience things to test our faith. God would not put anything on us that we couldn't bear, and keep in mind, God uses the ones who he chooses. Look into the mirror and sincerely ask yourself if you are one of the chosen ones. Please remember when you become a soldier for the Lord, you couldn't have answered a better call. There is a saying, You never know when the teachers are ready until the study arrives.

Now listen, statistics say we (as young black males) are safer in prison than out of prison. We know right from wrong. Also part of this solution is within the problem, maybe the cause can be our family structure. Once we did not have both parents in our life, especially the father, we fell victim to the streets and the systems! We must give our youth the escape route! Statistics also say by the time a young black male reaches the age 18, he will be in prison, been in jail or on probation. We need to come together as a village to raise a child, as they did in the neighborhoods. The whole projects and community as a whole needs to be the children's parents.

Listen, prison gives people the opportunity to look deep within themselves, to better know themselves. It gives them the opportunity to find God, to further educate themselves, as well as strengthen themselves in areas where they are weak. Prison opens people's eyes. Some have found themselves and have found God. Prison actually saves some people's lives because when one doesn't have any hope, then they have no future.

Brother IBN was a young brother trying to work his way into the knowledgeable circle. He was on a journey to becoming a universal builder. IBN became awakened to the fact of not limiting himself to knowledge and not drawing a circle around himself, meaning establishing perimeters to knowledge. Knowledge was meant to be sought from the cradle to the grave, from the womb to the tomb. IBN searched outside himself to find what good he could do for the people, but one thing Brother IBN overlooked about himself was to go inside self and get to know self. Once Brother IBN did that, he would master everything outside himself with this knowledge, wisdom and understanding by translating it through his newly found gift which is by writing.

Brother Omar had a good heart and a deep concern for the people. He believed in the narrow ways that he could bring about a change for the people. He believed that old methods would work in a modern daytime.

You have to let soldiers be soldiers, and Brother Omar one day would realize that and just play his part as the good soldier he was.

Brother Curtis can be described as a young brother with older folk's knowledge and wisdom. He's dedicated to move the teaching today through the Honorable Elijah Muhammad that were being ministered to the people today through the Honorable Minister Louis Farrakhan. The brother is sincerely about bringing these teaching forward to the people.

Brother Larry True X was extraordinary in history. He had a little of something about lots of events that took place in history... and the things that he didn't know he could direct you where to go to get that information.

Mr. Pete was a brother that if a person had to define in the least words category, they would come up with two words: The Truth... because he was concerned about the youth. Mr. Pete strongly believed in giving the young generation better choices. He was really concerned about replacing the youngsta's negative way of life with something positive. Mr. Pete is serious about brothers in the servitude condition have, and still are paying the way for the upcoming and forth running young generation. Mr. Pete preaches it, lectures it, means it and meant it... their brothers who are on the path leading astray should not want their seeds, or anyone else's children, to walk in their footsteps. Everything came from the heart and from the soul.

My blessings and prayers go out to all of the single mothers and will-be mothers. May Allah, may God, may the Creator, may our Lord protect and guide their sons to a brighter and bigger blessed future.

Inshaa-Allah, meaning if it's the will of Allah.

About the Author

This novel is only for entertainment people. Some of us had to be held accountable for the game. Some were successful and many others unsuccessful. So, young generation, I strongly advise you not to incorporate my characters' characteristics. The game is old , but brand new to a sucker. So please stay within reality, because this content is only for music, movies, novels, and TV. I wrote this serious just to escape my reality and to be perfectly honest, it was my comfort zone. I told myself that it can be educational for the youth, because it paints a picture as well as give them the blue print.

The whole layout is that they are like putty in someone else's hand. Finding themselves in a no win situation. Tupac said it best, "Me against the world." Yeah, you against the world. Now if it is the will of God, I have unhypnotized you.

AVAILABLE NOW

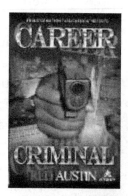

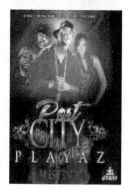

COMING SOON

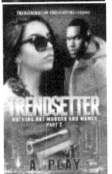

Order Form

Make **Money Orders** PayableTo:
KBA Publications
PO BOX 2863
Phenix City, AL 36868

QTY	KBA Publications Available	Price
	A Daughter's Cry	$15
	Career Criminal	$15
	Ridaz – Part II of Career Criminal	$15
	Trans-4-ma-tion Part I	$15
	Trans-4-ma-tion Part II	$15
	Atl's Finest Part 1	$15
	Atl's Finest Part II	$15
	Port City Playaz	$15

Ship To:

Name: _____

Address: _____

City:_____ State: _____ Zip: _____

For Shipping and Handling: Add $3.75 for 1st Book. Add $1.75 for each additional book. All books are also available on Amazon and Kindle. All titles coming soon, also can be pre-ordered.

What is the Holy Day of Atonement?

Atonement is the seeking of forgiveness and guidance from Almighty God. The process of atonement includes the recognizing of the wrong and acknowledging the wrong, confessing to it, repenting from it, atoning for it, forgiving, reconciling and making a perfect union with Almighty God. Please note, however, that the process begins with recognition. We must recognize the value of human life.

Atonement is the prescription for moral and spiritual renewal. Black, Hispanic, Native-American, Asian, Pacific Islander and White American families should engage in the Eight Steps of Atonement.

Eight Steps of Atonement

1.   Someone must point out the wrong.
2.   Acknowledge the wrong.
3.   Confess the fault. First to God, then to those offended.
4.   Repentance - a feeling of remorse, contrition, and shame for the past conduct which was wrong and sinful.
5.   Atonement - meaning to make amends and reparations for the wrong.
6.   Forgiveness by the offended party - to cease another for the harm done.
7.   Reconciliation and restoration-meaning to become friendly and peaceable again.
8.   Perfect union with God.

Made in the USA
Middletown, DE
23 May 2022